THE LAST MISSION
Steven Bussey

Seven Siblings | Melbourne, FL - *Publisher*
ISBN: 978-0-692-85630-7
Card Catalogue Number: 2017904176
Title: The Last Mission / Steve Bussey
Digital distribution |Seven Siblings, 2017
Paperback |Seven Siblings, 2017

Cover art by Carving Smiles Graphics and Designs

DEDICATION

Catherine Mae Jolley Bussey, Mom
Happy 82nd Birthday

Veronica Ann Carroll Bussey, My Wife
Happy 40th Anniversary, Honey
Thank you for staying

To America's military veterans silently suffering, you are not alone and you are loved.

Another Old Soldier
By Steve Bussey

Day and night—stress intense
Enemy abound outside the fence
Friend today tomorrow's number
The cries I hear within my slumber
Guns fall silent—aircraft land
Ticker tape and marching band
Calendars change—decades done
But a mind still under the enemy sun
Day and night - stress intense
Enemy abound inside the fence
Intrusive thoughts uncontrolled
Another old soldier not paroled
Once a friend now a number
Cries still heard within my slumber
M-16 to a bottle of rum
Another old soldier, society's bum

PROLOGUE

"In my dreams I hear again the crash of guns, the rattle of musketry, the strange, mournful mutter of the battlefield." —Douglas MacArthur

A single beam of moonlight pierces the darkness through the window blinds of the sprawling East Coast beach house and lands at the foot of the bed, minute particles of dust visibly dancing in the moonbeam. A baritone mumbling breaks the silence. It has been a very long time since he's had a peaceful night's sleep and this night was no different.

It begins slowly and then builds. Intrusive thoughts throughout the day. He tries to focus on more pleasant things but the demons persist. The alcohol makes it worse.

Thoughts morph into bad dreams - not too bad at first—unpleasant memories that turn the quixotic hope for peaceful slumber into fidgeting - tossing and turning.

Cold drops of sweat roll off his body like rain from a tin roof, soaking the sheets and pillow. The anguished mumbling begins to crescendo until the man is yelling at the demons in the night with a full throat, "Covering fire - covering fire god damn it!"

He violently thrashes as he yells, his arms swinging wildly and his legs flailing away, ripping the covers from his naked body.

He rolls from the bed onto the floor and grabs his Glock from the nightstand as he pushes his back against the bedroom wall for protection. His heart racing, breathing rapid and shallow, hands shaking and wet he holds his .40 caliber like a seasoned professional and peers into the darkness for his attackers. There is no one there - there is never anyone there. He carefully places his Glock on the floor beside him, hangs his head in shame and disgust, reaches for the bottle of Jack Daniel's in the nightstand...he won't need a glass.

His right hand rubbing his head, left hand clutching the whiskey - he quietly sobs as he whispers to the universe, "You always knew what to do, Honey...you could always bring me back..."

He very gently and unconsciously fingers the Glock as he takes a deep, long pull straight from the bottle of Jack.

CHAPTER ONE

"War is what happens when language fails."
—Margaret Atwood

Sarah Tomzewski was an outdoorsy girl who usually relished the beautiful Los Angeles fall weather, loved the warmth of the autumn sun on her face and the feel of the air as it washed across her athletic body, but this day was different as she walked west on 5th Street toward the 73-story U.S. Bank Tower for a meeting with her agent.

She brooded as she walked; her usually upright square shoulders demonstrating her self-respect and determination were now slouched, almost limp. She struggled to smile back at the fans that recognized her, pointed at her, acknowledged her with a look and a nod, but could only manage a stiff, almost plastic grin.

The beautiful young blonde actress from New Zealand had good reason to feel self-confident. She studied acting and dance as a young girl growing up just outside of Auckland and, when the time was right ten years ago, the then 25-year old actress sent an audition tape to Hollywood for a role in a new television show, packed a suitcase, and flew half way around the world based solely on a "maybe." She was beautiful *and* gutsy.

But on this *Chamber of Commerce* day in downtown LA, Sarah was not feeling beautiful, glamorous, or courageous. Her world had been shattered, or so she thought. "I'm done with men," she muttered.

I really—really hate meetings; Sarah thought to herself as she made her way through the opulent cavernous lobby of the Bank Tower to the elevators. In fact, on this particular day, she'd much rather be curled up on her couch with a good book, cuddling her rescue puppy and sipping a little Chamomile. Well, she'd probably prefer a couple of bottles of red wine today instead of her tea, maybe even a little whiskey, but the couch, book and puppy all sounded good to her.

"Hello, Ms. Tomzewski, Anne is on the phone right now but she said to show you right in."

Anne Campbell's secretary got up from her desk in the outer office on the 53rd floor and motioned for Sarah to follow her.

"Thank you." Sarah's response was flat and emotionless, her characteristic warm, toothy smile replaced by a scowl - her brow furled and her deep blue eyes narrowed to a squint.

Subconsciously, Sarah admired the secretary's toned, tanned body—typical LA beach bunny, she thought, bleached blonde hair, no doubt, pulled back in a girlish ponytail, but pretty and fit, happy and dressed appropriately for high profile office work. Sarah liked people who took pride in their appearance and took care of themselves physically.

Sarah walked into her agent's office, dropped her purse on the floor with a thud next to an overstuffed armchair positioned across from a white leather couch, plopped down as if exhausted from a full night of filming action scenes, and groaned. I hate meetings, she thought, and today is just not the day for this crap.

"My God, Honey, who pissed in your cereal this morning? You look like crap," Anne Campbell said as she hung up the phone, her voice made raspy and deep by decades of smoking and drinking.

"I don't want to talk about it, Anne. Let's just get this meeting out of the way so I can get home and relax a little." Sarah's voice cracked with a combination of anger and anguish as she spoke.

"Damn girl, I know you've been working hard but you're the most energetic actress I've ever rep'd and I've never seen you get tired and pissy like this. What's up?" Anne asked, as she landed her robust 50-year old frame with precision on the couch opposite Sarah.

"I said I don't want to talk about it, Anne, please." Sarah's voice now had an air of control. "You know that I don't like meetings. I'd much rather be camping, or jogging, or surfing or even walking on a bed of hot coals right now instead of sitting here with you - nice as you are and as much as you've done for me...I just..." Sarah stopped herself because she felt her anger building and knew she was about to get a little insulting. She liked Anne and didn't want to insult her. Nothing was Anne's fault.

Anne Campbell had dealt with it all during her 25-years as a talent agent, moody actors, drug addictions, broken marriages, scandals, even the occasional murder. She knew Sarah was not moody, not drug or alcohol addicted and not lazy or slothful. She suspected something serious was afoot, but didn't want to push.

Sarah worked regularly since arriving in Hollywood ten years before, and amassed a comparatively small but multi-million dollar fortune. She wasn't a super-star yet, had not caught the attention of the tabloid press, but was famous enough that people routinely recognized her on the street any time she left the house for shopping or a night out with friends. Whenever asked, she always happily and graciously signed autographs and posed for pictures with fans. She loved people in general, but she really loved and appreciated her fans.

"Honey," Anne said, "I think you need a mini-vacay, maybe some time with your parents in Auckland. You've worked hard these past two years and I know you're tired. Maybe you need to recharge your batteries a little, take a little time off."

"This is personal, Anne, not professional, and personal follows you no matter where you go - working or vacationing. I'll deal with it."

"We're not going to read about it in the tabloids, are we, Honey?" Anne asked cautiously.

"No, Anne, we're not. You know I'm always careful about keeping my personal and professional lives separate."

There was a brief but uncomfortable silence as Anne Campbell tried to read Sarah's face and understand her tone. Her curiosity was about to get the better of her, not because she worried about her "meal ticket" imploding or otherwise going crazy, but because she had a true affection and admiration for Sarah.

"Crap! What the hell was that?" Sarah said, as the building shuttered slightly and the windows rattled - the fire alarm sounded an ear-piercing whine.

"Earthquake?" Anne asked questioningly, almost childlike, looking at Sarah for confirmation.

The building public address system crackled to life, "*Shelter in place*," the anonymous voice commanded. "*Active shooter on the first two floors - shelter in place.*"

Sounds of gunfire replaced the voice on the public address system, followed by another loud explosion as the fire alarm system continued the intense ear-splitting whine. Screams suddenly filled the hallway outside Anne Campbell's office.

Another explosion somewhere below the 53rd floor office, then another. The lights flickered and then failed, the office now illuminated only by the warm LA late afternoon sun entering from the large office window behind Anne's executive style desk. An acrid smell of gunpowder and explosives wafted up through the elevator shafts and stairwells causing Sarah and Anne to cough and convincing them their worst fears were real...this is not a security drill!

Sarah and Anne looked at each other for comfort, or answers, or understanding only to find extreme fright in the other's face—all blood drained from each, eyes wide and mouths agape.

Broken and bloodied dead bodies and shattered glass dotted the Bank Tower lobby as gunshots and explosions continued to echo throughout the building. Blood oozed from the wounded finding the path of least resistance to flow from one body to another, the blood of innocent victims unceremoniously commingling.

Body parts dismembered by explosions littered the floor - flesh and bone and hair devoid of human context lay as if having never been alive. The wounded whimpered their anguished cries - groaned as they crawled toward death in the once spectacular sun-lit lobby as a thin layer of pale blue and white smoke hung low in the air as a pall.

Three men clad in one-piece black jumpsuits, ballistic vests, their heads and faces covered with ski masks, walked the lobby almost mercifully putting the wounded out of their misery with one shot to the head from their AK-47s.

Twenty-five other men similarly dressed fanned out through the building, some shooting, some throwing grenades, but all looking for innocent people to kill during the blitzkrieg attack.

Several men made their way up the interior fire escape stairwells to the floors above, shooting fleeing building occupants as they moved with purpose, while others began to line the lobby and entryways with explosive charges linked by det-cord...each man with a clear, pre-planned mission to complete. They went about their evil methodically.

The unmistakable sounds of war were continuous. Automatic weapons fire and explosions resounded without interruption as innocent men and women crumpled to their deaths one by one.

Many were able to escape before the terrorists secured the exits, some on the lower floors breaking windows with office furniture so they could jump to the ground below.

Those who landed without injury, or only slight injury, shouted up and encouraged others to jump.

The faint sounds of explosions and automatic weapons fire made their way from the lower floors to Sarah and Anne's ears as the fire alarms whined their urgent call. The sounds of panic were all around.

Another explosion—more automatic gunfire, this time closer, maybe a floor or two below.

Anne Campbell scrambled to the outer office - her young, bleached-blonde secretary was gone. Through the windows Anne saw people running in the hallway, heard their panicked screams. With a deep breath for courage, she locked the door in order to "shelter in place," and watched in amazement as people ran to and fro in the hallways, not knowing which way to run or where to hide - not following the orders from the anonymous voice over the PA system.

"We'll be okay, Sarah, I know we'll be okay," Anne said, almost pleading with the universe, a slight hint of prayer in her voice as she pushed her secretary's desk against the glass doors. "The cops will get here and stop them before they ever reach us."

"The police are here!" Sarah shouted back to Anne from the inner office with relief in her voice, while looking out of the window down onto South Grand Avenue.

Sarah was understandably scared to death, but she was not a coward. Not only was she a courageous woman, but she was also born of courageous parents and raised to be tough and independent.

As very young newlyweds, Sarah's parents escaped from East Germany, from behind the Iron Curtain, and eventually fled to New Zealand. Courage coursed through her veins. But she was also no fool. She knew the roles she played in movies and on television were make believe and not real. She suffered no delusions regarding her own abilities.

The two women looked at each other in horror as they realized the automatic weapons fire was now in their hallway...just down from Anne's plush office.

"Get in the closet, Anne, now!" Sarah demanded. "Move over and get down - get down!"

CHAPTER TWO

"I believe in God for many reasons, but chief among them is that I have seen the face of Satan and I know one cannot exist without the other." —Steve Bussey

The afternoon sun was waning as the first responding LAPD officers realized they had neither the firepower nor the manpower for what they were facing. The older officers immediately understood they hadn't faced a threat like this since the North Hollywood Shootout in 1997 when they faced two heavily armed bank robbers wearing ballistic vests, a shootout that took over thirty minutes injuring 12 officers and 8 civilians before it ended with the death of the two gunmen.

Officers sought cover behind the engine blocks of their cars as 7.62 millimeter AK-47 rounds fired from inside the building easily pierced the sheet metal, plastic and glass of their vehicles. Car tires exploded, glass shattered and flew aimlessly around them.

As one police officer lay slightly wounded behind his cruiser, he shook his head and muttered, "Damn it," as he recalled a briefing he received years earlier. The U.S. Bank Tower was one of the original targets on 9/11 and the feds had preempted two additional planned attacks against it. So, it's finally happened, he thought.

The U.S. Bank Tower commands the LA skyline. There are 2 floors below ground and 73- floors above. The Tower is an imposing cylindrical structure with a long, sweeping exterior ground floor staircase and its floor to ceiling glass facade on the first floor gave the terrorists inside a clear view of the responding law enforcement units.

Without warning or apparent reason, the gunfire stopped. Only the mournful wail of distant sirens getting closer and the constant squawking of police radios pierced the air. Suddenly, hostages began to appear in the windows, they lined up next to each other one-by-one, shoulder to shoulder, facing outward, their hands bound behind their backs with zip ties, mouths gagged with bloody clothing, eyes wide and faces frozen in horror.

Their blood lust temporarily satiated, the terrorists inside the building went about the business of rounding up the survivors as hostages. They methodically moved floor by floor and room by room, checking even the smallest nooks and crannies that could possibly hide someone. They separated male from female hostages and placed some in front of ground floor doors leading into the building for use as human shields.

Terrorists draped the ISIS black flags—the Islamic State—outside of broken windows and down onto the exterior facade all around the Bank Tower, firing celebratory shots into the air from their AK's as they went about their work proclaiming the takeover of the 11th tallest building west of the Mississippi - the tallest building in one of the world's most famous cities.

Police officers held their fire for the twenty minutes it took for the terrorists to throw the mangled dead bodies of their victims out of windows and doors.

Sarah and Anne fidgeted in the dark closet as Anne mouthed the words, "Oh my God...someone's out there," pointing to the closet door. They moved closer together, trying not to make the slightest sound...not even breathing.

Sarah was raised in a religious family but had not prayed in years and wasn't sure she remembered how. She thought about her parents in New Zealand and tried to remember the last time she called and spoke to them. She tried to think positive, tried to remember good times but the only memories she could manage were her regrets.

The two women screamed in terror and covered their heads as the door flung open.

"Get out!" a tall man with a thick Middle Eastern accent and dressed in all black military style clothing, his face covered with a ski mask, commanded as he motioned toward the office with his pistol. "Get out!"

"No!" Anne screamed as she placed her left arm against Sarah's chest to protect her and hold her back while slapping at the man with her right hand and kicking with both feet like a toddler throwing a tantrum. "No, no, no!"

The terrorist fired one shot into Anne's forehead, her blood spraying on Sarah as she cried out. The man pointed his pistol at Sarah and commanded, "Get out," as he again motioned with his pistol.

Sarah struggled to get to her feet, her legs rubbery from fear and the horror of seeing Anne killed. A second terrorist reached in and grabbed her, threw her onto the floor in the middle of Anne's office and placed the muzzle of his AK-47 to the back of her head as she wept.

"Why, my God, why..." Sarah sobbed.

"There is no God but Allah!" the man who shot Anne screamed in his thick accent as he kicked Sarah in the ribs with his black combat boot.

The second terrorist grabbed Sarah by her long blonde hair, dragged her out of the office, down the hallway, and threw her into the elevator. When they arrived on the 24th floor, they took Sarah to a large executive conference room with fifteen other women.

A very large Middle Eastern-looking man walked in the room and surveyed each woman. Holding them by the chin, he checked each side of their face, their eyes and then looked at their clothing and bodies without saying a word. He simply nodded as he found each one acceptable.

"Ah, I know you," the man said as he looked at Sarah. "You are that whore actress, the one who parades her body around and has sex on television and in the movies," he said as he looked up and down Sarah's body.

"I am not a whore!" Sarah yelled, briefly overcoming her fear to defend herself - her reputation. "The movies are pretend—they're just movies—they're not real," her voice now more calm, almost pleading, Anne's murder still fresh in her mind.

"They are real enough to corrupt our men," the man said sternly. "They cause our men to commit sin against Allah. Take her back upstairs to my new office. We will save her for later." He motioned to one of his men to remove Sarah from the others.

"All you other whores," the man said very loudly to get the attention of the women. "You will now strip to your underwear and put on the shirts you are given. If you argue, if you refuse, I will shoot you and bring up another woman in your place. You are our wives now and it will be your pleasure to be the wives of Allah's army," he said, as one of his compatriots gave each woman an oversized man's dress shirt.

CHAPTER THREE

"Patience is bitter, but its fruit is sweet." —Jean-Jacques Rousseau

The sun was low on the horizon and ready to make its exit as Special Agent Craig Buckley, FBI Deputy Director for Counterterrorism, in LA for an unrelated meeting, pulled up to the Joint Terrorism Task Force's mobile command post on Wilshire Blvd. He paused and took a deep breath before opening his car door. Bowing his head, he silently said a brief prayer. He worried that his presence would ruffle the feathers of the Special Agent in-Charge of the LA office, as well as state and local authorities.

Craig Buckley was a small and disarming man, standing only 5' 7" tall and weighing 160 pounds. His sometimes-rough South Philly accent and direct approach with people belied his easy manner. After his 25 years in the FBI, he was tired, he was tired of the long days and nights, but he was mostly tired of the bloodshed and the new threats materializing day after day with no end in sight. He was ready to be nothing more than the best husband and grandpa in the world.

"Good afternoon, Director," Bob Sherman, FBI Special Agent in-Charge of the LA office greeted his boss as he walked into the mobile command post. "You here to take over operations?" he asked with a somewhat aggravated tone.

"No, Bob, I'm just here to be your conduit to the head shed and make sure you have all the assets and resources you need - keep the boss and bureaucrats in

D.C. briefed." Craig tried to disarm Bob and the local authorities in the command post. "Bring me up to speed, what are we looking at here?"

"We have approximately forty ISIS terrorists in the building - near as we can tell - with about two hundred or so hostages," Bob Sherman started. "As you might remember, the Bank Tower was one of the original targets on 9/11 and Homeland Security has thwarted two additional planned attacks against the building."

"Yep, I remember," Craig nodded slowly as he answered.

"The terrorists are using most of the hostages as human shields around the glass facade and windows on the ground floor and have the entire floor rigged with explosives. We stopped trying to establish contact with the terrorists because each of the three times we tried, they shot a hostage in the head and tossed them out a 20th floor window, so we have no idea what in the hell they want. We do know that the shooting inside the building has stopped, except for those three executions when we tried to make contact."

Craig Buckley's mind wandered as he tried to listen to the briefing. He drifted mentally to his last fishing trip with his grandson—the excitement his 8-year old grandson showed when he caught that first fish. His shoulders drooped as he listened. He noticed the odor of sweat, bad breath, and stale coffee commingling in the air of the cramped command post.

"We have snipers positioned as observers in adjacent buildings here, here, here, and on several floors here," red dots illuminated on the video screen as Bob Sherman spoke and Craig nodded his understanding. "We're also trying to place every video and audio surveillance device known to law enforcement in and around the building but we don't have any audio or facial recognition yet."

"So, what's the plan...anyone...someone?" Craig asked.

"Patience, Director Buckley, patience - we wait them out until they either tell us what the hell they want or force our hand," the LAPD on-scene incident commander spoke up.

"I understand patience, but what in the hell are you going to do if they force your hand, execute a direct frontal assault through the explosives and hostages?" Craig's South Philly direct nature began to get the best of him.

"We have every S.W.A.T., every FBI and Homeland Security counterterrorism team west of the Mississippi either here or on the way," Bob Sherman interrupted. "LAPD, LA County Sheriffs and California Highway Patrol have every road blocked, every intersection controlled - nobody gets in or out," he continued.

"Look, guys, I'm going to get out of your way and let you do your work," Craig started hesitantly, almost apologetically. "But, my initial assessment is that this is beyond regular law enforcement capabilities - even SWAT and federal CAT teams. We can't call in the military because of the Posse Comitatus Act and the last time federal agencies used the National Guard we had that debacle in Waco where more than seventy people died in that conflagration and a whole lot of agents killed. I'm not trying to rush you or take over, but we're going to have to make some decisions and get some wheels in motion here real quick."

The late afternoon sun dissolved into the Pacific Ocean with brilliant splashes of red, yellow, and orange, rays breaking through scattered clouds as Craig's briefing continued amidst the constant low hum of voices in the command post, distant sirens, and the crackle of police radios. His mind raced with different scenarios - all bad - and then wandered back to his wife and kids, his grandkids.

After the briefing, Craig leaned back against the interior wall of the mobile command post and watched, listened, as melancholy washed over him. He tried not to admit to himself what was going to happen. He told everyone he wasn't there to take over but he knew he was going to have to make the call. He was going to have to call Washington and give the FBI director his advice, and nobody, not even Craig Buckley himself, was going to like it. We're going to have to call *them* in, he thought; we're going to have to call the contractors.

Craig knew what even most officials in state and local law enforcement didn't know...yet. After 16 years at war, there were a lot of former and retired Navy SEALs, Special Forces soldiers and others who were not quite ready to leave the battlefield and found jobs with private contractors. The federal government used some of the contractors to provide security and bodyguard services for the State Department and other government officials in warzones, and other countries contracted with them as well for the particularly difficult and bloody operations. But there was more to it than that.

Many senior intelligence officers in the federal government knew the terrorist threat in America was increasing far beyond that which local law enforcement could handle. It was apparent to many from what was happening in Europe and other places around the world, as well as the "lone wolf" attacks in America. But Craig, and others, knew for years that actual ISIS or al-Qaeda fighters would eventually make it to the shores of America, and now, that day had arrived.

Mike Hampton had trouble collecting his thoughts as he sat astride his 9-foot long surfboard in the Atlantic Ocean just off the coast of Virginia Beach. His mind wandered to every violent event he'd participated in over the past 37 years or so like a rapid fire slide show, the blood, the broken bodies, all of the needless death, the deaths he had caused and the deaths he was unable to stop. He bobbed gently in the chilly October water as the sun struggled to crest the horizon - soul surfing the dawn patrol - alone in the water at daybreak. With his back to the beach, he squinted against the morning sun as he stared at the horizon looking for his next wave.

Mike knew there was trouble somewhere in the word when he saw Angela, his senior executive assistant, standing on the beach as he turned and paddled to catch what would become his last wave of the day. Angela only showed up unannounced when his services, his contractors, were needed somewhere in the world - needed to stop something violent by committing violence themselves, horrendous violence.

Wearing his short john wetsuit to stave off the autumn cold, Mike Hampton guided his white long board with black flames painted along the rails, up and down the face of the chest-high wave. The waves were unusually nice, breaking to the left with just enough power for a good, long, ride but not too choppy - not too much work at all. Out of the corner of his eye as he rode and closed in on the beach, he saw Angela's impatience manifest in toe tapping, her right hand waiving over her head signaling for him to come in. As he approached the shallow water, he jumped from his board and allowed what was left of the wave to take his board to the sand, reaching down and disconnecting his leash as the board pulled at his ankle.

"What's up, Angela?" the 55-year old Mike Hampton asked, his voice made thick and raspy from his drinking and screaming in his sleep the night before...most nights. "Where we going this time?"

"Craig Buckley called, there's a hostage situation in LA—about 40 ISIS terrorists have taken over the U.S. Bank Tower in downtown LA and have dozens of hostages...they released a lot of them over night—it's a pretty bloody scene, according to Craig, but there's another little twist, there's a high profile hostage, an actress," Angela Montero briefed Mike as he peeled the top of his wetsuit off down to his waist and poured a gallon of fresh water from an old milk jug over his head to get the salt water off his skin.

Most people considered Angela Montero tall for a woman at 5'8". She was a slender 35-year old married woman from New York City with olive complexion skin and very outspoken with Mike when she needed to be. She was about the only one left in his life that could speak to him, as he sometimes needed.

"Craig also requested that you lead this operation yourself."

"Of course he did," Mike responded with an annoyed tone. "He probably wants to have lunch or something when it's over."

"Did Craig forward a briefing package?" Mike asked as he toweled off. He wasn't worried about Angela seeing his physical scars, old bullet and shrapnel wounds, surgical scars. Angela had been his executive assistant for more than four years and she knew his whole story, knew what he had been through in his life.

"Yes."

"Let's walk up to the house. I need some eggs and coffee. I'll look at the briefing package after I eat."

Mike Hampton had been around the block and back more than just a few times, and felt rode hard and put away wet, as the old saying goes. He was tired of his line of work but felt it was the only thing keeping him alive...even though it presented the greatest opportunity for his early death. Maybe, somewhere in the back of his mind, he did have a death wish. He would never eat his own gun, never really felt suicidal, but quite often felt like death would be a final release.

Mike and Angela silently trudged through the 50 yards of sandy beach to the sprawling beach house on 65th Street at the north end of Virginia Beach, a couple of miles from where Atlantic Avenue turned into Shore Drive. Mike loved the area because it's where he did most of his growing up as a "Navy brat" before he graduated high school and went into the Air Force, but mostly because it was where he'd met his high school sweetheart - his wife - and the two of them had so many great times, so many important memories. He returned and bought the beach house after her death, as well as two adjacent beach houses so his kids and grandkids would be comfortable when they visited.

"I need a shower, Angela," Mike said as he started his 6'2", 205-pound muscular frame up the stairs to the second floor of his house, running his fingers through his somewhat long and shaggy wet brown hair. "Leave the briefing package on the table and go ahead and make the calls—alert the teams. We'll leave for LA in three hours."

CHAPTER FOUR

"A hero is no braver than an ordinary man, but he is braver five minutes longer." —Ralph Waldo Emerson

Sarah couldn't sleep that first night in captivity. Every time she closed her eyes, she saw Anne's murder, and wept. She could still feel Anne's dried blood on her face. The day was no better, with only occasional sips of water from her captors and a few stale crackers for a meal.

Sarah sat alone in the corner of the dark, spacious 53rd floor office as the second day passed into evening, her hands bound behind her back with zip ties, her ankles bound and her mouth gagged with remnants of someone's bloody shirt. She was clad only in her thong panties, bra, and the oversized man's button down shirt her captors forced her to wear.

Only the emergency lights that hang in every hallway now illuminated the inside of the U.S. Bank Tower. The acrid smell of sweat, gunpowder, and death added to Sarah's difficulty breathing. She wondered as she quietly sobbed, how many men will rape me tonight, tomorrow. Will I die from the violent rape or will they just kill me when they're finished using me.

Sarah tried to shift her weight to find even the slightest comfort, she tried to move her feet to reposition the zip tie holding them and rubbed her hands together. She struggled to ignore the smells as she took deep breaths through her nose trying to get some air, at least a little air, through her mouth around the gag.

The man Sarah believed to be in-charge, the head terrorist, walked into the darkened room, walked over to

Sarah and knelt before her. She tried to kick him in the groin to inflict a little pain, or get him to kill her quickly, but he deflected her feeble attempt.

He just knelt before her and stared at her for what seemed like an eternity, saying nothing; then, with his knuckles, he gently rubbed her cheek as he stared into her wet, frightened blue eyes. He unbuttoned the top button of her shirt, then the next, and then a third, until her shirt was open to just down below her bra line, as she squirmed and silently tried to object, only able to indicate her hate with her eyes.

"You are worth 100 hostages to us," he said in a whisper. "Since we have you, we can free some others so that the crusaders will not attack us in this building until our work is done. And very soon now, you will be my whore. You will serve me as I serve Allah. And when I am done with you, in one more day or five more days, as Allah decides, we will kill you in front of the world on live television. We will put acid on your face to cleanse it and then take off your head." The man, who had yet to identify himself by name to Sarah, simply stood and walked away without another word, leaving her more confused and frightened than before.

Sarah was exhausted and as time passed she felt herself nodding off but then suddenly jolting awake as she heard gunshots and explosions in her mind and saw Anne's head exploding again and again, a morbid slideshow with a cruel projectionist. When she forced herself awake, she waited, waited for the rape and the murder, and she prayed. She prayed for a quick death, asked God to take her before being gang raped, to take her before they threw acid in her face, before whatever horror was next. She cried for her parents and their impending loss of their only child.

As Sarah's head slowly nodded up and down from exhaustion, her eyes opened and closed like a drunk not quite finished partying, she thought that she saw something new in the darkness—something had changed.

Two terrorists armed with AK-47's stood near the door of the office and spoke to each other in Arabic, their voices low. They weren't there before, Sarah thought to herself. Sarah didn't know what they were saying, but they kept looking at her and motioning to her. This is it, she thought, the rapes start now.

Sarah looked around the room hopelessly, looked to her right toward the large floor-to-ceiling windows, and then to her left, to her captors—her guards. A single red dot appeared on each guard, and then without a sound, each man fell limp to the floor, dead, small holes appearing in the windows. The snipers found their marks.

Sarah took a deep breath through her nose as tears began to stream down her face. She squirmed, tugged at her restraints. Her mind raced...was this her rescue, she wondered? Was it going to be violent, would she be injured or killed?

Mike Hampton opened the door, walked into the office, knelt, and checked the two terrorists to ensure they were dead. Dressed similar to the terrorist in black military style clothing, ski mask with a large oval opening revealing his eyes, ballistic vest, Kevlar helmet with attached night vision goggles, he walked over to Sarah and knelt in front of her, moving his silenced rifle around to his back as he bent down.

"Shhhh, don't make a sound," Mike Hampton said as he placed his gloved index finger to his lips, motioning for Sarah to remain silent. "I'm the good guys," he winked.

Sarah nodded slightly, hesitantly, unknowingly, as Mike Hampton removed his gloves and reached into a kit bag attached to his web gear.

"Just nod yes or no. Are you hurt anywhere?" Mike asked as he used a pair of wire cutters to free Sarah's ankles. Sarah very slightly moved her head from side to side, indicating "no," even though her ribs were still sore from the earlier kick, her ankles, and wrists raw from the zip ties.

The sounds of gunfire reverberated through the building once again, causing Sarah to tense her body and squirm, her eyes widened in renewed fear as Mike worked to gently free her gag.

"Oh my God," Sarah whispered, her voice thick with fright. "They're coming for us...they're coming, we have to get out of here! We have to get out!"

"Shhhh," Mike repeated as he gently clutched both sides of Sarah's face with his hands. "I need you to trust me - sit very still and don't make a sound. I have to hear the radio through my earpiece and I don't want the bad guys to hear us if any of them are outside that door. Those are my guys downstairs fighting and freeing the other hostages." He looked directly into her deep blue eyes as he spoke. "Do you understand me?" Mike asked firmly.

Sarah nodded once, "Yes."

He didn't really care if Sarah talked or not, he knew there were no terrorists within earshot. In fact, he was a fan and loved to hear her New Zealand accent, wanted to talk to her. But for the time being, he needed her to get used to following his instructions without question. He needed her to listen to him, do what he said, and not question him.

"Now, before I free your hands, I have to check you for injuries. I know you're uncomfortable, but I need you to just sit still another minute or two and do what I say," he whispered as Sarah nodded again.

Mike took Sarah's bare feet into his hands and checked each toe and her ankles, and then gently moved his hands up to her knees. He did a blood sweep by running one hand under each leg up to her buttocks.

"Please don't think I'm getting fresh or trying to cop a feel, Miss Tomzewski, but I have to check," Mike said, as his brown eyes narrowed and he smiled slightly with just the right corner of his mouth under his ski mask. Sarah braved a slight smile as she slowly nodded, "Okay."

Mike slowly moved his hands farther up the top and sides of her legs and to the top of her thighs, and then her waist, applying gentle pressure as he went to see if she would react with any pain.

"I promise, Miss Tomzewski, I'm really not trying to cop a feel," he smiled again, trying to break the tension.

"Sarah," she whispered.

"Excuse me?"

"Please, I'm just Sarah, just call me Sarah," she whispered again as she dropped her head and looked at the floor feeling embarrassed and ashamed for reasons she could not yet understand. She couldn't understand the many mixed emotions welling up inside her. Her emotions ebbed and flowed faster than typhoon driven waves in the Pacific, and confused her as she raised her head and watched Mike. How is he so calm, she wondered?

Even as constant gunfire and occasional explosions continued to echo throughout the building, Sarah felt her emotions ebb and herself relaxing, breathing easier, and beginning to trust her rescuer. She wasn't sure if it was her fatigue, or Mike's small attempts to make jokes about touching her body as he checked for injuries. She fidgeted in place a little, as he touched her, and glanced at the door on the other side of the office.

"Don't worry, those are my guys out there, and they're the best at what they do," Mike said as he applied slight pressure to Sarah's ribcage, causing her to wince slightly in pain.

"Not injured, huh?" Mike whispered with a little smile, almost nose to nose with Sarah. "Lean forward a little for me." She did as he said until her head was resting on his shoulder as he moved his hands up to her armpits.

"Oh, second base," Sarah teasingly whispered in Mike's ear. Her body went limp as she sighed deeply. In that moment, she felt safe for the first time in almost two days.

Mike's shoulders slumped and his body bounced a little as he chuckled silently. He reached behind her with his wire cutters and freed her hands, leaned back as he pulled her arms in front of her, checked each finger, her elbows, her skin for cuts and bruises, and her shoulders.

Mike reached into his pocket and took out a small container of handy-wipes. He pulled one out and very carefully and gently washed the blood from the side of Sarah's face with one hand while his other hand checked her head for bumps. Sarah arched her back and squared her shoulders, twisted a little from the tickling as he ran his fingers down the length of her spine to ensure there was no swelling.

When Sarah was free from all of her restraints, and Mike was sure she was mostly uninjured except for a few very sore ribs, he moved to her right side and sat on the floor next to her. He reached up to the radio mic attached to his web gear on his left shoulder, and keyed the mic.

"Eagle Control, Eagle 9-9," Mike called in a very low and soft baritone voice.

"Go ahead, 9-9," a voice squawked through Mike Hampton's earpiece.

"Time hack."

"Eagle 9-9, time hack is 0130."

"Copy, Eagle Control, Eagle 9-9 plus one ready for egress," Mike advised.

"Copy, Eagle 9-9, hold your position, you have hostiles retreating up, moving floors toward you."

"Copy."

Mike Hampton leaned back against the wall, tilted his head back slightly, and smiled to himself. He shook his head as he thought about how he was able to collect his thoughts and stay focused during an operation as opposed to when he was doing office work, surfing, working out or trying to sleep and the intrusive thoughts and nightmares always interrupted. And, he thought, he was sitting in a dark office next to a nearly naked young actress of whom he was a big fan. He watched every television show and movie she was in, including the bad ones.

Mike had rescued many people during his career, had protected foreign heads of state, diplomats and even presidents. He advised military officers of all rank, generals, on operational matters and he was never star-struck or impressed by rank or status. Everyone wipes their own ass, he thought. But he was starting to enjoy sitting on that floor with Sarah Tomzewski even with gunfights raging just floors below them and the immediate future uncertain. He felt more at home during a mission than anywhere else.

As she sat next to Mike and tried to make herself believe that everything was going to be okay, Sarah began to sob quietly as she thought about Anne Campbell's death and the ten years they knew each other. Anne was sort of Sarah's American mom since her actual mom lived in New Zealand. She occasionally disagreed with Anne Campbell over which part in a movie or television show was best, but she respected her and followed her guidance on how to protect her reputation, how to stay out of the tabloids.

"Sarah," Mike said in a very low and comforting tone of voice as he reached into his kit bag with his right hand and took out a small silver flask while he put his left arm around her to comfort her. "I know you're exhausted and scared, but how about a shot of red wine for your nerves?"

"Oh my God," Sarah answered, "you have wine? I would love that!" Sarah said, as she wiped the tears from her cheeks.

"It's not the most expensive red wine on the market, but wine drinkers in my family, my sisters and daughters, and some friends, tell me it's pretty good," Mike said, as he opened the flask and handed it to Sarah.

"Oh, here," Mike continued as he reached into his pocket. "Here's one of those little snack things with cheese and crackers, it isn't much, but I know you have to be starving. Besides, my grandson loves them," Mike said as he opened the package.

"Are you kidding me?" Sarah asked with a little sarcasm in her voice. "Cheese, wine and crackers? Do you do this for all the girls?"

"Well, no," Mike said, "but no matter what else happens this morning, I'm always going to be able to tell people that I had wine, cheese and crackers with Sarah Tomzewski." Mike couldn't help but start chuckling before he finished the sentence because even he knew how lame it sounded as he said it. But, he also knew that Sarah was thirsty and starving and a little wine would help relax her, steel her nerves for what might be about to come.

CHAPTER FIVE

"No battle plan survives contact with the enemy." —
Helmuth von Moltke

Mike allowed himself to relax as he and Sarah sat silently
in the dimly lit office, listening to the sounds of war below
them as Mike's men fought the ISIS terrorists and freed
the other hostages. His eyes though, glued to the office
door in front of him and to the left. He went over the
egress plan time and again in his mind as he listened to
his men on the radio through his earpiece, thankful that
Sarah couldn't hear the play-by-play.

Normally, there would never be time to relax during a
hostage rescue. Speed and precision timing, the element
of surprise were key to all hostage rescues. Mike
Hampton was a professional and he would usually never
bring wine to a rescue or even consort with hostages in
any way, but this mission was different. He knew there
would be waiting during this rescue as his men worked
their way to free the hostages on the lower floors of the
building and fight the terrorists. This was one of the most
unique situations Mike Hampton and his men had ever
faced.

"So, can I ask, who are you, what's your name, what do
I call you, are you a cop, military?" Sarah finally asked
after several drinks of wine from the flask.

"I'm sorry, but I can't tell you my name. You can call
me anything you want," Mike didn't take his eyes off the
office door as he spoke.

"Well, what do your men call you?"

"To my face or behind my back?" Mike asked sarcastically, causing Sarah to laugh quietly.

"Yeah, to your face," she replied as she took another drink of wine from the flask.

"Well, it's really not necessary for you to call me anything, not now anyway."

"Why can't I know your name," Sarah leaned her body into Mike's and looked up at his masked face as she spoke, his left arm still around her shoulders.

Mike Hampton usually wouldn't put his arm around a hostage during a rescue or even sit with one the way he was sitting with Sarah. But, like most fans, the amount of things Mike already knew about Sarah due to her public career made it seem as if he already knew her to at least some extent. Most fans feel like they have some connection to the actors they follow. And, Sarah was younger than three of Mike's kids were, so at this moment, he thought of one of his daughters being in this situation, he felt like "the dad" rather than the rescuer.

"Man, this is going to sound lame, like something from Batman or Superman," Mike paused, shook his head and chuckled softly. Hostages being rescued never have this many questions, he thought, they just want the hell out and do what they're told.

"Have you ever watched the news when local law enforcement did a drug bust and the cops had their ski masks on, or when they show Navy SEALs on television overseas they always blur their faces out?" Mike asked.

"Yes."

"Well, I'm not a cop or a SEAL, but it's kind of like that. My guys and I work all around the world and our anonymity is very important to us. We have to be able to move around freely doing surveillance, following people, and things like that without being recognized," he explained. "It also helps keep our friends and families safe."

"How about if I promise not to tell anyone who you are," Sarah asked sheepishly.

"No," Mike replied, "that wouldn't work. You're a public person and I have no doubt that you're going to have to give a press conference after this is all over, and then you're going to be interviewed ad nauseam on all the talk shows about this whole thing and if you know who I am then you're either going to have to lie and say you don't know, which is unacceptable, or say that you do but aren't allowed to tell, and that's unacceptable. In the first case, a gentleman would never ask a lady to lie and, in the second case, if people know that you know who I am then that makes you a target of my enemies, and a gentleman certainly wouldn't put a lady in *that* position."

"So, you and you're men are going to risk your lives to save me and I don't ever get to know who you are?" Sarah asked incredulously. "Not even just a first name?"

"Well, maybe one day after I retire, if I think it's safe for you," Mike said in a very matter-of-fact tone of voice hoping to end the uncomfortable conversation. He kept his eyes glued to the office door as he spoke, but could feel Sarah staring at him.

Sarah again rested her head on Mike's shoulder, and wondered silently. She couldn't see much of his face, but even in the dimly lit office, she could tell that Mike was an older man from the crow's feet around his eyes and the texture of the skin on his hands. And, she thought, he referred to a grandson. His voice was comforting and soothing, but also betrayed his age. She reached up, took his left hand that was around her shoulder into her left hand, and noticed there was no wedding ring. But, she thought to herself, he mentioned having daughters. Divorced or widowed, she wondered, or maybe he just took his ring off for the rescue operation.

What has a man like the one sitting next to her, saving her, done in his life, Sarah wondered. What has he seen and experienced? If he's not a cop and not military, then why is he the one sitting next to her risking his life for her? Her eyes closed as she began to nod off, the fatigue and wine taking their toll on her.

"Eagle Control, Eagle 9-4, 9-4 Alpha and Bravo are pinned down in the southeast stairwell and Eagle 9-9 has 5 hostiles moving on his position, copy?" The radio squawked in Mike's left ear.

"Eagle Control, copies...break...Eagle 9-9, Eagle Control..."

"Eagle Control, Eagle 9-9, I copy. Have any available units move to support 9-4, I'll handle my end," Mike responded in a whisper as he carefully moved his left arm from around Sarah and tried to stand without waking her. She groaned slightly and shifted on the carpeted floor as he moved.

Mike moved to the office door and brought his rifle to a firing position as he crouched, radio still squawking in his ear. He reached up, turned the doorknob, and opened the door enough to see down the hallway to the south, propping the door just slightly open with his foot.

Mike glanced at his watch, 0210. The operation was behind schedule. "No plan survives first contact with the enemy," he muttered as he dropped his night vision goggles into position and peered down the dimly lit hallway.

CHAPTER SIX

"I learned that courage was not the absence of fear, but the triumph over it. The brave man is not he who does not feel afraid, but he who conquers that fear." —Nelson Mandela

Mike brought his silenced M-4 rifle to bear as three figures carrying AK-47s appeared from around the corner at the end of the hallway, and waited, let them close on his position as he glanced back into the office to check on Sarah.

Sarah jolted awake, placed her hands over her mouth in shock as Mike fired several 3-round bursts down the hallway at the terrorists, hitting and disabling two of the men. Several bullets from the remaining terrorist's AK-47 violently impacted the door and doorframe around Mike as he fired another burst from his M-4. Sarah gasped and jumped into a low crouching position as Mike and the terrorist fought.

Bullets continued impacting the doorframe and wall around Mike, some flying into the office and striking furniture. Mike dropped his empty magazine with one hand as he grabbed a fresh one from his vest and reloaded his weapon, ducking and moving his head as the terrorist continued firing at him.

Mike fired several more 3-round bursts before two bullets impacted his ballistic vest just below his sternum, knocking the wind out of him. He kept the door propped open with his foot as he fell back slightly onto the office floor from the force of the impacts.

"Oh my God!" Sarah yelled in horror. She slowly started to crawl in his direction, reached her left hand out as if to grab him, but he motioned for her to stay put.

Mike continued to fire into the hallway as bullets continuously impacted around him, wood splinters flying into the air, some sticking to his ski mask.

Mike's left arm momentarily fell limp as a bullet found the unprotected flesh in his upper arm, blood slowly soaking his shirt. He quickly regained his firing position and continued the fight. Another bullet grazed his hip below his vest, but the adrenaline racing through his veins kept him from noticing. Sarah watched the scene unfold in horror, worried for Mike's safety...for her own safety.

Mike continued firing until the remaining terrorist was dead and the incoming fire stopped. He looked to his left and motioned for Sarah to move to his position.

"Oh my God, you've been shot—you're shot!"

"Get behind me, Sarah—move!" Mike demanded as he used his left hand to force Sarah behind him, his voice no longer sympathetic and comforting.

"You need a doctor...is there anything I can do?"

"Just stay behind me, grab my belt and go where I go, do what I say...no matter what happens just stay behind me and do what the hell I say!" Mike knew there were two additional terrorists somewhere close.

Mike stood up into a high crouch, flung the office door open, and carefully moved into the hallway with Sarah in-tow. He slowly moved toward the three terrorists, knelt, and made sure they were dead. Arriving at the corner at the end of the hallway, he peered to his right down the next hall leading to an interior fire escape...all clear, he thought to himself.

Mike paused, turned to his left, used his hand to move Sarah and they both sat with their backs to the wall.

"Listen to me, Sarah; we have to make our way to the roof. You have to stay right with me unless I tell you otherwise—you have to do exactly what I say, when I say, and how I say, do you understand?"

"I understand, but you've been shot. I mean...you're hurt," Sarah's voice was just above a whisper and thick with concern.

"They just winged me Sarah — just nicked me up a bit," Mike's eyes and voice softened as he answered Sarah, trying to reassure her.

Sarah was trembling as she looked at Mike Hampton's increasingly bloody clothes. She wanted to reach up and touch his arm, squeeze it and try to stop the bleeding, but she didn't dare. He hadn't "told her" to do anything.

"Eagle Control, Eagle 9-9," Mike said into the radio mic.
"Go ahead, 9-9."
"Eagle 9-9 plus 1 moving to position bravo, two hostiles still active in my area, copy?" Mike reported.
"Control copy, 9-9...break...Eagle Control, all Eagle units, 9-9 plus one moving to position bravo. Let's wrap this up."

Mike stood back up into his high crouch, reached back, grabbed Sarah's hand, and firmly placed it on his web belt, shaking it slightly to indicate that he wanted her to hold on to him right there. The pair moved cautiously down the hallway to the fire escape door, Mike checking for broken glass and other debris as they walked so that Sarah wouldn't injure her feet.

Mike peered through the window of the fire escape door, first up the stairs and then down, as far as he could see. He reached back, removed Sarah's hand from his belt, and motioned for her to stay where she was. He slowly opened the door and checked the stairwell landing...clear, he thought to himself as he nodded. He motioned for Sarah to re-attach herself to his belt.

The sound of gunfire continuously echoed up the stairwell as Sarah and Mike made their way upstairs toward the roof, his M-4 in a firing position as they walked, aiming up the stairs ahead of them. Sarah walked carefully and stayed as close to Mike as she could without tripping him.

As they walked, Sarah thought to herself how strangely calm she had suddenly become since watching Mike in that gunfight back at the office—watched as he was wounded. Thinking about the range of emotions she had been through over the course of the past two days confused her. Some of her emotions seemed misplaced to her, inappropriate for the moment. She should be in fear at that very moment as they walked, she thought, but she was somehow confident in Mike and his abilities, his determination, and she felt safe.

Mike abruptly stopped and dropped to one knee while looking up the stairs as he and Sarah approached the 70th floor landing. He held his rifle with his left hand, reached down with his right, removed Sarah's hand from his belt, and motioned for her to sit still. He slowly crept up to the stairway landing, and then knelt again. He glanced back at Sarah, now 10 feet away from him, and again motioned for her to stay put. He refocused his attention to the top of the stairs.

Two ISIS terrorists appeared at the top of the stairs, "Allahu Akbar!" they shouted as they began firing at Mike. Mike returned fire, several 3-round bursts from his M-4, 7.62 rounds impacting the floor and walls around him. One terrorist immediately went down, dead, as the other dropped to a knee wounded.

One of the terrorist's bullets impacted Mike's M-4, shattering the upper receiver and knocking the weapon from his hand. Another bullet struck his ballistic vest on his right side in the middle of his ribcage, momentarily squeezing the air from his lungs.

Mike rolled out of position for cover, drew his Colt 1911 .45 from the holster strapped to his right thigh as bullets narrowly missed him. He rolled back into position and again returned fire. He dropped his empty magazine with one hand while reloading with the other hand. Two more shots from Mike and the last terrorist was down.

Mike Hampton kept his .45 trained up the stairs, waiting, watching as his heart raced, his breathing rapid and shallow. He braved a moment to take his eyes from the staircase in front of him to glance down at Sarah as he struggle for deep breaths to slow his heart rate, worried that the incoming fire could have ricocheted and wounded her.

Sarah's entire body was stiff with fear, but she managed a slight smile as Mike looked at her. He nodded to her, silently asking if she was okay, and she nodded back, yes. He moved his head, motioning for her to join him up the stairs. Sarah immediately moved up the stairs, crouched next to Mike, and grabbed the back of his web belt. Mike stood, and the pair started up the stairs again.

"Crap," Mike said with frustration as he stopped in the stairwell one floor down from the roof. "There's broken glass on the stairs and landing, and you're barefoot. Come here," Mike motioned for Sarah to move in front of him. "I'm going to have to carry you the rest of the way," he said as he bent down to pick her up.

"You can't carry me, you're hurt...you're shot, for Christ's sake."

"I'm fine, Sarah, they just winged me."

"Yeah, yeah, I know, just nicked you up a bit...right?" Sarah said sarcastically.

"Right," Mike replied approvingly.

Mike reached down and picked Sarah up in both arms so she was across his waist and chest, one hand under her bare thighs and buttocks, the other behind her back, her head to his left, and carried her up the last two flights of stairs to the door leading out to the roof.

"I swear, Sarah, I'm not trying to cop a feel here, but there really is no other way to carry you...I promise," Mike pleaded embarrassingly as he walked, thinking about how Sarah was only slightly older than his youngest daughter.

"Don't worry," Sarah replied softly as she teasingly moved her buttocks in his arms, squirmed a little, playfully smiling at him.

Mike opened the last door and carried Sarah to a corner of the roof where there was a pre-positioned equipment bag. He gently placed her on the roof and motioned for her to sit with her back against the high wall. He sat next to her on her right side, his back against the wall as he watched the doorways in front of them.

"Eagle Control, Eagle 9-9," Mike said as he keyed his radio mic.

"*Go ahead, 9-9,*" the voice answered through his earpiece.

"Eagle 9-9 plus one at Bravo, time hack."

"*Copy, 9-9, time hack is 0253.*"

"Copy. Operational status?"

"*Eagle 9-9, remaining hostages are out—four wounded—Eagle units...five wounded, zero dead, repeat, zero dead. Approximately 15 enemy remaining on various floors...some moving high toward you.*"

"9-9, copy."

Sarah stared at Mike as he talked. It bothered her that she could only hear his side of the conversation. She wanted to know what was going on, how his men and the other hostages were. She also pondered the enigma sitting with her. She couldn't put her finger on what it was, but there was something about him that was beyond intrigue.

"We're going to sit tight for just a few minutes, Sarah," Mike said. "Then we'll get you out of here," he nodded to her.

"Well, if we have a few minutes then let's do something about that bleeding," Sarah said as she reached for Mike's wounded shoulder.

"I'm fine," Mike reiterated.

"Good Lord, you big strong man...I know, I know, they just winged you, just nicked you up a bit," Sarah's voice was thick with sarcasm.

"Well, it's true," Mike said somewhat sheepishly. It reminded him of past conversations he'd had with his wife over the years, when he was still a special agent with the Air Force Office of Special Investigations and working tactical counterintelligence in the Philippines.

"Let me see your arm," Sarah ordered as she twisted her body to face Mike and look at his shoulder. "I wish I had some bandages or gauze or something."

"I have some first aid stuff in that pocket on my left thigh, if you insist on nursing me."

"Why didn't you tell me that before?" Sarah snapped.

"Um, because we had someplace to be and people to kill," Mike replied somewhat playfully. "Besides," he said, it's just a through-and-through wound that barely even found some meat—didn't hit any bone or organs...not a problem."

Sarah reached into Mike's thigh pocket and pulled out four small packages of gauze. She carefully found the hole in his shirtsleeve and tore it open, revealing his long sleeve spandex shirt underneath.

"Really? Spandex?" she looked at him disapprovingly.

"What can I say...it's functional and makes me feel pretty," Mike smiled at her beneath his ski mask.

Sarah packed both sides of his upper left arm with the gauze, reached back into his pocket, retrieving a small bandana and tied it around his arm.

Mike wasn't used to the attention and it made him somewhat uncomfortable as he sat beside Sarah, but he had to ignore it and concentrate on the last part of his mission. The mission timeline was off, late. He had planned for the shooting in the building to be finished, or at least seriously subsided, by the time he made it to the roof with Sarah so a helicopter could pick them up, but his men were still fighting ISIS on many of the floors below, making it too dangerous for the helicopter. He knew it was risky, but it was time to get her away from the building. It was time for plan "B."

"Let me ask you something, Sarah," Mike started. "Have you ever been skydiving or base-jumping?"

"No, I haven't. Why do you...oh no," Sarah said as her shoulders dropped. "Don't tell me, please don't tell me..."

"Yep, today's your lucky day."

"Oh, hell no."

"Yep."

"Well do you at least have more wine before we go?"

"Nope."

"Damn it."

Mike reached into the large equipment bag he prepositioned when he parachuted onto the roof of the building earlier in the morning. He took out two personal harnesses and a parachute designed for base-jumping, and then stood as Sarah watched intently.

Mike took his weapons off, his web gear and then his ballistic vest, neatly placing them all in the equipment bag. He took off his black fatigue blouse revealing his muscular body beneath the tight spandex, folded the blouse, leaned down, and placed it in the bag. Sarah took a sudden deep breath, silently gasped a little, as Mike took off his Kevlar helmet and goggles hoping that he was about to finally take off his ski mask. He placed his helmet in the bag and left his ski mask in place.

Sarah watched admiringly as Mike put on his harness without saying a word and as if he'd done it a thousand times before. She had been apprehensive at first, when he first mentioned base-jumping, more than she revealed, but suddenly felt calm again as she watched Mike work. He put his parachute on and adjusted the harness.

"Okay, Sarah," Mike said as he stepped in front of her with her harness in his hand and knelt down. "We can do this one of two ways. I can connect the back of your harness to the front of mine, like I'm supposed to do with a tandem student jumper, or I can connect you face-to-face with me...your choice." Mike said, matter-of-factly as he held out the harness toward Sarah. "If I connect your back to my front, then you're going to be looking straight down over 1,000 feet onto South Hope Street for a few seconds when we jump."

"Oh, face-to-face," Sarah replied, emphatically. "Definitely face-to-face."

Mike squatted in front of Sarah and helped her into her harness, careful not to touch her inappropriately as he worked. He tightened the harness around her upper thighs, moving her shirt as he needed and accidentally revealing the front of her panties. He turned his head and looked up at the stars in the early morning sky, finishing his work without looking as a young, girlish smile creased Sarah's lips. This man is a real gentleman, Sarah thought, truly chivalric.

He cinched the harness until it was snug, but before, he hoped, it was uncomfortable on her bare skin. He then adjusted the top of the harness around her shoulders and chest, again careful not to touch her inappropriately.

Mike stepped back, squatted, and motioned to Sarah, "Sit on my lap, right here on my thighs facing me." He patted his thighs as he spoke.

Sarah stepped toward Mike, spread her legs around his, and sat on his thighs as she wrapped her arms around his shoulders and placed her cheek next to his masked cheek.

"I have to reach down between us and connect our "D" rings, Sarah," Mike said as he reached down low into the very small space between their waists.

"Oh," Sarah said as she squirmed a little. "Third base!" she answered teasingly, with a tone of approval.

Mike just dropped his head and chuckled, his shoulders bobbing up and down as he tried to work.

"I guess I asked for that."

"Yes, you did."

"Okay," Mike said, as he put his arms around Sarah and stood up. "Slide your hands around to my back and under my parachute. Don't reach over the parachute, hold it, or get in its way. Put your face against my neck," Mike instructed. "Wrap your legs around my waist and lock your ankles."

Mike carried Sarah across the roof to some scaffolding left by construction workers days before, near the edge of the building. He used the scaffolding to get onto the ledge of the U.S. Bank Tower's crown and, without warning to Sarah, jumped into the darkness.

Sarah clutched Mike as she had never clutched anything or anyone before in her life as the pair floated down in the early morning LA darkness to the street below. Mike guided the parachute away from the Bank Tower and adjacent buildings during their decent, skillfully driving toward a preplanned landing zone where some of his men and FBI special agent Craig Buckley would meet them, and away from the prying eyes and cameras of the media.

Four of Mike Hampton's men and several FBI agents ran to Mike and Sarah as they landed in the middle of the intersection of South Hope Street and West 4th. Sarah was startled as men very roughly reached between her and Mike and disconnected the D-rings connecting her to Mike as she unwrapped her legs from around his waist, and stood on her own. She looked questioningly into Mike's eyes, almost pleading.

Mike simply nodded to Sarah as two men helped collect his parachute and remove his harness, two other men removing her harness in the dimly lit street. She protested as the men pulled her by the arms toward a waiting ambulance. She tried to pull free and walk back toward Mike, but to no avail. The men were determined to put her in the ambulance.

"No!" Sarah yelled. "No! *He* needs the doctor, not me! He's been shot—he needs a doctor!"

A black Lincoln Continental pulled up and stopped near Mike. The front passenger door swung open, and Craig Buckley motioned for Mike Hampton to join him as Mike's men and FBI agents took Sarah to the ambulance. Mike smiled and again nodded to Sarah, as he removed his ski mask giving her one brief glimpse of his face through the darkness.

CHAPTER SEVEN

"In my dreams I hear again the crash of guns, the rattle of musketry, the strange, mournful mutter of the battlefield." —Douglas MacArthur

Every light in Sarah Tomzewski's modest Hollywood Hills home was on except in her bedroom, the dimly lit room illuminated by the hall light just outside her bedroom door. Sammy, her small, 6-year old black and white rescue puppy lay next to her, cuddled up against her.

Three months after her harrowing ordeal in the U.S. Bank Tower, after watching Anne's murder, the sleepless nights were mounting. On this night, it began slowly at first. Intrusive thoughts at work made her forget her lines while filming her new movie. She tried to focus, but they persisted. She often excused herself from the movie set, walked to a dark corner, pulled out a small silver flask, and took a drink of Pinot Noir. She tried to refocus on her work during the day, but the demons persisted.

At one o'clock in the morning, a dimly lit room inside a brightly lit house, the intrusive thoughts morphed into bad dreams...every night, her quixotic hope for peaceful slumber again turned into fidgeting, tossing, and turning. The drinking made it worse.

Cold drops of sweat rolled off her body like rain from a tin roof, soaking the sheets and pillow. The anguished mumbling began to crescendo until Sarah was yelling at the demons in the night with a full throat, "No! No! My God!"

She violently thrashed as she yelled, her arms swinging wildly and legs flailing away, ripping the covers from her naked body as she tried to slap the gun away from Anne's head in her dream, she screamed again, "No!"

She rolled from the bed onto the floor and pushed her back against the bedroom wall for protection. Her heart raced, breathing rapid and shallow, hands shaking and wet as she reached for her silver flask, eyes scanning the bedroom for her attackers, she peered through the bedroom door and listened.

There was no one there—there was never anyone there. She took a sip of Pinot from the flask, closed it, clutched it to her chest, and sobbed quietly.

"Where is he?" she mumbled through her tears. "Who is he? Anne..." She cried as she tried to wipe Anne's dried blood from the side of her face, blood long since washed away.

Sarah dried her eyes and looked around her room, still sitting naked on the floor. The room was modestly but neatly appointed; a four-post double bed with satin sheets and a comforter, a padded bench at the foot of her bed—a Key Largo South to the Sea dresser with a distressed Sienna finish and mirror across the room from the bed and against the wall. She glanced at her pictures and art hanging from the walls. Stuff, Sarah thought, just a bunch of junk, pretentious junk at that.

Sarah took another sip of Pinot from the silver flask, his silver flask, and checked the clock again...1:20 AM. After a little quick math in her head, she reached onto the nightstand beside her and grabbed her phone—9:20 PM in Auckland, she thought

"Hello, Sarah," Sarah's mother answered the phone in her mixed Polish-New Zealand accent. *"How are you?"*

"Oh, you know me, Mum, can't sleep...always the night owl."

"You can't lie to me, Sarah. You've been crying again—I can hear it in your voice."

"I'm okay, Mum, just normal crap at work. The director's stupid, the script is stupid, the whole damn movie is stupid, and I don't know why I signed on in the first place," Sarah lied again.

"Sarah, my dear, you have to talk to someone. You have too..."

"I am talking to someone, Mum, I'm talking to you, I talk to my friends, I talk," Sarah objected.

"You know what I mean, Honey."

"I don't need a shrink or a therapist, Mum, I'm fine...I'll be fine...I can handle this. There's no problem. I just couldn't sleep tonight so I thought I'd call. That's all."

"I know you're a strong and smart woman, Sarah, your father and I raised you to be that way. But remember, Honey, everybody needs somebody sometime."

"Really, Mum," Sarah chuckled. "You're quoting Keith Urban song lyrics to me now? Really?"

"You know I'm right, Honey, you need somebody right now, you need to talk to a professional. You yelled at your father when we were there after your rescue, you yelled at poor little Sammy and you're cutting yourself off from the world. Now you're having trouble at work."

Sarah knew her mother was right; she had isolated herself, holed up in her Hollywood Hills home, only going to work at the studio lot and back home again, and her new security guards always drove her. As often as they invited her, she never went out with her friends, not since her second week home after the rescue. She ordered her groceries on-line, including her wine, and had them delivered. She made no public appearances since her initial press conference three months ago and she was no longer active on social media. Her fans missed her and were restless.

"I'll be fine, Mum, I promise. It's all just temporary...it'll pass," Sarah conceded trouble to her mother.

"Sarah, do you remember what I told you when you were a little girl in dance classes? I told you then, Biedny tancerz będzie przeszkadzało nawet przez rąbek spódnicy, my little honey."

"I know, Mum, I remember... A poor dancer will be disturbed even by the hem of her skirt," Sarah repeated the Polish to English translation.

"You are a poor dancer right now, Sarah, because you cannot concentrate on your work. You have things you must attend to, things you must talk about and resolve, Honey. Your movie, your director, your script are only stupid because everything bothers you right now, even the hem on your skirt. You must heal so you can be a good dancer again. I want to see you dance again, Honey"

"*Kocham cie, Matka,*" Sarah paid her mother respect by speaking to her in Polish.

"I love you too, Sarah," her mother repeated the Polish to English translation.

Sarah lay in bed staring at the ceiling, watching the ceiling fan go round and round, the blades perfectly balanced and spinning smoothly. She didn't dare close her eyes, not again. She peered towards the bedroom door and wondered if she should close it for protection or leave it open so she could see "them" coming. Should I turn off the lights so I can hide in the darkness if they do come? She looked at the curtains on her bedroom window and saw the reflection of the blazing white floodlights outside that the security company installed two months before.

Sarah knew there were two men in dark suits, squiggly little wires running up the back of their coats, out through the collar and to their ears, security guards, patrolling her yard, keeping watch over her through the night...big men, armed men, Secret Services types. She felt stupid, childish, and ashamed. She was better than this, she thought, tougher. "I can handle it," she muttered to the universe. "I can handle it."

Sarah glanced over to the clock...3:30 AM. She got out of bed and threw her robe on over a pair of yoga pants and a skin tight workout shirt, shuffled to the kitchen and put on a pot of coffee. As the coffee pot gurgled and belched, she called her new agent, Burt, and left a message.

"Hey Burt, this is Sarah, see if you can book me on any of the LA based talk shows—I'll do them all—fit them in with my shooting schedule for the movie...I'll send you the latest call sheets for the movie if you need my schedule. It's time for me to get back out in the public again."

Sarah had no desire to do any of the talk shows, no interviews because she knew what they would all want to talk about, what the public wanted her to talk about, and she didn't know if she could hold herself together during an interview like that. But, she had a different thought this time. Maybe, just maybe, she thought, she could draw "him" out by doing interviews. She wanted to find him.

When the coffee was finished, she poured two large mugs and walked them out the front door to her two security guards. She liked them and figured she could spend a little time with them without either of them asking her a thousand questions about her ordeal. But she also had a few questions of her own.

"Good morning, Jack," Sarah started. "Coffee?" She held one mug out to Jack.

"Thank you, Miss Tomzewski. I have a thermos, but your coffee is always better."

Jack Byler was a robust black man, somewhere over 6'5" tall, and about 280 pounds of muscle. Sarah didn't know it, she never bothered to ask, but he was a former Army Ranger with several tours of duty in Iraq and Afghanistan. He had a sort of high-pitched voice that didn't match his massive size, and a very distinctive Southern drawl.

"Where's Sam?" Sarah asked.

"He's round back. You can set his coffee down, Ma'am, and I'll make sure he gets it."

"Let me ask you something, Jack. The LAPD and the FBI both told me that you don't work for them, you're private security guys, right?"

"Ma'am, you know I can't answer a whole lot of questions," Jack said as he slowly sipped the hot coffee.

"I know, Jack, and I don't want to make you uncomfortable. But if you are private security then why don't I get a bill, how come I'm not paying for it? I mean, I know the studio isn't paying for it, so who is?"

"Miss Tomzewski, all I know is that Sam and I have the night shift and we're going to protect you from everything and everybody. I don't get involved in paperwork, business stuff, or who's paying for what. I just know that nobody's going to hurt you while I'm here."

"Okay, Jack," Sarah said. "Just to let you and Sam know, I'll be ready to leave for work around 6:30. Oh, and please call me Sarah and not ma'am or miss...okay?"

"Yes Ma'am, Miss Sarah," Jack spoke with his lips just touching the rim of the mug, looking down at Sarah with a little playful smile in his eyes.

Who in the world is paying for my security, Sarah wondered as she walked back into her house. Who does Jack work for if he's not a cop, not FBI. "Yep, time to do some interviews, some talk shows," Sarah muttered to Sammy. "Time to start getting some answers, Sammy, time to start trying to find that man, yes it is," Sarah nuzzled her puppy as she walked to her room to clean-up and dress for another day of shooting a stupid movie, with a stupid script, and a stupid director.

Mike squirmed in the big, over stuffed leather easy chair in the den of his spacious, two-story, 6-bedroom, 4-bath home on the southern tip of Merritt Island, Florida, as he watched television, trying to get comfortable with his cracked and bruised ribs...two cracked ribs and three bruised when the 7.62 millimeter bullets fired from the terrorist's AK-47s slammed into his ballistic vest three months before.

"Crap," he muttered to himself as he shifted in the chair trying not to spill his Jack Daniel's.

Mike Hampton hadn't planned on "snow birding" in Florida for the winter, but the bullet holes in his left shoulder and hip changed his plans. He had originally planned on splitting his time between his two houses, one in Virginia Beach, the other on Merritt Island. He wanted to spend Christmas with his daughters and two grandsons in Florida, but then head back up to Virginia because he loved the cold Mid-Atlantic winters, a little snow and ice, but not too much. But a little time to convalesce meant a few months longer in the Eastern Central Florida warmth at his spacious house nestled between the Banana and Indian rivers, and lots of time with his two grandsons.

Mike saw Sarah as he channel surfed past the entertainment network channel, and quickly flipped the channel back. He recognized the car she got out of, and the two-burley men in dark suits who got out with her, his men, as she walked toward a store on Rodeo Drive. He watched as the cameraman approached her on the sidewalk trying to get a live interview with the now elusive star. His men moved closer to her and assumed a protective stance.

"Miss Tomzewski," the entertainment reporter said, "do you have a minute for us?"

"For you? Of course I do," Sarah answered happily as she walked toward the camera, her entire face smiling a plastic smile, eyes covered by sunglasses. She knew she was "playing a part" and hoped the camera, and her fans, wouldn't notice.

Mike smiled, she looks happy enough, he thought. That's good. But his investigative nature, 20-plus years in military law enforcement and his counterintelligence days, kicked in. His instincts caused him to automatically check her clothes to see if she was dressed as she normally dressed, was she herself, was she really ok, or were those just words?

Mike's men gave him regular reports of her leaving the lights on inside her house nightly, all of them, and bringing them coffee at all hours of the night and day. He knew she wasn't sleeping.

"What can I do for you gentlemen?" Sarah asked.

"Tell us how you are, Sarah, tell your fans how you are and what you've been doing."

"Well, I took a little hiatus and vacationed with my parents in New Zealand, rested up a bit, and now I'm shooting a new movie." Sarah began to move toward the store entrance, not wanting to prolong the interview, but just give a tease and pretend to be ok, pretend that all was normal.

"In your press release three months ago you talked about the man who rescued you and how you didn't know who he was, have you found out, have you talked to him since?"

"No, I haven't," something in Sarah's voice changed as she answered.

"What do you know about him, Sarah, anything?" the cameraman asked.

"I just know he's a wonderful man with wonderful, gentle, revealing brown eyes."

"So you haven't had any contact with him—don't know anything else about the man behind the eyes?" they pressed.

Mike grunted and took a drink of his Jack Daniel's. "The man behind the eyes," he mused. "That's gonna stick."

"Can you tell us anything else, how you're doing," they asked.

"Well, I'm taping the Ellen Show tomorrow so you'll just have to wait for that to air I guess," Sarah turned and walked into the store, Mike's two men trailing her.

Mike switched off the television and stood up. I guess I'm healed up enough for a nice long bike ride, he thought.

Wintering in Florida also meant that Mike Hampton would get a lot more hours on his Harley Fat Boy, riding Highway A1A south from Satellite Beach, through Vero Beach, and down to Ft. Pierce. At Ft. Pierce, he usually liked to cross the river back over to U.S. Highway 1 for the drive back home. He'd cross from the mainland over the Pineda Causeway and back to his house on Merritt Island. It was always a nice ride that took him about half a day, with stops to eat and look at the scenery. Unlike the Virginia law, he didn't need a helmet in Florida, and he especially loved that.

Mike stopped on his way out to the garage, sat at the dining room table and pulled out his phone.

"Yes Sir, Mr. H.," Angela Montero said when she answered Mike's call.

"Do me a favor, Angela. Sarah is taping the Ellen Show tomorrow...send two dozen long stem roses to the studio, marked for Sarah and I'll email you a note I want attached later."

"Wow, Mr. H., been a long time since you sent flowers to anyone," Angela teased. *"But its way past time you started thinking about dating again, it's been a year and a half now, Mr. H., and I think Sarah Tomzewski is perfect for you!"*

"Save it, Angela, don't start on me," Mike said with a little aggravation. "It's just an apology for causing her so much consternation over the past three months. You just order the flowers and I'll email the note to you after my bike ride."

"Yes Sir, but...."

"Goodbye, Angela," Mike hung up and walked out to his garage for his afternoon ride.

CHAPTER EIGHT

"Death's random touch; bullets missed by fractions, a millimeter here and a whisper there confuse the mind and wound the survivor's soul." —Steve Bussey

Wardrobe, hair, and make-up done, Sarah very nervously stood next to the producer backstage waiting for Ellen to introduce her to the audience. She closed her eyes, lowered her head, and attempted to steal herself for the interview, praying for control over her emotions. She had always described herself as a crier, but standing and waiting at that moment, she felt as if she was about to completely fall apart and questioned her decision to do interviews. It's just too soon, she thought.

Sarah worried about how she looked, more for the entertainment tabloids than for the audience, and for "him." Two nights before, she placed her under-eye moisturizing gel in the refrigerator to chill it so it would better reduce the puffiness under her eyes, the dark, puffy circles from too much wine and not enough sleep, the dehydration. The make-up artist at The Ellen Show spent extra time airbrushing Sarah's face to hide that puffiness and to contour her cheekbones and chin, using a bronzer to give her some color and bring her back to life, a Hollywood attempt to make a young, beautiful actress look herself again in the age of high definition television. The cosmetologist ensured Sarah's long blonde hair had a little extra body and, parted on the left side, framed her face in the best way possible.

"Ladies and gentlemen," Ellen said, "please help me welcome the incredibly talented and beautiful Sarah

Tomzewski to the show in her first interview since the horrific events at the U.S. Bank Tower in downtown LA three months ago."

With a deep sigh, her shoulders rising and falling with her chest, "I've got this," Sarah muttered, softening her fake plastic smile, as she walked out from behind the curtain. The audience erupted with applause as she walked toward Ellen in her knee length, form fitting winter-white dress with a plunging neckline with gold lace framing her ample cleavage, leopard print Louboutin stiletto heel shoes.

"Now, tell us how you are, Sarah," Ellen started the interview.

"Thank you Ellen, and thanks to your audience, what a wonderful group and such a warm welcome, thank you all," Sarah tried to act as naturally as she could.

"I'm doing so well, Ellen, it's so wonderful to be home after...you know...and the little vacation in New Zealand with my parents for the holidays...back to work, back to normal." Sarah lied.

"Wow, that's wonderful," Ellen followed-up, "but I can't imagine being back to normal after what you went through. I'd be a basket case. Can you tell us about it?"

Sarah clinched her lips and breathed deeply through her nose, sighed again as she felt her emotions welling up inside her. She unconsciously scanned the audience, not knowing for what or who she was looking. She tried to turn slightly to use the corner of her eye to look to the curtain backstage, and was relieved to see her big, burly bodyguard. Her eyes checked each cameraman, each producer, and the director. She fidgeted in her chair, not knowing why she was uncomfortable.

"I'm sure everyone can understand that some things are still too difficult to talk about right now, at least with much detail. Some of the emotions are still kind of raw. Let's just say that it was horrific, terrifying, but turned out a lot better than it could have, better than it should have...for me anyway."

Ellen didn't want to interrupt as Sarah paused and thought. Up close, Ellen could see the wetness in Sarah's eyes as she spoke and the very slight shaking of her shoulders, almost a shiver. She could see the make-up artist's work on Sarah's face.

"So many wonderful people, moms, dads and quite a few children were killed that day and for some reason, I don't know why, but I was spared...I was rescued. But Anne, poor Anne Campbell, my agent, didn't make it, she wasn't rescued," Sarah's voice lowered as she spoke, cracked as she looked away from Ellen and at the floor, then the audience.

Sarah sat with her knees together and at an oblique angle to the audience as she and Ellen talked, her hands neatly folded in her lap, occasionally dabbing tears from the corner of her eye with a tissue. She took deep cleansing breaths when she felt her emotions welling up as she described Anne Campbell's murder, the sounds, and smells in the building—the panicked screaming in the hallways during what was now classified the single worst terrorist attack on U.S. soil since 9/11.

"It's all just so confusing when you think about the randomness of it all," Sarah said softly, looking out toward the audience, but over their heads.

"I was in that lobby just moments before it all broke out, what if I had still been there, why wasn't I still there?" she dabbed her tears. "And then, I was sitting right there in the bottom of that closet with Anne. Why Anne and not me, why not both of us? Why did I survive?" Sarah's voice cracked, she cleared her throat and tried to work up a little moisture in her mouth. She sensed an unfamiliar taste on her tongue and in her mouth that she just couldn't place. She thought about it as Ellen spoke to the audience for a minute and decided it was kind of a metallic taste.

Sarah suddenly felt herself become agitated. She noticed the heat from the studio lights and felt as if they were making her sweat unnecessarily. She dabbed the tissue across her forehead. Her chair was stiff and hard. She shifted her position, squirmed a little trying to find a modicum of comfort. Why is that stupid director flashing hand signals at Ellen, she wondered - that's idiotic, the entire audience can see the moron.

And that audience, she thought as Ellen talked, what in the hell is that woman wearing, Sarah wondered, that doesn't even match - who the hell goes out in public like that?

"Sarah...dear...are you with us?" Ellen said. "Sarah?"

"Oh yes, I'm sorry, just day dreaming a bit, I guess," Sarah snapped back into reality.

"So," Ellen started, "tell us about this man who rescued you, parachuted off the top of a 73-story building with you hooked to his chest...the man behind the eyes as that one entertainment network called him."

Sarah took a deep breath again. This is it, she thought, the only reason she wanted to do an interview, this one question. She shifted in her uncomfortable chair again, sat a little more upright, shoulders back, chin up, eyes serious but soft. For the first time during the interview, Sarah looked directly into the television camera with the red light atop it.

"He's a wonderful man," Sarah said. "And so paradoxical, such an enigma."

"And I understand that all you could see were his eyes, right?" Ellen Said. "You could only see like this much of his face," Ellen used her hands to form an oval around her own eyes from the top of her nose up and around her eyebrows."

"Yes, that's all, "Sarah answered." Until the very end when he took off his ski mask and I got a quick glimpse of his face from a distance and in the dark as some guys pulled me into the ambulance." Sarah took another deep breath through her nose and again adjusted her posture, fidgeted in her chair.

"He is a very muscular man, very well built, and I guess over six feet tall, maybe 6-2," Sarah continued. "With a sexy, deep, comforting voice. But those eyes, those soft brown eyes, they were so comforting and so revealing. He had little crow's feet in the corners of his eyes...I guess he's an older man and he's probably been out in the sun a lot, seems like a real outdoors guy. I can only imagine the things those eyes have seen, the danger, the death, the horror."

"Ooh, sexy baby! What do you mean he was an enigma, such a paradox?" Ellen asked.

"Well," Sarah started, "you have this man who is risking his life, ended up killing five terrorists during the rescue and I guess he's done that before because he really seemed like he knew what he was doing, but his touch was so gentle, his voice was so comforting—so violent yet so gentle. When he first came into the room where I was held, he had to check me out to see if I was injured—checked my whole body by, you know, touching..."

"Okay," Ellen said, "you've got my attention now...you've got all our attention," Ellen teased and tried to lighten the mood.

Sarah recounted the entire scene for Ellen and her audience, how her rescuer had touched her checking for injuries, how she could see him smile under his ski mask, the way he joked with her while everyone's life was on the line, "cop humor," he called it. She described how he kept apologizing for touching her, almost pleading for her not to think he was touching her gratuitously, or "trying to cop a feel," as he put it. She had an excited quality to her voice as she spoke with enthusiasm and the words just flowed as if professional writers scripted them all.

"Now remember," Sarah explained, "this is a man who risks his life, I don't know how often or how many times, a man I watched fight and get shot, but his touch was so gentle, his manner so easy and his only focus seemed to be making me feel safe and comfortable. I just thought it was all so paradoxical."

"Well, since we're talking about your man behind the eyes," Ellen started," there is a little something here for you, something that was sent to the studio today." Ellen waved to her producer to bring the package out.

"This package was delivered to our studio today by messenger, with a note addressed to me and asking me to give this to you, Sarah, after having it checked out by the bomb squad"...the audience laughed..."I'm serious...the note said after I had the package checked out by security and the bomb squad," Ellen joined the audience in laughter as Sarah sat with both hands covering her mouth.

The producer handed a very long rectangular box elegantly wrapped in silver paper and tied with red ribbon and a large red bow, to Sarah. Her mouth was slightly open as she looked in stunned silence first at the producer, then Ellen, then shot her eyes toward the camera with the red light atop, and the audience. She was both speechless and breathless.

"Now, before you open that," Ellen said to Sarah," let me assure everyone that the package was fully checked by security and the LAPD bomb squad...and, let me read *my* note before you read yours, Sarah."

Sarah dabbed the sweat from her forehead, a few small tears from the corners of her eyes. She shifted in her chair again, and thought. She wanted to tear into the box, wanted to read the note, she knew, she thought, she hoped, it was from "him." Does he want to meet, she wondered. Does the note tell me who he is or anything about him, how I can find him, where I can find him? She felt the emotion welling up inside her as her mind raced.

"Okay Sarah, everyone, here's the note that came to me and my producers with the package. Dear Ellen, I do not mean to impose on your show...isn't that so sweet?" Ellen interrupted herself and looked up from the note to make a brief comment to her audience.

"However," she continued reading the note. "Would you please give this package to Sarah when she tapes your show? I will of course leave the logistics of it up to you, your producers, and Sarah—whether you give it to her before the show, during or after—after having security and the LAPD, maybe the bomb squad, check it...your choice. Very respectfully, Sarah's man behind the eyes."

Sarah's emotions overtook her and she began to sob. Her shoulders and chest bobbed up and down as she tried to catch her breath. She ran her fingers over the silver wrapping paper as a slideshow flashed in her mind—him kneeling in front of her and explaining, "I'm the good guys," his gentle touch as he checked her for injuries, his jokes, his eyes. Her mind raced with memories and questions, then fear. What will the note say? she wondered. Can we finally meet, or is this the final no?

Ellen looked to her producers and then threw in an unscheduled commercial break during the taping to let Sarah collect herself. She leaned across, placed her hand on Sarah, and rubbed her shoulder while the audience sat in silence. Sarah dabbed her tears and apologized to Ellen. She pulled out "his" note and read it silently.

"Okay, Sarah, do you want to share the note with everyone?" Ellen asked when they came back from the commercial break.

Sarah sighed deeply, her hands trembling, tried to clear her throat and fix her voice.

"You know, Ellen, if you don't mind, I think I'll keep this private for right now, keep it just for me for a little while. I apologize to your audience, to my fans, but I think I'll keep this just for me right now."

"I understand, Sarah," Ellen replied. "And I don't think the audience minds at all, I think we all understand," Ellen craned her neck and scanned the audience as they applauded, individual audience members nodded their heads in agreement.

Sarah trembled as she folded the card and placed it back into its envelope. She removed the ribbon from the long rectangular box, and then the silver wrapping paper. She took the lid off the box and held the box up for the audience to see the beautiful two dozen long stem roses.

She forced her lips to smile as she held back the cry, knowing her face was betraying her, her cheeks and chin quivering.

"Oh my God," Ellen said. "You mentioned that during the rescue he told you that you might be able to meet when he retires, right? He's still working?" Ellen asked Sarah.

"Yes, maybe when he retires."

"I guess we'll all just have to hope he lives long enough for Sarah to meet her man behind the eyes," Ellen said to the audience and the camera with the little red light on top as Sarah again wiped her tears away.

Sarah shivered with fear as Ellen spoke those words. She had never thought of that, never considered it, that he lives long enough for her to meet him. Will the randomness of death take him away from her the way it took Anne? She shuddered.

CHAPTER NINE

"Thus fought the heroes, tranquil their admirable hearts, violent their swords, resigned to kill and to die." —Jorge Luis Borges

Mike Hampton and his twenty-five men worked feverishly to load as many Christian families as they could into the trucks parked just outside the small Iraqi village 250 miles north of Baghdad on that cold March morning, the sun threatening to crest the horizon and expose their operation. Mothers holding small children wrapped in woolen blankets, crying, some screaming, clambered onto the old deuce and a half trucks with some assistance while the sounds of artillery and small arms continued closing in on them. Old men scurried around, checked every house, every building along the dried out dirt roads to ensure nobody was left behind as the town priest prayed and gave thanks.

His shoulder still sore from the wound sustained four months earlier, Mike carried the meager belongings of several families out of mud-brick shacks and scrap metal buildings, loading them onto trucks. The smell of the place bothered him, reminded him of the Philippines over two decades before, the smell of feces, urine commingling with charcoal smoke and diesel fumes...sickening, he thought, acrid. "At least it's not one hundred degrees and humid," he mumbled, "nice and cold."

"Bobby! Get these trucks the hell out of here!" Mike ordered. "Me and Tom will make a final sweep for stragglers," Mike said as he moved his M-4 rifle from his side and back to his chest, atop his ballistic vest.

"Eagle 9-9, this is Eagle 9-1," the radio crackled to life through Mike's earpiece.

"Go ahead, 9-1."

"We got trouble, Boss...ISIS has advanced units moving on your position from the west and north, looks like light mounted infantry—moving under artillery cover...copy?"

"I copy, 9-1...you just make sure the Peshmerga keep that road south open damn it!" Mike ordered.

"Bobby!" Mike shouted. "Get those fucking trucks rolling south baby—let's go, let's go! Pray faster, Padre, pray faster," Mike said to the village priest standing near-by.

A mud-brick house two blocks away suddenly exploded north of Mike's position as the first truck roared to life pumping thick, black diesel fumes into the already acrid air, and began to roll south, raining debris as civilians screamed and children cried. All of them had already heard what ISIS did to other Christians in Iraq and Syria—the murders, torture, sex slaves, hell on earth. Mike recalled a Bible passage from his youth—*then they will deliver you up to tribulation and put you to death, and you will be hated by all nations for my name's sake.*

Buildings continued to disappear in violent explosions of fire, mud-brick, and sheet metal—abandoned family heirlooms, evidence of family life covering centuries...gone. The debris rained down like fiery hail, almost biblical, as truck after truck roared to life taking 125 Christians, old men, women and young children to safety. All males in the village of fighting age long since killed by ISIS or converted to Islam and conscripted. Smoke from the now rapid explosions, one after another filled the air and mixed with the dust kicked up by the trucks on the dried out dirt road leading south. ISIS fought their way through the Peshmerga and to the outskirts of town.

"Eagle 9-9 to all Eagle units—fighting tactical withdraw—keep those rat bastards from reaching the trucks...keep their god damn heads down... I don't want any small arms fire hitting those kids in the back of the trucks..." Mike ordered.

The incoming artillery fell quiet, never a good sign, Mike thought. Members of ISIS clad in all black, faces covered, carrying their banners and flags, moved into the small Iraq Christian village. Fighting intensified as the sun broke the horizon, Mike's men engaging, and snipers providing over-watch from any elevated vantage point they could find. Several small units of five ISIS fighters each moved street by street, five man units supporting each other as they checked mud-brick homes and sheet metal buildings for Christians.

"Eagle 9-9 to all Eagle units—staggered withdraw to the Humvees—Eagle 9-3 on point, Eagle 9-6 take drag. . .snipers down. . ."

Mike and his men fought their way to the outskirts of the village and took cover in a washed out ravine about 100 yards to the south. Mortar fire and RPG rounds rocked their position as they returned fire, the fighting rapidly escalating. In-coming artillery shells began crashing around their position, close, too close for Mike's liking.

"Allied 1, Allied 1, this is Eagle 9-9, over," Mike squawked into his radio.

"Good morning, Eagle 9-9," Allied-1 responded. *"What can I do for you boys this morning?"*

"Allied-1, we could use a little close air support right about now. Screw the artillery coming from our west and just take those bastards out in the village."

"Eagle 9-9, pop smoke for identification."

"Allied 1, popping smoke...identify," Mike responded.

"Copy, Eagle 9-9...I have green smoke, repeat I see green...you and your boys are a little close there, brother...you sure?"

"Copy Allied 1, danger close, repeat, I copy danger close. Just take those bastards out—take out the village!" Mike replied firmly.

Within a minute from Mike's last radio transmission, the entire village began exploding from east to west. Dust, dirt, debris blew into Mike and his men's position with hurricane force as two U.S. Air Force F-16s streaked high across the sky. They held their heads and covered their ears from the repeated violent concussions as the debris-filled shock waves washed across them in the early morning twilight.

"Let's roll out!" Mike shouted to his men as he stood in a high crouch. He felt dizzy, the effects of the shock waves from the explosions he thought. "Shit, got my bell rung," he muttered.

He watched as his 25 men moved toward the five Humvees, counting each one as they moved, ensuring all his guys were moving. He looked back toward the village, looking for bad guys, looking for any of his men straggling.

As he started to move toward the last Humvee in line, a 7.62 round from an ISIS AK-47 struck the middle of his back in his ballistic vest, violently shoving him forward as if hit in the back at full force with a bat by a major league baseball player. Another tore through the skin and muscle of his upper right thigh just below his buttock. He went down hard, his head spinning. He struggled to keep his eyes open as he began crawling toward the Humvee, struggling to grab enough earth to pull himself along, struggling for the strength.

"9-9 is down...9-9 is down!" Bob Morton motioned to another Eagle team member as he ran back toward Mike. Bob knelt and checked Mike, started to tear his pant leg open to check the wound.

"Just get me in the god damn Humvee, Bob," Mike said as he winced in pain, struggling for breath and trying to keep his eyes open. "Just get me in the fucking truck," he whispered.

Bob Morton and Tom Beck dragged Mike Hampton to the last remaining Humvee as sporadic small arms fire from one or two remaining terrorists kicked up sand and dirt around them. Artillery shells in coming from the west began falling around their position again. Mike succumbed to his concussion, closed his eyes, and passed out.

"Boss is out cold," Bob Morton said as he began to administer first aid to Mike's leg inside the Humvee.

"How bad's he hit?" Tom Beck asked as he started up the Humvee and headed south down the dirt road.

"Oh hell, he's just shot in the ass," Bob gave Tom a quick glance. They both smiled and then broke out in full-throated laughter.

"Son of a bitch is going to hear about this for ever, I'll make damn sure of that," Bob laughed uncontrollably, barely getting the words out.

"Well, at least he'll go to a hospital this time," Tom said.

"No shit, only way this asshole ever goes to a hospital is if he's unconscious."

Bob Morton was a 32-year old former Navy SEAL. He was a solid 6-feet tall and 205 pounds of muscle and mean with too many tours of duty in Afghanistan and Iraq to count. During his eight years as a Navy SEAL, Bob deployed an average of 250 days a year, including deployments to the central Philippines and several parts of Africa including Somalia, and Libya. He looked the part; body scarred with old bullet and shrapnel wounds, like Mike's body. As most SEALs do, Bob let his black hair grow long and scraggly for deployments and wore a full-face beard, his beard stained from spitting his chew into an empty soda bottle and leaving little drippings down his chin.

The Humvees finally made it outside the range of ISIS artillery and small arms fire, on the road south to the joint forces base at Erbil, Iraq while Bob Morton continued to administer first aid to Mike. Bob really liked working for Mike Hampton over the past two years an often thought of that first chance meeting.

Three years ago, the Navy gave Bob Morton a general discharge for smacking an Afghani warlord. The man lied to Bob and Bob could not abide a liar, especially when that liar placed an entire operation at risk. After his discharge, Bob bummed around Virginia Beach, stayed close to the Navy bases where he'd served, Dam Neck and Little Creek Amphibious Base—stayed around the sailors he served with, some of his SEAL team members. After losing several jobs, his apartment, and his marriage temporarily, he started to drink. And then he drank more, and more. Mike found him sitting on a curb in front of a low-rent motel with not enough money for a room gave him a beer and asked him his story.

Before long, Mike rented Bob a room and sat outside while Bob showered and cleaned up, then took him for a good meal. They talked during the meal and Mike hired Bob on the spot, gave him a signing bonus so he could buy some new cloths, and set him up with a realtor to get a new apartment. Bob respected Mike a great deal for giving him another chance, but he also loved him like a father and would do anything for him, including loading him onto a C-17 medical evacuation flight from Erbil even when he knew it would piss off his boss.

Mike Hampton woke up at 35,000 feet lying on a bed anchored to the wall of the C-17. He felt weak and it was difficult to open his eyes, and keep them open for very long...stupid drugs, he thought. He craned his neck slightly and tried to inspect his surroundings; his ballistic vest and all of his gear was gone, IV in his left arm, naked under a sheet, bandages around his right thigh. In the shadowy belly of the C-17, Mike saw Air Force personnel in their desert tan flight suits attending to civilian casualties of the continuing war in Iraq, IV bags hanging from walls of the airframe and poles attached to gurneys and stretchers. He heard the low murmuring voices of medical personnel. Then, to his left, he saw Bob sitting in a jump seat grinning like the cat that just ate the canary.

"What in the hell are you smiling at, you smug bastard," Mike asked with a very aggravated tone.

"Who, me?" Bob replied happily. "I'm looking at my boss getting medivac'd for the first time since I've known him—

hard as hell to get you to even go to a damn doctor, much less get in an air ambulance."

"The rat bastards only winged me—you assholes couldn't just have Doc patch me up?"

"Yeah, yeah, yeah . . . they just nicked you up a bit...I know, I know . . . right in the ass baby! Concussed and shot in the ass!" Bob could barely get the words out before bursting into laughter. "Just relax, Boss, it's a long flight to Landstuhl, Germany.

Mike took a deep breath and thought for just one quick moment.

"I'll tell you a secret, Bob, just between you and me," Mike started as Bob just sat and looked at him.

"I'm getting too old and too slow for this shit. I've been hit now on our last two missions and, to be honest with you, I really think I'm starting to put you guys in a little needless danger, becoming a liability to you" Mike lay back on the bed and looked at the ceiling of the C-17 cargo bay as he spoke.

"You ain't slow, boss," Bob said with his Texas draw. "You just ain't lucky," Bob chuckled quietly. "You know me and the guys would fight the fires of hell with a squirt gun to face the devil himself with you because you never take stupid risks and you always have a plan," Bob's tone was more serious.

Thanks asshole," Mike replied sarcastically. "But the truth is, you and Tom had to come back for me and that put both of you at risk."

"You've gone back for people plenty of times, Boss, we all have. That's what we do."

"Well," Mike said thoughtfully, "I think it's time to retire from the operational crap and leave it all up to you guys," Mike's voice tailed off as he spoke, the drugs winning out and putting him back to sleep.

Sarah Tomzewski stood in stunned silence in the middle of her darkened living room, a glass of wine in her left hand, her old white robe thrown over her yoga pants and skintight workout shirt as the news anchor announced breaking news from Iraq.

"We have breaking news out of Iraq... an exclusive report from our Pentagon correspondent concerning a group of about two-dozen Americans who apparently conducted some sort of private operation in Northern Iraq...Jennifer, what can you tell us?"

"Dan, sources in the Pentagon speaking on condition of anonymity, have told us exclusively that a group of about two dozen Americans, all former servicemen, have conducted a private rescue operation in a small Iraqi Christian village in Northern Iraq, just outside what was once Iraq's largest Christian enclave in Qaraqou, but was destroyed by ISIS in 2014. Now, details are sketchy, at this point, Dan, but our sources are telling us that the group of Americans has successfully rescued over 100 Christians. The operation, however, was apparently not without casualties; sources told us that at least one American was severely wounded during heavy fighting and may have been killed, and they released this blurry photograph of medical personnel loading a man on a gurney onto a C-17 for medical transport to the U.S. Military hospital in Germany..Dan."

Sarah gasped, carefully placed her glass of wine on the end table with a shaky hand, stood back up and cupped both hands over her mouth. "It's *him*, she thought, I know it's "*him*." Please don't be dead," she muttered—"don't be dead...."

CHAPTER TEN

"Some things scratch the surface while others strike at your soul." —Gianna Perada Carini

Mike Hampton twisted, turned, fluffed his pillow, and tried everything else he knew of to get comfortable in his hospital bed, but nothing worked. His IV tube, oxygen, and wires to all the monitors kept tangling as he moved and agitated him. Landstuhl Regional Medical Center, the American hospital in Germany, was nice but he hated all hospitals, and doctors, and officers, and being laid up. Bob Morton was right; the only way to get Mike Hampton to go to the doctor or a hospital was for him to be incapacitated in some way. He usually had his private doctor travel with him to take care of him when he was injured, even shot, and it drove Dr. Welker crazy. He always tried to get Mike to go to an emergency room and always failed.

"Good morning Master Sergeant Hampton, how are you feeling today," Major Thornton said as he walked in Mike's brightly lit hospital room.

"I feel like crap, Doc... And I haven't been Master Sergeant Hampton since 2002. Just call me Mike, or Hampton or dumbass or something."

"You're ID card says Master Sergeant retired, and this is a military medical facility, so you'll receive the respect of your rank that you earned, *Master Sergeant*," the doctor placed a little emphasis on the last two words. "And you'll also show me the respect I know my oak leaf clusters have earned."

"Well yes sir, *Major*," Mike mimicked the doctor's emphasis.

In his own not-so-humble opinion, Mike Hampton served under some pretty bad officers during his career. One young lieutenant almost got him stabbed due to a very bad decision while breaking up a knife fight in the barracks in 1982 as a young base policeman. Another officer in 1989 almost got him and several of his men killed in the Philippines while working tactical counterintelligence and counter-insurgency. There had been other "bad" officers, but none of them had the opportunity to place Mike's life in jeopardy.

Major Thornton busied himself checking Mike's vital signs, inspecting his wound, checking his eyes, ears, and nose. He wrote notes on his clipboard as he worked, and Mike just laid there as if a baby monkey with its mother picking nits—annoyed.

"Let me ask you something, Master Sergeant," Major Thornton started. "It says here in your comprehensive medical file that you have PTSD symptoms."

"Don't bust my chops, Doc; I'm here because I got shot in the ass and my bell rung and not for foo-foo dusting."

"Are you enrolled at the VA or seeing anyone, going to counseling—anything?" the Major ignored Mike's protestations and continued.

"Sure, Doc, I go to counseling a couple nights a week at my local VFW. In fact, I go so often I have my own chair...right at the end of the bar where I can see the TV."

"Okay, Master Sergeant. I get it—big, tough guy like you can handle anything. It's nothing to be ashamed of or embarrassed by, you know."

"Who said I was embarrassed or ashamed?"

"I'm just saying, Master Sergeant, there's help out there for those who want it."

"Yeah, help from pill pushers after waiting a year for an appointment," Mike muttered.

The one thing Mike really was embarrassed about was his fear of needles. He absolutely hated needles. He'd rather fight an entire enemy battalion single handedly with nothing but a pistol than sit for a shot or an IV. And his regular doctor figured out a long time ago that getting blood from Mike Hampton for routine medical tests was nearly impossible. He always threatened to punch Mike in the nose to get a blood sample, and Mike returned the favor by threatening to kill his doctor.

Mike laid his head back on the pillow and stared at the fluorescent lights as the major babbled on and on about his PTSD. The problem was Mike knew the doctor was right. His late father, a military retiree, had PTSD and his little brother, a Desert Storm veteran, struggles with PTSD. He knew the doctor was right.

Mike would never admit it, except to himself, but he felt ashamed and embarrassed every single time he had a PTSD episode. He felt stupid. He felt that a man should be able to control his own mind and emotions. Whatever was bothering him, he thought. Whatever the details, he should be able to snap himself out of it, but he couldn't. He should be able to control it, but he couldn't. He sometimes felt less than a man, like a small child that can't control himself on the playground.

When he did listen, Mike heard the major express his concern that Mike lived alone and didn't have a service dog, or a cat, or a bird or even so much as a gold fish. Living alone, going home from work to an empty house, the major said, is not good for men and women with PTSD. They need companionship and some responsibility. They need love, even if just from an animal. People dealing with PTSD need to be involved and engaged or usually, they will isolate themselves from society to the extent possible for them, from society and family. Mike knew it was all true because it was exactly what he did in his own life.

"Okay Master Sergeant, I'll leave you alone," the major said. "Oh, one last thing, you're CT-scan came back and your bell wasn't rung too badly, brains are hardly scrambled at all...for a crusty old NCO that is."

"Thanks Doc, I love you too."

Mike spent the next two hours lying in bed scanning television channels, Armed Forces television, and German television. Nothing appealed to him until he saw Sarah Tomzewski giving an interview on one of the morning news programs in New York. He looked at her and checked her out. He tried to discern any evidence that she was still struggling, having a hard time in any way. He didn't like the updates he received from his men providing her security. Other than finally deciding to do interviews, she still wasn't going out, except for the movie she was shooting. At home, she still left every light on at night, left the television in her room on all night, and barely bothered to clean herself or get dressed on her days off, just wearing an old robe over some yoga pants and a shirt. She rarely had visitors, not even her close friends or former co-stars, just the grocery deliveryman.

Mike shook his head as he listened to Sarah talk about the rescue and him, his eyes...the man behind the eyes, everyone repeated. She kept talking about how she wanted to meet him, to thank him, to get to know him. But he picked up on something else that bothered him. Sarah seemed stuck on why the terrorist spared her, why she was rescued, why she survived, and her agent didn't. Why had she not been in that lobby when the terrorist attack happened but all those other poor, innocent people were? In his heart, Mike knew what was bothering her...one of the same things that bothered him since 1987.

"Hey Mr. H!" Mike's senior executive assistant, Angela Montero, bounded into his hospital room with a spring in her step and a smile on her face. "What's shakin', how ya feeling?"

"Oh, I feel just peachy, Angela, how was your flight over?"

"My flight was fine and I brought everything you wanted."

"Christ, I've been here for three days. I thought maybe your flight got hijacked or diverted to Paris or something, spending my money sightseeing and touring."

"Oh stop it. You know I can't just pick up and take off like you can. I still have family at home and I still have a life, you know," Angela knew Mike was teasing her, but shot back anyway. It's what he expected, a little playful conflict.

"How are Brad and the boys?"

"Oh they're fine. They told me to tell you hi, so hi—and the boys are wondering when Mr. Mike might send them another video game. Don't worry though, I told them never," Angela smiled at Mike as she sat in the chair next to his bed and handed him an electronic tablet and some files.

"Call of Duty? Really? Call of Duty for 8 and 10 year old little boys?" Angela expressed her motherly displeasure with Mike's last gift to her sons.

"Well at least I didn't give them Grand Theft Auto, even though I think they would loved it," Mike chuckled his low, gravely chuckle as he spoke, intentionally needling Angela.

Mike really liked and respected Angela. As his senior executive assistant, she ran the New York office and supervised three other executive assistants, three secretaries and two administrative specialists. The office handles all of his personal and professional correspondence, screens incoming letters and packages, prepares outgoing letters, takes all phone calls, and keeps his schedule. Angela updates his electronic calendar on the tablet nightly and makes sure he receives regular updates to his call list, the list of phone calls he has to make every day, both personal and professional. She even keeps track of family birthdays, anniversaries, and other special events in his life. Angela Montero gets Mike Hampton where he needs to be, when he needs to be there, and ready to do what he's supposed to be doing.

"You know, Mr. H, I saw Sarah Tomzewski on your television when I walked in. She has such a crush on you and you have her just hanging out there twisting in the wind with your Clark Kent, Bruce Wayne—can't meet me attitude."

Mike put down the folder he was reviewing, took off his wire frame glasses, and glared at Angela.

"She doesn't have a crush on me and..."

"Oh pul-eese," Angela interrupted. "You are so naive when it comes to women. All those divorcees and widows at New York social events, and the young girls in your club in Virginia Beach who try to slip you their phone numbers...you are so naive!" Angela laughed and shook her head. Few people outside his immediate family could speak to Mike Hampton that way.

"Those widows and divorcees are after my money and those young girls are looking for a temporary sugar daddy and I'm nobody's sugar daddy," Mike protested. "And I am certainly *not* naive."

"Yes you are, you are so naive and cynical—turning into an old curmudgeon."

"I'm not old. Hell, I'm only 55...I won't be old for another ten or fifteen years. I may be an ass but I'm not a curmudgeon...and I am not naive! And anyway, Sarah Tomzewski doesn't have a crush on me. You know damn good and well that it isn't unusual for people we rescue to develop an affinity for us. It happens all the time, and she's just curious...just normal curiosity."

"You always have an excuse, always an alibi."

"And I'll tell you another thing, Angela. I look out at the dating scene today and it isn't anything like the 1970s. It all looks so emotionally complicated; people are so bitchy with each other these days and needy. It all just looks so damn confusing and complicated and I don't need that crap."

"So what then, you're just going to stay alone and celibate?"

"I'm not alone, Angela, I have plenty of family and a few close friends."

"Very few," Angela muttered under her breath.

Mike put his glasses back on and returned to reading the file. He took a deep breath, his chest and shoulders visibly rising for dramatic effect, and let out a disapproving grunt for Angela's benefit. After reviewing his new call list, approving a few expense reports, and signing a few letters, he handed the brown leather folder back to Angela and took his glasses off.

"I want you to do something for me, Angela," Mike said in a very serious tone of voice.

"Yes, Sir."

I want you to get with Mac and the other attorneys and start the process for me to retire from all operations, all of them. No more missions, no more operational stuff. Okay?"

Mike made his decision and settled the issue in his own mind. He was comfortable with his decision, he thought. The rescue operation in Iraq should be one of his last missions, even though retiring for him would be more of a process than a one-time event.

"Are you serious, Mr. H?" Angela sat up straight in her chair and closely inspected Mike's face for any signs of indecision. "Are you sure?"

"Yeah, I'm sure. And one other thing, have the lawyers find my DD-214 in my important papers—request all my medical files from the Air Force." Mike took a deep breath and returned his gaze to the fluorescent lights above his head. "I think it's time to check in with the VA."

Angela sat in stunned silence for just a moment. She knew Mike's family and close friends had been on him to retire since his wife passed away a year and a half before. One year after her death, his family began trying to get him to at least think about dating again. Some of his close friends tried to set him up on blind dates or introduce him to women, but he always used the excuse of his work to say no. And now, Angela thought, he would no longer have that excuse. What she didn't know, is that Mike was lying to everyone about why he wasn't dating.

"So, Mr. H., are you finally going to put Sarah Tomzewski out of her misery and let her meet you, let her know who you are?"

"Yes."

CHAPTER ELEVEN

"Being deeply loved by someone gives you strength, while loving someone deeply gives you courage." —Lao Tzu

The morning sun set the Atlantic horizon ablaze with fiery shades of red and orange mixed with yellow and purple as Mike Hampton sat in the sand behind his beach house contemplating his new semi-retirement. June finally arrived and it had been long enough since the ISIS terrorist shot him in the leg during the rescue mission in Iraq that he could finally surf again. But true to form, Virginia Beach failed to serve up even a modest wave, the ocean flat as a lake as high pressure dominated the weather pattern.

His head fuzzy from Jack Daniel's and no sleep, Mike unconsciously drew abstract shapes in the sand beside him as he stared blindly over the still ocean and thought about his life, his late wife, and all that he'd seen...all that he'd done. Some said his life was about courage and heroic acts, but he knew it was about death and destruction. The needless loss of innocent life as men committed the most heinous acts possible against each other, men, women, and children, innocent children...true, hellish evil. Like so many military men and women before him, and sure to come after him, so many first responders, Mike had seen and done things no man should ever see or do, and he took them all to bed with him every night of his life, a mistress forced upon him.

Mike drew in a long, cleansing breath through his nose and released a deep and thoughtful sigh, dropped his head, and closed his eyes as he muttered, "You always knew what to do, Honey, you always knew what to do."

At that moment in his life, Mike was at his daily crossroad and had to make a decision. He could sit there on that beach, a beach that remained mostly devoid of people during the day, and drink the other half of the Jack Daniel's bottle, or he could clean up, get his Harley Fat Boy out of the garage, and go meet his VFW friends for breakfast at the diner. He picked up the bottle of Jack with his left hand, twisted and pulled at the cap with his right, leaned his head back and looked at the last remaining visible stars in the morning sky..."I'm going to go get some eggs at the diner and then take a little ride with my friends, Honey...be back a little later," he whispered.

As was usually the case, Mike was one of the last riders to arrive at Mom's Kitchen diner on Holland Road, and the long parking lot of the strip mall shopping center was already filled with all manner, size, shape and color of motorcycles. He swung his Fat Boy around in a semicircle and carefully walked it back into a parking space next to a bright, metallic blue three-wheeler. He doffed his helmet and hung it from his handlebars, threw his fingerless leather gloves inside it, but kept his sunglasses on as he walked toward the diner. Beautiful day for a ride, he thought.

Mike walked into the diner and spied Jim and his wife, Pat, sitting in a booth together along the wall opposite the counter. Jim and Pat were two of the only people in the world Mike trusted with personal conversations, his darkest secrets, fears, and even hopes and dreams. What few hopes and dreams he had anyway. Mike loved his family dearly, but there were things he would never reveal to them and he was always very guarded around his mother. There were things he just wasn't ready for them to know.

Mike loved and trusted Jim and Pat because he knew their history, their story, and they had always been straightforward with him. He was always comfortable around them, since that first night he met them shortly after to moving back to Virginia Beach, after his wife's death, and Jim saw Mike sulking over his beer while sitting at the bar in the darkened VFW.

Jim Patterson was an overweight, 66-year old Vietnam veteran with a prosthetic left leg from the knee down that caused him to limp. He wore his gray hair very short and a white and brown full-face beard. His leather motorcycle vest plastered with an array of patches from bike week in Daytona Beach all the way north to Sturgis and all points in between. It was Jim's metallic blue three-wheeler Mike parked beside in the lot.

"What's shakin' baby?" Mike said as he leaned down and kissed Pat on the cheek.

"Same old crap different day," Pat said. "What's new with you, haven't seen you in a while."

"Nothing much," Mike said as he sat in the opposite side of the booth from Jim and Pat.

"But I'll tell ya this, I don't think I've seen this much leather since my last trip to the whore house," Mike grinned at Pat as the little brunette waitress placed a cup of coffee in front of him.

"You've never been to no damn whore house, boy," Jim chuckled in a low tone as he sipped his coffee.

"Well, apparently I need to go," Mike replied. "People tell me I'm at risk of being celibate if I don't. Going to be a dried up old curmudgeon pretty soon."

The Army drafted Jim for Vietnam in 1969, the moment he turned 18 years old and graduated from Princess Anne High School, the same school Mike and his wife graduated. His then girlfriend, Pat, waited another year for her graduation, and then a second year for Jim to finish boot camp, school, and then return home with part of his leg left somewhere in the jungle north of Da Nang.

"There's a beautiful young actress who's been all over the television talking about you and looking for you, Mike." Pat said as she looked at Mike over the top of her granny glasses, her long thin gray hair falling down her shoulders and around her face.

The waitress saved Mike by walking back over to the booth and taking their orders, refreshing their coffee cups.

"She's kinda cute, why don't I just jump her bones?" Mike said sarcastically when the waitress walked away, trying to lighten the mood back up. He knew where the conversation was going and he also knew he could never lie to Jim and Pat, or make excuses. Jim and Pat were fun people, good people, but they didn't like excuse makers and they called Mike on it every time he tried.

"That actress is cute and she really wants to meet you," Pat continued.

Mike sighed and shot a quick glance to Jim hoping he would rescue him as the waitress had. Instead, what he saw in Jim's face was a lecture coming; the kind of lecture a big brother gives a little brother when the little brother has screwed up.

"Look Pat," Mike stopped and thought for a moment, struggling for a way to diffuse the conversation, a way to placate Pat and Jim.

"Here come the excuses," Pat leaned over and whispered to Jim.

"There are real life considerations here, guys. How in the hell could I bring a new woman into my life when I was still running around the world getting shot at and blown up? I mean, hey baby, nice to meet you, thanks for the hump, gotta go to Iraq now, maybe I'll call later and maybe I'll be dead...see ya."

"Didn't you just retire?" Pat asked as she laughed at Mike's comment.

"Yeah, I sort of retired," Mike said. "Still some things hanging out there that I'm going to have to be involved with. But there are more considerations...like all these damn scars, and the nightmares. I can see it now, welcome to my boudoir baby, don't get excited if I wake you up with a blood-curdling scream or smack you in the mouth because I think your attacking me in my sleep...yeah, that'll work. What woman wants to take that on?"

"The scars are not the man, Mike," Pat said with a loving, almost motherly tone in her voice.

"You think I'm stupid for standing by Jim when he came back from Vietnam with only a leg and a half? You think he didn't have nightmares of rice paddies and deltas, booby traps and bullets. You think he didn't scream out in the night?"

"No, Pat, I don't think you're stupid. I meant no disrespect. Look, maybe there's a woman in my future, maybe not. I don't know. But I do know, whoever she is, she won't be a drop-dead gorgeous Hollywood actress younger than three of my kids, who can have any man she wants—her own age—to build a life with. Besides, she doesn't even know me, she's just curious about who rescued her is all. All this crap about her looking for me is all about curiosity and a hostage developing an affinity for her rescuer. But, I'll meet her, put her out of her misery, as Angela said, tell her I'm a fan, and answer her questions. Should be able to do it over lunch one day."

The conversation ended when the cute little waitress brought the food to the table. Jim, Pat, and Mike ate mostly in silence, only exchanging mundane conversation as Mike contemplated everything said to him so far that morning. He knew he was still in for a lecture from Jim, he could feel it coming. Jim gave pretty good lectures too, tough lectures; Mike thought to himself and chuckled slightly under his breath as he shoved steak, eggs over easy, hash browns and buttered toast into his mouth to sop up last night's Jack Daniel's still in his stomach.

Jim leaned back in the booth, arched his back until both shoulder blades were touching the red plastic covering on the padded bench. He pursed his lips and wiggled them a little as he sucked a piece of steak from between his teeth, his cheeks moving from side to side and his beard wiggling. He took a deep, contemplative breath and exhaled.

"Let me tell you something, little brother," Jim said as he reached for a tooth pick."

"You got this anger inside you, eating you alive the way you just inhaled those eggs. And you got that anger inside you because you're just ate up with guilt, and I know that guilt, little brother, I know it and what it does to a man. You got a cloud of guilt hanging on you like that Pig Pen character in those Charley Brown cartoons has a cloud of dirt following him around," Jim paused and looked Mike over to ensure he was listening.

"Guilt?" Mike said. "Pray tell, Obi-Wan," Mike tried to joke.

"You got a guilt because you've seen the devil's work...you've seen it and couldn't do anything about it. You got a guilt because you looked right into the face of evil itself and were helpless to stop it, helpless to save them, all of them," Jim leaned forward in the booth, placed both elbows on the table, clasped his hands together, and pointed his finger at Mike.

"Somewhere inside you, you gotta know the truth, Mike," Jim continued softly. "Those people are dead because they're supposed to be dead. You couldn't save them because we all have a destiny, and those people are dead because that was their destiny, that was their fate. I don't know who the hell you think you are, Mike Hampton," Jim waged his finger at Mike. "But you gotta understand you ain't Superman and you sure as hell ain't God almighty Himself. The truth is there's been evil in this world since Adam and Eve ate that damned fruit and there's gonna be evil in this world till Jesus Christ Himself rides back down on that cloud with those trumpets blowing - you can bet your ass on that one, little brother," Jim nodded definitively at Mike as he finished, leaned back into the booth.

Mike took a deep breath and lowered his eyes from Jim, lowered his head and nodded in agreement. He knew in his heart that everything Jim was saying was truth. He hated it, but he knew it. His eyes welled up as he continued to nod.

"Mike," Pat said. "You meet that young actress with an open mind, no preconceived notions, no agenda...don't blow her off, or just feel like you're checking a block on a form and letting her go. She's one of the ones you did save—fate—her destiny was for you to save her and she feels like she has some unfinished business with you, whatever it is, it's unfinished and she needs to finish it so she can be whole again. You owe her that much."

Mike insisted on paying the check as the three of them stood mostly in silence and prepared to leave. Mike kept thinking about what Jim and Pat said, the lectures, and knew they were right. He wasn't a psychologist or therapist, but he was an educated man and knew a lot about PTSD. Jim was especially right about the anger and the guilt. Mike was on the verge of hating the world, he could feel it in him, and it burned.

Jim walked over to Mike in the parking lot as Pat put on her motorcycle helmet and prepared to leave. Jim was fastening the Velcro strips at the top of his fingerless gloves around his wrists as he limped around Mike's Harley to where Mike was standing.

"You get to the VA, little brother, you get there," Jim said. "You take care of that guilt and the anger will go with it. Once the guilt and anger are gone, those nightmares will stop...mostly stop, anyway. And I'll tell you something else," Jim continued. "I don't give a rat's ass if it's that pretty little blonde actress or not, but I do know you deserve love in your life again and need it. I only survived after Nam because of Pat. We were partners and she knew how to take care of me and love me."

"I know, Jim, I know and I appreciate the advice," Mike said.

"Mike, your wife's dead because the cancer took her...that was her fate, her destiny. That ain't on you, little brother, that's on fate. And I know that your nightmares, and thoughts and anger weren't as bad when she was still here and lovin' you."

Mike nodded in agreement. Everything in his life got worse when his wife passed away. He had screwed a lot of things up when she was still alive, bankrupted the family, and lost the house due to his drinking and not being able to concentrate on things, on work. But he was just drifting through life the past two years without her, going from one mission to another while thinking about how death could be a final release.

"A man can't walk through this life alone, Mike, no man can. You need and deserve love in your life and I don't mean your kids and grandkids. I mean a partner, like Pat is my partner. You find the right woman and she'll understand the nightmares, your past, give her half a chance and she'll love you because you'll be worth it to her." Jim shook hands with Mike and walked over to his three-wheeler.

"Hey Mike!" Jim shouted as he climbed astride his three-wheeler. "You're a good man, Charley Brown, just get back about the business of livin'. You go through life looking in the rearview mirror and you're just gonna bump into walls all day." Jim hit the electric starter on his trike, threw it into first gear, and rode off with Pat.

CHAPTER TWELVE

"Love looks not with the eyes, but with the mind, And therefore is winged Cupid painted blind." —William Shakespeare

The Southern California afternoon summer heat blazed outside Sarah Tomzewski's house in Hollywood Hills, the sky clear and a brilliant blue, as she busied herself with mundane housework. She shuffled around in her white robe, black yoga pants and skintight workout shirt only opening her front door for grocery deliveries, or to give her security guards a mug of hot coffee. She liked her security guards, especially the night guys, Jack and Sam, but hated that they had to be there, that she needed security guards. It made her uncomfortable, unsettled and she hated feeling that way.

Normally when she finished shooting a movie she would vacation with her parents in New Zealand, explore the Outback with some old friends and a guide, hiking and canoeing, and all the other outdoor activities she used to love so much...used to. But now, her last movie project wrapped, she isolated herself from friends and family, kept her house dimly lit in the daytime, fully lit at night, and the air turned way down low and cold.

Sarah walked over to her couch and plopped down, pulled her legs and bare feet up under her buttocks, leaned to her left against the arm of the couch, and poured herself a glass of Pinot. She grabbed the remote control, clicked on her 52" plasma screen television, and leaned back against the couch. "Sure," Sarah grunted to herself, "why not a few bonbons and Oprah."

"Damn," Sarah said when someone knocked on her front door. "I just got comfortable." She shuffled to the door, peered through the peephole, and opened the door.

"What's up, Bill?" Sarah asked one of her daytime security guards standing on her front porch in his light, tan suit, a squiggly little wire running up his back and to his left ear, gun bulging inside his suit coat just beneath his left arm.

"I'm sorry to disturb you, Miss Tomzewski, but your mail came," Bill said as he handed Sarah a stack of envelopes.

"Oh, thanks, Bill." Sarah nodded as she closed and locked her front door.

Sarah shuffled back over to her very large black leather couch, and plopped down with her mail. She grabbed her glass of wine and finished it in one gulp, then poured another. She took another drink, about half the glass, and then set the glass back on the end table and began to thumb through the envelopes as Oprah mumbled in the background.

As Sarah thumbed through the stack of envelopes, she ran across one very elegantly addressed to her, but with no return address. There was just one word neatly printed in the spot where a return address would normally be..."Me." Sarah slowly stood, envelops falling from her lap and onto the hardwood floor. Her hands began to tremble as her eyes welled up. "Oh my God," Sarah muttered. "Is this...is it..."

Sarah nervously touched the side of her face with a shaky right hand, left hand holding the envelope. She stared at it, afraid to open it but wanting to open it more than any Christmas present she had ever received. Her mind raced wildly with scenario after scenario. She shook her head briskly to straighten herself up. "My God, she muttered," What the hell am I afraid of. I'm a successful, 35-year old grown woman and not some damn teenage girl in school..."

Sarah grabbed the television remote and turned off Oprah. She picked up her glass of wine and walked over to the dining room table, pulled out a chair, and sat. She took a deep breath and opened the envelope.

"My gosh, what wonderful handwriting, Sammy, very nice penmanship, yes it is," she said to her puppy as she began to read.

Dear Sarah,

I hope all is well with you. Please allow me to apologize again for causing you so much concern and consternation over the past eight months. I know the curiosity has been aggravating at times, to say the least, and that is my fault, so I offer my sincerest apologies.

As I told you I might do last October, I have now retired from working in the field and I want to keep my promise to you. But, I still have a business to run and some work to do here on the East Coast, so I will not be able to make it to LA any time soon.

"Crap," Sarah said as she read that last line, disappointment building again.

If you're up for it and not too busy working, I would like to invite you and some of your friends, as few or as many as you like, your choice, to visit Virginia Beach at your earliest convenience. I can arrange your transportation on one of our company planes, and I have a beautiful beach house right next door to me, where you can all stay, my treat. The beach house has six bedrooms and four full baths, if that helps you decide how many friends you might like to invite.

"Yes, yes, yes, Sammy, yes!" Sarah pumped her arm and fist as she read.

I would be happy to show your friends and you around Virginia Beach, maybe Williamsburg and some of the other historical sites, and answer all your questions. When you decide, please just let my security guys outside your front door know yes or no, and if yes, when you would like to travel and the number in your party.

Warmest regards,
Mike Hampton...Your man behind the eyes

Oh my God, Sarah thought. I can't go to Virginia Beach now, I look like crap...my face and eyes are puffy...I'll need an entire make-up counter just to look presentable, she thought as she ran through her house excitedly opening all the drapes and curtains.

"Crap, I have to call Beth, and Robin...I have to tell them," she muttered. "Why does he want me to bring friends? Does he want me to bring friends? Maybe he just thinks I'll be more comfortable bringing friends, Sammy," Sarah said to her puppy. Her mind raced. I need spa time, she thought, I need my hair done, nails, a mani-pedi, oh my God this skin, my face is a wreck.

Sarah took Mike's letter, poured herself another glass of Pinot, plopped down on the couch, pulled her long legs and bare feet up under her buttocks again, excited to share her news. She dialed Beth Mullaney first, her former co-star from the old romantic comedy they worked on for five years when they were in their twenties, when Sarah first arrived in America from New Zealand. When Beth answered, Sarah put her on hold and three-way dialed Robin McKenna, another former co-star from the old show.

"What's up girl," Beth answered. "Haven't heard from you in a while."

"Hang on, Beth," Sarah said. "I want to tell both of you this at the same time. Are you there Robin?"

"I'm here, what's up?" Robin answered.

Sarah took a deep breath and looked back at the letter, made sure she remembered it correctly.

"Hang onto you hats, ladies...I heard from *him*!"

"Yay!" Beth exclaimed. *"Finally!"*

"Hot damn," Robin said. *"So, what's the word? Who is he, how old is he, is he married, when are you going to meet? Oh my God, did you already meet?"*

"Hang on, Robin, hang on." Sarah said. "No, I haven't met him yet. I got a letter from him today—an apology and an invitation."

"Ooh...what kind of invitation?" Beth joked and Robin laughed.

"Well, he invited me and as many friends as I want, or as few, to fly to Virginia Beach on his corporate jet and vacation at a beach house for as long as I want, as long as we want, all expenses paid and he said he would answer all of my questions...all of them."

"Are you going?" Beth asked. *"Did you call to tell us or invite us? Are we going?"*

"Yes! I want you both to come, please, if you can, if you're not too busy working. I'm so nervous; I don't want to go by myself. Can you guys please come?"

"Hell yeah, I'm in," Beth said. *"I'm on hiatus for the summer."*

"Me too," Robin said. *"I'm in. When are we leaving? I can be ready in an hour."*

Sarah and her friends made plans for a spa day and then planned to leave for Virginia in three days time, Saturday. She told her daytime security guard, Bill, their travel plans and the number of people in her party, as Mike asked.

"Two weeks in Virginia with him, Sammy, two whole weeks!" Sarah nuzzled happily with her puppy.

Mike Hampton sat at the desk in his home office that Saturday afternoon making phone calls, going through his updated call list from Angela. He hated the phone calls; hated talking on the phone, but much of it was a necessary evil for his business. He didn't mind the calls to charities and the foundation he ran in Virginia Beach, his foundation for homeless and struggling veterans. "To whom much is given, much is expected," Mike remembered from his days attending religious studies as a kid growing up. But in addition to knowing he was supposed to be charitable, he just wanted to do anything he could for struggling veterans.

"I can't believe that you're sitting here working this afternoon and not picking those ladies up at the airport," Angela said derisively.

"You're the one who gave me the damn call list with all these calls on it for me to make."

"Hey, don't blame me, buddy boy," Angela said. "You're the one who decided to prolong your morning workout, then go surfing, and get started late," Angela snapped back at Mike.

"Don't worry, Angela, the guys are picking them up in a long, shiny white stretch limo and bringing them straight here. Then I figure they'll want to rest up a little before dinner and I put a dinner invitation for all three of them on the coffee table in the living room next door," Mike said confidently, as if he'd thought of everything.

"Yeah, because Sarah Tomzewski isn't excited or in a hurry to meet you or anything, she's probably ready for a nice nap," Angela scoffed as she turned and walked out of the office shaking her head.

"Jesus, I can't win for losing," Mike muttered to himself. "I put fresh cut flowers on the dining room table myself for crying out loud...didn't farm it out or ask anyone to do it for me...geez..."

Mike got up from his desk and walked out to the pool deck, around the outdoor kitchen and bar, and looked next door. He stood there in his tan cargo shorts, white surfer tee shirt and slaps, and watched as the long, shiny white stretch limo pulled up. He took a sip of his coffee as he watched his guys open the back door to the limo - Beth, Robin, and then Sarah Tomzewski stepped out and the security guards showed them the way into their vacation beach house.

After the three women went into the house, Mike opened his gate and walked the path through the sand between the two houses. He stood on the front porch momentarily and motioned with his head for his security guys to take off. He took a deep breath and rang the doorbell. It opened almost immediately.

"Hello Miss Mullaney," Mike said when Beth opened the door. "I'm Mike Hampton. Is Sarah busy or is she freshening up from her long flight or something?" He suddenly felt like a teenage boy in high school at *that girl's* house for the first time. Jesus Christ, he thought, what the hell's happening to me...let Jim and Pat and Angela get inside my head with their crap.

"Oh my gosh...you're *him*—the man behind the eyes," Beth said.

"I guess—that's what they say anyway. Is Sarah here?"

"Oh, I'm sorry, come in... Come in."

Mikes eyes immediately scanned the open rooms for Sarah, the large living area that opened into an almost equally large dining area with a long, wood table and eight wood chairs, then a wide-open kitchen separated by a breakfast bar, a cliché beach theme to every room.

"Hey guys, who was at the door?" Sarah asked as she walked through the long hallway and into the living room, looking at her hands as she rubbed them together after having washed them. She abruptly stopped about one third of the way into the living room and looked at Mike. Her mouth went dry and she trembled slightly.

"Hello, Sarah," Mike said. "I apologize for coming over unannounced, but my senior...um...Angela Montero, a lady who works for me, said I was rude not picking you up at the airport, so I wanted to come over and apologize," He stepped farther into the room toward Sarah as he spoke.

"Oh, hi," Sarah said sheepishly as she quickly waived with one hand down by her waist.

"I hope you don't mind," Mike said as he stepped closer to Sarah. "Oh, I'm being rude again, I'm Mike Hampton," Mike nodded as he introduced himself.

Sarah, wearing a pair of designer blue jean shorts, a white spaghetti strap blouse that just barely covered her belly button, and tan, flat sandals, smiled her signature toothy smile, one she had not flashed anyone for the past eight months, and extended her hand toward Mike.

"Hi Mike, I'm Sarah."

Sarah's eyes darted over toward Beth and Robin, rolled in their sockets as she discretely tried to motion for them to leave the room.

"Well, I don't know about you Robin," Beth said, "but I need to unpack." Beth widened her eyes and nodded toward the hallway ever so slightly.

"Oh, me too, we're going to go unpack," Robin followed Beth down the hall. "Very nice to meet you."

Mike nodded at Beth and Sarah.

"So," Mike said as he shook Sarah's hand. "If I remember your appearances on those talk shows correctly, I'm supposed to get two things when we meet."

"Two things?" Sarah said, her voice trailing up as she spoke. "Two?"

"Yep, two things," Mike said confidently, "a kiss on the cheek and a big old hug."

"Are you sure it was just two things?" Sarah said.

"Well, yeah," Mike said. "But let me see...let me think a minute...a big old hug...kiss on the cheek..." Mike cocked his head, looked up, and counted on his fingers as he pretended to think. "Yep, I'm sure it was two things."

Sarah reached over and punched Mike in his left shoulder, almost where the ISIS terrorist shot him during her rescue. She stepped back, cocked her head to the left, and gave him a look of disapproval. She stepped back forward, toward Mike, embraced him with a big, lingering hug, noticing his muscular body, the muscular body that held her when they parachuted off the top of the Bank Tower, and then gave him a kiss on the cheek.

"Oh yeah," Mike whispered as he put his arms around Sarah and returned her hug. "*Three things...punch in the arm*, big old hug, and a kiss on the cheek...three things."

"Thank you for saving my life."

"You're welcome, and thank you back for being such a good sport about all the groping I had to do and being such a good rescuee."

Mike and Sarah embraced a moment longer and she tightened her arms around him.

"Oh, I have to change our dinner plans a little, if you don't mind. Instead of going out, how about you all come over to my place for a cookout on the pool deck. Some of my family dropped in and some of the other guys from your rescue are coming over with their wives and girlfriends so you'll get to meet them too...should be about 30 people or so—music, steaks, seafood, the works."

"That sounds great, but about dinner," Sarah said. "Beth and Robin just wanted to order in and relax a little from the trip. So, if you didn't mind, it was just going to be you and me for dinner. But I'll let them know about the cook-out."

"OK, dress comfortable and bring a bathing suit if you want—there'll be people swimming in the pool and using the hot tub so, whatever you guys want to do...come over anytime you want."

Even though she wanted some alone time with Mike and conspired with Beth and Robin to get it, she liked the idea of a cookout with some of his family and guys from the rescue because it afforded her an opportunity to ask questions about Mike from people who knew him well, questions she might feel uncomfortable asking him directly...questions he might feel were inappropriate or just none of her business.

"There's another reason for the change in dinner plans, Sarah," Mike said as he walked toward the front door, "there's a chance I might have to go to work tonight."

"Oh? I thought you retired? You might have to fly off to Iraq or someplace tonight?" Sarah said.

"I did, sort of retire...mostly retire...there's just a couple of things left hanging out there that I have to be involved with and no, not Iraq or somewhere...this one's a local operation."

"OK," Sarah said with some trepidation in her voice. "I'll let Beth and Robin know the plans and we'll be over in a little while."

CHAPTER THIRTEEN

"The family is one of nature's masterpieces." —George Santayana

The late afternoon sun set high in the sky over Virginia Beach as Sarah Tomzewski, Beth Mullaney, and Robin McKenna found the path between Mike's beach house and theirs. The path of small rolling sand dunes surrounded by mature sea oats ran sixty feet from the north side of the actress' beach house to Mike's, the emerald blue Atlantic Ocean to their right and more houses and a side street to their left as the three women walked. Typical for the Atlantic Ocean off Virginia Beach in June, the ocean was as flat as a lake with only small ripples of waves barely breaking on the sand and lapping at the feet of a few sunbathers 100 yards from the houses.

Sarah led the group over the path, wearing her cut-off blue jean shorts that barely covered her bathing suit bottom and a white cotton shirt unbuttoned over her bikini top, sleeves rolled loosely up her forearms. Her brown flat sandals made the warm white sugar-sand spray up around her muscular legs each time she took a step.

"Good Lord, Sarah, could those shorts *be* any shorter? They're up your butt crack!" Beth laughed as she spoke.

"Shut up, you...I'm nervous enough as it is."

Sarah thought as she walked and tried to understand why she was nervous. Sarah Tomzewski was never really nervous about meeting anyone or making new friends. She was never even nervous working with so-called

Hollywood "A-listers" for the first time. She just wasn't the nervous type. She was always self-confident and unafraid.

Sarah originally developed a girlish crush on Mike's revealing brown eyes, about all she could see of him during the rescue, his soothing baritone voice, and his gentle manner but she really didn't know enough about him, she thought, to have any romantic feelings for him. She made sure her two friends didn't see her face contorting as she thought to herself, her lips pursing and brow furrowing. During the walk, she decided that she might be nervous because she had built Mike Hampton up so much in her mind's eye, in her delusions that nobody could ever meet her expectations, and that bothered her. Getting to know Mike Hampton, she thought, was destined to be a letdown for her.

Oldies rock music from the 1960s and 70s blared from over the eight foot tall wooden fence as Sarah, Beth and Robin approached the bottom of the steps leading up to large wooden deck and the gate to the pool area. They heard laughter and water splashing mixed with the music and smelled food cooking over a charcoal fire as they walked up the steps and to the gate.

Mike Hampton's beach house was elevated above the sand dunes and the back faced the ocean to the east and the side of the house with the pool, hot tub, and outdoor kitchen faced south. A large twelve-foot wide and twenty-five foot long elevated wooden deck framed the exterior of the house outside the pool deck, separated from the pool area by an eight-foot high wooden fence with a gate.

"Hello Ms. Tomzewski, I'm Mike's senior executive assistant from New York, Angela Montero," Angela said as she reached out to shake hands with Sarah, Beth, and Robin as the walked in the gate. "It's so nice to finally meet you—all of you. Please come in and make yourselves at home."

"Thank you," each woman replied as she shook Angela's hand.

"Let me give you the lay of the land before you start mixing and mingling. Of course, Mike's over there in the outdoor kitchen manning the grill," Angela pointed to Mike fifty feet to the west at the other end of the pool deck as she spoke. "You already know your two nighttime security guys from back in LA, Jack and Sam," Angela motioned. "Those two guys with their wives right over there are two of Mike's most trusted guys, Bob Morton and Tom Beck, and the older guy with the prosthetic leg they're talking to, and his wife, are Jim and Pat, two of Mike's best friends. Oh, and that's Mike's five year old grandson going down the slide into the pool r-i-g-h-t...now. I guess everyone else can introduce themselves as the night goes on."

Mike happily cooked burgers, hotdogs, sausages, steaks, and seafood in his outdoor kitchen next to the wet bar using one large charcoal grill for the meat and seafood, and a gas grill for the sides. A little sweat caused his white surfer tee shirt to stick to his torso and his tan cargo shorts to stick to his thighs as he cooked. Spatula in his right hand, a bottle of water in his left, kitchen towel over his right shoulder, Mike sang along to the music, laughed as he watched people drink and tease each other, play in the pool, and beautiful young women relax in the eight-person hot tub. Mike loved the beach life, his friends, family, and always enjoyed a good party.

"Hey you," Mike said as Sarah walked over. "How're you doing?"

"I'm good, how are you?"

"Perfect," Mike answered as he tended the food on the grill. "If you need a place to change, that's a changing room and bathroom right there." Mike used his spatula to point to his left at the outdoor changing room. "There are towels in there and more in the storage room next to it. That's my youngest daughter tending bar over there if you're ready for a drink," Mike pointed to his right. You and your friends feel free to come over and use the pool and hot tub anytime you want while you're here, even if I'm not here. Just come up those back steps."

"Thank you," Sarah said. "So, when do I get to have all my questions answered...remember, you promised?"

"I sure did and I'll keep that promise. Why don't you get a drink, mix and mingle, meet and greet, swim a little if you want while I cook and when I'm finished, we'll sit and eat together and I'll correct everything all these other morons tell you about me. How's that?" Mike smiled and winked at Sarah.

"Deal," Sarah pronounced and walked over to a long, white plastic deck chair next to the ones Beth and Robin chose. She set her bag and towel on the chair and peeled off her shorts, and then her shirt, revealing her skimpy light blue bikini and athletic body as Mike watched from the corner of his eye while singing along with a Three Dog Night song.

"Humph," Mike grunted and then chuckled at himself. "Dirty old man," he muttered. "She's younger than your own daughters, dummy. Some dirty old man looks at your daughters like that and you'd knock them out," he continued to mutter to himself.

As he continued cooking, Mike watched Sarah, Beth, and Robin in the pool to make sure they were having fun. They stood in the shallow end against the side of the pool sipping their drinks as they talked to everyone who walked or swam past them, and everyone stopped to talk to the actresses. Mike felt a little guilty, as if he'd set them up to be interrogated by a bunch of fans, but he was glad they were there and glad he wasn't out at a restaurant with Sarah, just the two of them. Mike knew a lot of people in Virginia Beach, old classmates and other old friends, and he didn't want anyone getting the wrong impression.

Before too long, Mike's daughter in-law, two sisters, and two daughters began moving food from the outdoor kitchen to the row of picnic tables on the far side of the pool deck closer to the house. Guests dried off, some dressed, and others stayed in their bathing suits, and moved to the tables. Some refreshed their drinks at the outdoor bar, and Mike began wrapping up his cooking duties as the sun moved a little lower in the sky and the afternoon heat and humidity began to abate somewhat. Sarah scanned the crowd to determine what most of the women were doing, dressing or not, and decided to just stay in her bikini.

"Sarah," Mike's youngest daughter, the bartender Amanda, said. "Would you mind sitting here at the end of the table and leave a little room to your right for Dad? He has to sit on the end with nobody on his right—his gun hand you know. It's a *thing* with him."

"Oh no, not at all," Sarah said. "And thank you, that's good to know."

Mike checked to make sure Sarah and her friends had food and found a comfortable place to sit, walked over, fixed his own plate, and sat in the empty space to Sarah's right, facing his daughters, daughter-in-law, and son on the other side of the table.

"Okay, Sarah, what did this wild bunch tell you about me that I need to correct. How did they slander me this time?" Mike said as he sat next to Sarah at the end of the picnic table. His family members groaned because they knew what was coming from Mike over dinner, some good-hearted sarcasm and teasing.

"Well let's see," Sarah started. "I don't think they slandered you," she said as she leaned to her right and bumped Mike with her shoulder. "You're 55, retired military, married your high school sweetheart and a widower now...and, Mike, I'm so sorry for your loss. That must have been so difficult after so many years together."

"It was tough, but it's been about two years now so, the emotions have scabbed over a little. But thank you."

"Let's see, what else..." Sarah Continued. "Oh yeah, you own your own night club and play guitar and sing in a band on the weekends and, by the way, Robin, Beth, and

I hope to see you play tomorrow night." Mike laughed as he bit into his corn on the cob.

"And according to your family, you hold the world record for dating dry spells having not had a date since the late 70's or 1980," Sarah chuckled because she knew Mike was married almost his entire adult life, but it was an inside family joke.

"Yeah, yeah, yeah," Mike said. "Everyone's so concerned with my love life."

"Or the lack thereof!" his family, Angela Montero, and a few other people at the tables shouted in well-practiced unison as Mike dropped his head and shook it from side to side, chuckling quietly to himself as Sarah again leaned to her right and bumped Mike with her shoulder again, teasing.

Shadows began to cover the pool deck as the late afternoon surrendered to evening, the sun falling lower in the western sky as everyone talked and relentlessly teased Mike. Mike's daughters began the process of cleaning up as Dr. Hook and the Medicine Show belted out "Cover of the Rolling Stone" through the outdoor sound system. Sarah, Robin, and Beth excused themselves from the table and walked over to the bar to refresh their drinks, even though Sarah knew she was on the verge of having too much to drink. She had promised herself before leaving LA that she was going to tone down her drinking, at least while she was in public, while she was around Mike.

Angela Montero reached into the pocket of her shorts and pulled out her cell phone. She read the text message and then looked at Mike and gave him a nod. Mike took a deep breath through his nose and nodded back to Angela as he placed his fork on his plate and then cleaned his hands with a napkin. Mike sat for a second and thought, and then made his decision. He motioned to Bob Morton with his head. Bob Morton's wife, Cindy, saw the communication and instantly knew what was happening—time for the men to go to work.

Almost simultaneously, Mike and all his men at the party stood and walked into Mike's house as Cindy Morton walked over to Sarah, Beth, and Robin at the bar.

"Excuse me, Sarah," Cindy started. "I want to tell you something that's very important," she said somewhat ominously. "I need you to listen to me now."

"Okay," Sarah said hesitantly as Beth and Robin watched and listened.

"Mike and the boys have to go to work now...they're all in the house dressing and getting ready...right now, this is very important," Cindy paused and took a deep breath as the other three women looked intently at her.

"Those men are loving, gentle men—they love their families and friends, puppies and babies and they love a good party. But make no mistake about it, they are tough, hard, and deadly men doing a very dangerous job and they can't do that job if they see fear in our faces or hear it in our voices. They know we hate it, they know we worry sick for them and their safety but they're able to get past it because we don't show it. Watch Mike's daughters and sisters, watch them, and see how they act, how they react. They won't even tell their dad, their brother, to be safe or be careful. They'll just say see you when you get back...that's it."

"But," Sarah interrupted. "What if something happens...I mean I just met Mike, what if...?"

"Stop that, Sarah," Cindy demanded. "Stop that right now—that's exactly what I mean. There's always what if with these guys, their whole lives are what if. Suck it up, just swallow it!" Cindy wagged her finger at Sarah.

"I know Mike thinks of you as a daughter so watch his daughters and how they act," Cindy continued.

"A daughter!" Sarah protested.

"Yes. Look, the world is a tough and dangerous place and it needs men like Mike and my husband to be mean and dangerous and to do mean things, brutal things, things other people aren't willing or able to do. But they can't do it...they *won't* do it if they see what it does to us, to their families, how it worries us. So we just have to suck it up and think about them as accountants going to the office for a late night reviewing tax returns or something. You understand me?"

"But," Sarah tried to interrupt again.

"There are not buts, Sarah, not now. If you go in that house right now you're going to see Mike and his guys dressing in all black and strapping weapons on all over their bodies because unlike other men, they don't keep their stuff at some office in town—they keep it with them at all times, either at home or in their go-bags because they never know, we never know, when they're going to get called out. And if you don't think you can use your acting skills to just suck it up then you stay out of that house."

Sarah took a deep breath to calm her nerves, looked at her two friends, and then back at Cindy. She quietly made her decision, grabbed her drink, and walked toward the French doors leading into Mike's house. Beth, Robin, and Cindy followed. As Sarah opened the door and walked in, she saw Mike, Bob, Tom, Jack, Sam and a few new guys standing around the dining room table in Mike's spacious beach house loading semi-automatic pistols into their holsters, checking silenced rifles, and putting on ballistic vests. Mike stood at the end of the table dressed in black military style pants bloused over his boots, and skin tight Under Armor on his upper torso revealing his muscles, muscles Sarah had seen before, his ballistic vest and black shirt laying on the table in front of him. Mike looked at Sarah and smiled apologetically, raising his eyebrows and nodding his head.

"Play the song, Boss!" Jack Byler said very loudly in his southern drawl. "Play the song."

"Yeah, play the song," Bob Morton chimed in... "It's time for the song."

Mike Hampton reached down, grabbed the remote control for his sound system off the table, and pressed play. A second later, a slow and almost mournful drum solo began and then a crying guitar joined. The orchestra chimed in a moment later and in less than a minute, Phil Collins began to sing "In the Air Tonight." Each mission for Mike was a moment he'd been waiting for his entire life, he thought, and Phil Collins perfectly set the mood. Mike and his men played the song before every mission to help get their game faces on.

The men listened to Phil Collins without speaking as they finished loading their weapons and dressing. As each man finished, he looked down at the table, closed his eyes, and gently bobbed his head to the beat of the music, listening to each word, each phrase intently.

Sarah looked on in disbelief while trying to summon her best *oh well* face, trying to fake it. She felt her knees try to buckle and her body quake as the drums began to crescendo and Phil Collins sang, the air conditioner blowing cold air on her nearly naked body clad only in her light blue bikini. She felt herself losing it, remembering Mike being shot, remembering him rocking back on his heels as the bullets struck his vest, struck his flesh...blood soaking his shirt...remembering...My God, this is all happening so fast, she thought.

CHAPTER FOURTEEN

"Our wounds are often the openings into the best and most beautiful part of us." —David Richo

Mike Hampton's men walked to the front door as Phil Collins' voice faded into oblivion and the mournful drums fell silent. Mike clipped his silenced M-4 rifle to the strap around his neck and let it hang across his chest and stomach, pointing slightly to the left. He picked up his gloves and walked toward Sarah and her friends, a Colt 1911 .45 in the holster high on his right hip and his Glock .40 caliber in the holster low on his right thigh.

"I apologize, Sarah, but I have to go to work now," Mike said. "I know I promised to answer all your questions, but..."

"It's okay, Mike," Sarah interrupted. "You'll answer them all another time, maybe tomorrow," Sarah took a deep breath as she talked, Cindy Morton's words reverberating in her head. "Will we see you later tonight?"

"I'll probably be out all night with the operation and then paperwork, meetings with local law enforcement and so on, but tell you what," Mike said. "Breakfast tomorrow is on me. You, Robin, and Beth come over around eight o'clock tomorrow morning, or whatever time you want, and I'll make you a big country breakfast with all the trimmings. In the meantime, you ladies feel free to hang out here with my family, have them show you around the house, drink, swim, whatever...enjoy yourselves."

"Deal," Sarah said while staring directly into Mike's deep brown eyes, acting as if she was playing a part in a movie, adlibbing the script. She reached out and gave his left arm a lingering touch.

Mike paused for a moment and held Sarah's gaze. Then he nodded briskly as if signing an agreement, turned and walked toward the front door. It was the second time she watched him walk off into the unknown.

"Oh yeah, girl's night!" Amanda said with a little song in her voice as she walked into the house waving a bottle of wine and several glasses over her head. "Let's turn the music on and get this party started," she twirled around in the dining room and set the glasses on the table.

"Oh my God," Sarah said as she slipped her cut-off blue jean shorts on over her bikini bottoms. "How can you do that—how can you be so cavalier? Your dad just walked out of here armed to the teeth ready to do battle and we have no idea what's going to happen and..."

"Okay, Sarah, grab a wine glass and sit down baby...we'll walk you through this," Amanda, Mike's youngest daughter and the family bartender said. Amanda was tall like Sarah, about five feet, seven inches, somewhat wild and only three years younger than Sarah.

Wine corks started popping faster than popcorn in the microwave as the women all gathered in Mike's spacious living room. Sarah looked around the room for the first time and thought about how Mike was somewhat of a minimalist like her when it came to decorating.

Mike had no desire to decorate his house, but his daughters and sisters insisted. They compromised with him on the "minimalist standard" and decorated the living room with a cliché beach theme, framed beach, and surf-themed art hanging on the walls along with a 55-inch flat screen television, one very large leather couch split the living area from the dining room, two over-stuffed leather recliners sat near the south wall near the French door. A drum set sat in the northwest corner of the living room near the front door, an acoustic guitar, electric guitar and a bass guitar all sat on stands near a piano and electronic keyboard.

Most of the women sat on the hard wood floor in a circle; some sat "Indian style," others with their legs tucked under themselves. The wine poured freely amidst the comfortable laughter.

"Here's the deal, Sarah," Amanda said. "There's always another mission. Dad always has some operation to go on and if you worry every time then you'll just drive yourself crazy."

"But I don't understand how you don't worry—how the hell do you do that?"

"Just ignore it, Sarah. We grew up with Dad wearing a gun to work every day and it was no big thing...we never really thought about it. There were a few times we had to visit him in the hospital, like when he was on his deathbed in the Philippines. Took him over a week to wake up that time and he actually died twice and stayed in the hospital for three months."

"Oh my God! How did your poor mum handle that?" Sarah said as Angela refilled her wine glass for her.

"Mom just never thought about it. To her, Dad was just a husband going to work like every other husband. She always knew in the back of her mind that something could happen, and often did happen with Dad. But she just didn't think about it."

"I can't even imagine," Sarah said as she sipped her wine.

"Mom and Dad dated in high school, Sarah and they grew up together as adults in Dad's law enforcement career so Mom was there every step of the way making career decisions with him and learning how to be a cop's wife. She kind of eased into it and had a chance to adapt. We were all born into it so it was always just our normal."

Sarah's body swayed slightly with the sound of the oldies rock and roll music playing low in the background. She glanced up to the ceiling and thought for a moment, then looked around the house and was struck by how "normal" it all was, how pedestrian. There were absolutely no signs of what the man who lived there did for a living. It was all just so normal, she thought.

Sarah didn't mind staying up past midnight with the other women to learn about Mike and his family—how they handled military and law enforcement service, and how the wives, husbands, and children handle the stress and danger. It occurred to her during the conversations and through her wine-clouded mind as the people around her told stories and laughed, that she had never known a police officer personally, or anyone in the military. Cindy Morton chimed in with her opinions and experiences being a military wife and how she personally dealt with Bob being off on missions. Most of the guests excused themselves and left Mike's house at 1 AM, including Mike's son, Mike Jr., and his wife, who went upstairs to bed.

"Score baby!" Amanda announced as she walked back into the living room and took her place on the floor next to Sarah. "Dad's photo albums!"

The pictures of Mike coaching his kids in Little League and youth football and other family photographs amazed Sarah. All she could think about again was "normal," he seemed so normal and everything about him seemed *normal*. Nothing indicated the man she met.

Sarah took a deep breath before she spoke. "I do have to ask you ladies one thing," she said. She hesitated and thought for a moment.

"Your dad, your brother, has done so much and seen so much...does it ever bother him? Does he have bad dreams or does he feel, you know...uneasy or something—I don't know how to say it or describe it." Sarah was slurring her speech as she talked.

"Honey," Amanda said. "Dad has nightmares the likes of which you've never heard of. He screams out in the night—get's up and paces the house...we all remember as kids, dad would be up all hours of the night after he retired from the Air Force. He quit one job after a year, tried to start a business, finally worked for a private investigations company for a couple of years—just bounced around for a while like he was lost, he just didn't know what to do."

"Oh my," Sarah said.

"It wasn't too bad when Mom was around because she knew what to do. And, it subsided a little bit after he inherited the money and started the company he has now, since he sort of got back in the field. But he still struggles."

Sarah moved up onto the couch, pulled her legs and feet up under her, rested her head on the arm, and watched as Mike's sisters and daughters looked at photographs and reminisced. It didn't take very long at all for her to succumb to the wine and fall asleep in Mike's living room.

CHAPTER FIFTEEN

"Success is not final, failure is not fatal: it is the courage to continue that counts." —Winston Churchill

Sarah awoke to the sound of stainless steel pots lightly clanging in the kitchen and the smell of coffee brewing. She took a long deep breath and felt herself relax as she exhaled and squirmed to adjust her position. She laid there with her eyes closed for just a moment, just the one moment it took for the wine from the night before to make her head throb around her temples and across her forehead. She tried to wet her lips with her tongue with only limited success. She opened her eyes and blinked slowly at first and then more rapidly, trying to focus.

As her blue eyes finally began to work, Sarah saw a drum set across the room in the far corner, several guitars placed neatly on their stands, and a piano. She noticed the pillow under her head and the blanket covering her, and tried to remember how they got there. She moved her bare feet and felt the soft, supple leather she was laying on. Near her head by the arm of the couch, she saw a small portable table with a glass of ice water and two aspirin. Oh my God, she thought. Am I still at Mike's house? She extended her arms above her head and her legs down the couch, groaned as she stretched her athletic body against the morning stiffness.

"She's alive!" Mike said playfully as he walked over and placed a mug of coffee on the portable table near Sarah's head, pausing momentarily. "I can have breakfast ready in fifteen or twenty minutes. Some eggs, sausages, hash browns, fresh fruit...whatever's your pleasure." Mike turned and walked back toward the kitchen.

"Oh my God, I'm so embarrassed. I must look horrid," Sarah said as she sat up and reached for the ice water and aspirin.

"Not at all," Mike replied. "You're a beautiful, sophisticated, glamorous young actress who just woke up the morning after a party, that's all. Everybody has to wake up and nobody does it gracefully," Mike smiled at Sarah as he leaned on the breakfast bar separating the kitchen from the dining room and grabbed his coffee.

"Thank you, but I really should go next door with Robin and Beth and get cleaned up a little to start my day," Sarah said as she sat up on the couch, wrapped the white cotton shirt closed around her bikini, and reached for her coffee.

"They're out on the beach."

"All ready? What time is it?"

"It's about 9:30, Robin and Beth are out on the beach and my family took off for the airport about two hours ago," Mike said.

"Oh my God, I'm so sorry," Sarah's shoulders slumped from embarrassment as she spoke and then sipped her coffee. "Oh, this is great coffee—perfect."

"Thanks," Mike said. "Jack and Sam told me how you like your coffee. If you want to, you can use the bedroom and bathroom upstairs at the end of the hallway on the right for your morning routine, my daughters and sisters keep all kinds of girl stuff up there and there's new toothbrushes and all that stuff for guests. Take your time and relax, no pressures, no worries, nothing to be embarrassed about. Just relax, we're all friends."

Sarah arched her back and shoulders, stretched again. She looked around and tried to remember the events of the last hour or two from the party, the photo albums, and the stories, the laughter. She watched Mike move around the kitchen and fought for that last little bit of focus from her eyes. She remembered lying up on the couch but had no memory of the pillow and blanket.

Sarah sighed deeply after taking another sip of her coffee, still embarrassed in spite of Mike's reassurances. She stood and walked over toward the breakfast bar as Mike turned and walked back toward the kitchen counter by the sink. She watched him closely as things his daughters, sisters, and friends had told her about him the night before began to flood her mind through the fuzziness of her hangover. After everything she learned about him, still a paradox, still an enigma, she thought... still so many unanswered questions.

She set her warm coffee mug on the breakfast bar and looked at Mike's back as he worked in the kitchen dicing up fresh fruit, the smell of fresh brewed coffee still permeating the air. For the first time, she really noticed his full head of long brown and gray wavy hair trailing down the back of his neck almost to his shoulders and covering the tops of his ears. Not very military, she thought. His broad muscular shoulders filled out his white surfer tee shirt without pulling it too tight and the openings of his Navy blue knee length cargo shorts left just enough room for his muscular thighs. His calf muscles looked as if he had just finished running a marathon. He moved with the ease of a professional chef and used his knife as if he'd been born with it in his hand.

Sarah marveled at the way Mike looked as comfortable moving around the kitchen as he had looked during the gunfight on the 53rd floor of the U.S. Bank Tower when he rescued her so many months before. Just so *normal*, she thought...he's just so *normal*. How can a man who has been shot so many times, been stabbed, blown up and on his death bed, died twice in one day, just be so normal, she wondered. Such a paradox. How is this man not a basket case or just a complete "hard ass?"

Mike cleaned his hands on a kitchen towel, threw the towel over his shoulders, grabbed the plate of fresh fruit, walked it over to the breakfast bar, and set it in front of Sarah.

"Dig in, if you're ready," Mike said as he walked back toward the sink and grabbed his coffee from the counter. "Did you decide if you want some eggs or something?" Mike sipped his coffee as he walked back toward Sarah.

"The fruit looks wonderful, so fresh." Sarah paused and took a bite of a peeled apple slice. "Mike," Sarah said. "I hate to ask this, but did I drool, or snore, or...anything...anything...when you...," Sarah hesitated, wondering how embarrassed she should be.

"None of the above, Sarah," Mike said absolutely. "None of the above."

"Oh good," Sarah said. She was worried she might have screamed out in the night with nightmares about Anne's murder or the rest of the hostage situation, as she did nearly every night, but wasn't sure how to ask, especially a man like Mike who she'd found out the night before had his own nightmares.

Mike set his coffee down and took a piece of cantaloupe from the platter as he stood directly across from Sarah and looked at her.

"Oh my gosh, you have a fat lip and a bruise on your cheek bone," Sarah said as she reached her finger toward Mike's cheek.

"Yeah," Mike said. "I got into a little tussle with one of the bad guys last night and he got in a couple of lucky shots. But its fine, it's all good."

"Nicked you up a bit?" Sarah smiled, remembering how Mike described being shot.

"Yeah," Mike replied. "Just winged me."

"Did the operation go okay?"

"Well, we rescued twenty-five preteen and teenage girls who were about to be sold into the sex-slave trade, and that's good. But, Bob Morton got shot up pretty bad and is in the hospital."

"Oh God! Poor Cindy. She must be falling apart right now! What happened, if I can ask?"

Besides Mike, Sarah never knew anyone who had been shot. And she had never been friends with the wife of a man who was shot before. She had tried but failed to imagine how Mike's wife might have felt all the times he'd been shot and injured. But now, she knew Cindy Morton, she had made friends with Cindy Morton and was heartbroken for her, imagining how she must feel sitting at her husband's bedside in the hospital wondering if he would live or die. I've lived such a protected life, Sarah thought.

"He'll live, they think, but in all probability he's going to be disabled and have to retire. The company will make sure he and his family is taken care of." Mike's voice was serious and professional as he told Sarah Bob's future. But, he did not elaborate on what happened, how Bob was shot. He didn't tell Sarah that Bob was shot saving his life during that "little tussle."

Sarah sat on a stool at the breakfast bar as she and Mike continued to talk. Mike explained that his company had information that the twenty-five preteen and teenage girls had been kidnapped from around the country, moved to an old warehouse near the commercial port in Norfolk, Virginia, and were going to be shipped out to North Africa, the Middle East, and Asia and sold into the sex-slave trade that morning. Mike felt bad that his company was not able to develop enough probable cause for law enforcement to get a warrant from a judge and take over the operation, to rescue the girls, causing him and his men to conduct the rescue themselves because they ran out of time. The rules for private investigators and security companies are far different from those for law enforcement agencies. But, Mike liked to turn things over to law enforcement any time he could.

Sarah was stunned. She knew nothing about kidnappings, the sex-slave trade, terrorists, men like Mike Hampton and Bob Morton, women like Cindy Morton, Mike's daughters and sisters—everything she was exposed to over the past eighteen hours or so, the conversations, the cavalier attitudes about death and danger, were so alien to her. Sarah played many roles on television and in movies and knew real events inspired some of the stories, but she never really took the time to sit and actually consider them. She hated politics and only watched the local news for the weather or inspirational local stories in LA. She always turned the channel on the television when stories about murder, mayhem, and terrorism were on.

"If you *really* don't mind, Mike, I think I will go upstairs and shower," Sarah said with a slight hint of melancholy in her voices.

"Don't mind at all, Sarah. Just let me know if you can't find something you need."

"Okay, I promise," Sarah said as she stood and walked toward the stairs.

"Hey Sarah," Mike called out as Sarah reached the bottom of the stairs. "Do you like motorcycles?"

"I love motorcycles. Why?"

"I'm supposed to meet some folks for lunch today at a diner in town in about two hours, at 11:30—so I'm taking the Harley out, probably go for a couple hour ride after that if you're up for it and don't think Robin and Beth will mind you being gone."

"Screw Robin and Beth," Sarah answered matter-of-factly. "I'd love to take a ride!"

Sarah stopped dead in her tracks half way up the stairs as she remembered something Mike's daughter said the night before, "nobody rides on the back of Dad's motorcycle—nobody. So many women have tried for a ride, but all have failed."

Chapter Sixteen

"Sometimes it's not the strength but gentleness that cracks the hardest shells." —Richard Paul Evans

After a long soothing shower and finding clothes, make-up, a blow dryer, and everything else she needed in Mike's upstairs master-guest room, Sarah bounded happily down the stairs feeling refreshed and ready for a motorcycle ride with Mike, her hangover tamed. She found a nice pair of tight fitting jeans and a white top in the closet and his daughter's form fitting leather boots that pulled up over her calf muscles outside her pant legs. She pulled her long blonde hair back into a low hanging ponytail as she walked.

"So, who are we having lunch with?" Sarah said as she walked over to Mike in the dining room.

"Jim and his wife, Pat. You met them last night."

"Oh I like them, Pat's funny. And they really like you, although, they're a little concerned about you being alone."

"Yeah, everyone has *their* opinion about *my* love life."

"Or the lack thereof, as they all say. They all love you so much, Mike, your family and your friends, and they're just concerned and think you should have someone in your life."

"I know, Sarah, they all mean well enough. But I've never been a bachelor before and figured I'd give it a try for a while. Vicky and I dated all through high school and got married when we were 18, so this past two years is all new to me, and I figured I wear it for a while and see how it fits."

"One of the benefits of being a bachelor, Mike, is dating, you know, playing the field a little."

"Yeah, so I'm told. But that seems like it'd get a little complicated. Do I call the day after a date, do I not call, what if I didn't like her or she didn't like me, or what if the date didn't go well...all that crap. I don't like complications and friction," Mike said as he put his wallet in his back pocket and picked up his keys.

It was a beautiful Mid-Atlantic day for a long motorcycle ride. It was 85 degrees outside and the sky was clear blue without a cloud in sight. Thankfully, the humidity was below 70 percent. Mike dressed in his usual Levi jeans, boots with the rubber soles for traction when he put his feet down on the pavement, white surfer tee shirt and his black vest with the few patches he'd collected over the years.

Sarah followed Mike through the dining room to the door leading out to the three-car garage. As the two stepped into the garage, Sarah noticed the immaculate, highly polished royal blue Ford Explorer, the shiny black two-seat BMW M4 convertible with fresh wax, and the perfectly chromed black Harley Davidson Fat Boy motorcycle with windscreen and leather saddlebags.

"Ok, let's put this brain bucket on you to protect that pretty little noggin...anything happens to you and I'll have about a million of your fans after me," Mike said as he stepped over to Sarah holding her helmet.

Sarah felt Mike's gentle touch on the side of her face as he put the motorcycle helmet on her and fastened the chinstrap, remembering that same gentle touch from the night of the rescue.

"And now let's put these sunglasses on to keep those baby blues safe," Mike said as he put the riding glasses on Sarah.

"Oh my God," Sarah said. "How do you do that?"

"Do what, did I do something inappropriate?" Mike said.

"No, no, I mean, look at your hands," Sarah reached down and took Mike's hands.

"Look at how rough and calloused these hands are—hands that were in a fist fight last night or a wrestling match or something, hands that shoot guns and parachute, rappel down buildings, fingers that look like they've been broken and mangled a few times, and yet your touch is so tender and gentle. How in the hell do you do that?" Sarah pumped Mike's hands up and down a little to emphasize her point as she spoke, careful not to hurt his knuckles swollen from last night's fight.

"I don't know, just years and years of practice I guess, raising kids and grandkids, changing diapers and wiping butts, and I do mean *years,*" Mike smiled and winked at Sarah as he moved toward the motorcycle and put his helmet on. He climbed astride the motorcycle and motioned for Sarah to jump on the back and hold on.

"Um," Sarah said, "are you wearing a gun under your tee shirt?"

"I always have a gun, Sarah. Does that bother you?" Mike said as he looked back over his left shoulder at Sarah.

"No, not at all," Sarah said. "Just wondering." Okay, first *not* normal thing, Sarah thought.

Mike hit the remote control to open the garage door and drove the Harley out. He took the long way to Mom's Kitchen in order to give Sarah the grand tour of the area. They rode south on Atlantic Avenue along the beach and through the tourist and hotel area, and then made the right turn onto Virginia Beach Boulevard. He pointed out landmarks to Sarah each time they stopped for traffic or at a red light. Sarah tightened her arms around Mike's waist as she leaned against his back, noticing the scent of his after-shave lotion.

The trip east on the boulevard took Mike and Sarah past some of Mike's old childhood stomping grounds and Sarah laughed as Mike briefly explained his teenage escapades when they stopped long enough to allow an explanation, chuckling as he remembered some of the funnier things he and his friends were caught up in back in the day. They drove past Mike and Vicky's old high school, Princess Anne, and then past Pembroke Mall. At the red light, Mike explained how he and Vicky loved the carnivals the mall used to host in the parking lot and described some of the rides. He looked off into the distance as he spoke.

The ride south on Independence Boulevard took them to Holland Road and Mom's, where they met Pat and Jim for lunch. During lunch, Sarah laughed as the three told stories about how they met and some of the conversations they shared. Jim and Pat were careful not to talk about Mike's PTSD or Jim's big brother, little brother lectures. They mainly talked about Mike's love life, or the lack thereof, as everyone said, and all the women who tried but failed to date Mike over the past two years. All three of them, Jim, Pat, and even Sarah teased Mike relentlessly as they ate and laughed.

"Oh Mike," Sarah said suddenly with a serious tone in her voice. "I forgot to tell you something and see if it's okay with you."

"Whatever it is, I'm sure it's okay. But what's up."

"Well, Robin and Beth's husbands are flying in tomorrow afternoon with the kids to stay at the beach house with us, if that's okay with you. And another former cast member from the old show, Adam, is flying in with his wife. I'm so sorry I forgot to mention it but, my head's been a little fuzzy today because, well, you know..."

"That's fine, Sarah, I told you in my letter to invite anyone and everyone you wanted. I don't mind at all but it's going to get a little crowded in that house," Mike chuckled a little as he finished his sentence.

"Nonsense, Mike," Pat chimed in. "If Sarah's the only one at the beach house without a husband or kids she should just move over into your upstairs master-guest room—didn't your family leave this morning?"

"Oh I couldn't do that," Sarah said. "I couldn't impose like that."

"Yes you can honey," Pat insisted. "Mike doesn't mind at all, do you?" Pat glared at Mike over the top of her granny glasses. Jim smiled and laughed quietly, fully aware of what his wife was doing, and how uncomfortable he knew Mike was at that moment.

"Nope, I think that's a great idea. That is," Mike paused. "That is if you don't mind risking your reputation and some tabloid finding out," Mike chuckled again. "I can just see the headlines now—rumors. Oh the scandal," Mike laughed.

"Stop it, you," Sarah said as she leaned over and bumped Mike with her shoulder. "If you're sure it's okay," Sarah said.

"Positive," Mike said. "It's settled."

The foursome finished eating and Mike again insisted on paying the check. Pat and Sarah walked out together before Jim and Mike and stood next to the motorcycles. They exchanged idle chitchat about how nice the weather was for a ride as they waited for the two men and other riders from the VFW who were riding with them to Emporia, Virginia and back for the afternoon to come out of the restaurant.

"Are you sure it's okay, Mike?" Sarah said as Mike walked over.

"Yep, it's fine. I do wish you'd told me they wanted to come though, because I would have sent a plane for them."

"The man has ten airplanes, Sarah," Pat laughed as she spoke. "He has the 757 you and your friends flew in on, an Airbus A-380 for long international flights and about eight other corporate business class jets...he's even got a 600 foot mega yacht he calls his *boat* and a 15,000 square foot penthouse in Manhattan he calls his *apartment*," Pat said derisively as she and Jim both laughed.

"Oh my God—how rich are you?" Sarah gasped at her own question and quickly put both hands over her mouth trying to keep the words in. Mike shrugged his shoulders and tilted his head.

"Dirty, filthy, stinking," Pat and Jim said in unison and laughed again. "That's all he'll ever tell anyone.

"It's all for corporate use, Sarah, and my family uses them all far more than I. I just use them when I have to, for business mostly," Mike was embarrassed. He had never gotten used to the rich lifestyle after inheriting his money and never liked to talk about it or the things he owned. He always tried to play it down.

The two-hour ride to Emporia and two hours back took longer than expected with stops for bathroom breaks, gas, and shopping, and a long, leisurely dinner on the road. Mike and Sarah arrived back at his house at 9:30 PM, long after Mike had expected to be home. They were both exhausted from the long ride and lack of sleep the night before, and Sarah's buttocks and legs felt as if they were still vibrating.

Sarah had plenty of time to think during the ride and was more intrigued than ever. A dangerous and deadly man that seems so normal and gentle, she thought, and now an incredibly wealthy man who doesn't live like an incredibly wealthy man. He grows his hair a little long, unmilitary, and rides a Harley, loves parties with his family and friends and does his own cooking, lives alone with just a daily maid service but no real servants.

Sarah thought how Mike could obviously retire in comfort and play golf or tennis or just ride the entire country on his motorcycle, but kept risking his life anyway, risking death. She was perplexed, intrigued. She also realized that she had just spent her first pleasant day since her rescue without any stress or fear, no intrusive thoughts. She was comfortable again for the first time in eight months. She was happy.

"You're welcome to stay here tonight, Sarah, if you want, since it's already getting late. We can move your stuff over here tomorrow," Mike said as the two walked in the dining room door from the garage.

"Are you sure you don't mind, Mike? I know Pat kind of pushed you into it."

"Not at all, Sarah, I don't mind at all," Mike said as he threw his keys and wallet on the dining room table. "It's kind of nice to have company and... Well...after all, it's you," Mike said as he shrugged his shoulders and motioned to Sarah. She laughed a nervous, embarrassed laugh.

"Okay, if you're sure."

"Positive. If you need to freshen up, just keep using that upstairs master-guest bedroom. There's some of my dress shirts in the closet in that middle bedroom up there if you need something to sleep in."

Okay," Sarah said as she started up the stairs.

"Oh," Mike said, "I'm going to get ready for bed but my new nighttime routine is to have some hot decaf green tea with honey before bed. Would you like some or some orange chamomile or something, some Pinot maybe?"

"Oh, some chamomile sounds wonderful," Sarah answered as she continued up the stairs. "Thank you." Sarah bounded up the stairs with a new excitement.

CHAPTER SEVENTEEN

"Have enough courage to trust love one more time and always one more time." —Maya Angelou

Sarah dialed Beth on her cell phone, put it on speaker, and laid it on the vanity in the upstairs bathroom as she began peeling off her clothes. When Beth answered she asked her to put her phone on speaker so Robin could listen, and told them about her day with Mike and that she was moving into his house for the remainder of their vacation.

After the phone call, Sarah washed up and then brushed out her long blonde hair and left it hanging down over her shoulders, bangs parted in the middle and pulled back. She refreshed her make-up but made sure not to use too much, just covered the dark circles under her eyes and highlighted her cheekbones. She thought for a moment, and then decided against wearing a bra under the light blue button down dress shirt she found in the closet of the middle bedroom.

Sarah stood in front of the mirror and checked herself. She decided only to button three middle buttons on the shirt and left the top and bottom of the shirt unbuttoned. She rolled the sleeves up to the midpoint of her forearms, and then rolled them back down again, cocked her head and looked in the mirror. She rolled them back up, but to her elbows this time and decided she liked it that way. The light blue cotton dress shirt fell just about to her mid-thighs. She was satisfied.

"Oh my God, what in the hell am I doing?" Sarah muttered to herself as she looked in the mirror. "I'm acting like a little school girl—a teenybopper, geesh. Get a grip Tomzewski."

Sarah bounced down the stairs and found Mike sitting on the couch in the dimly lit living room, his head back and eyes closed as if meditating, his hot tea and her mug of chamomile on the table beside him. She paused at the bottom of the stairs, wondering if he had fallen asleep and if she should just quietly turn and go back upstairs to bed.

"Hey you," Sarah finally said to Mike as she walked over and sat at the opposite end of the couch. "Sleeping already?"

"Nope," Mike said. Just listening to the music and clearing my head from the day's activities." Mike picked up Sarah's mug of orange chamomile, leaned over, and handed it to her. She used both hands to take the warm mug from Mike carefully.

"So Mike," Sarah started. "Do I get to ask you some questions now?"

"Sure. I told you I'd answer all your questions and I guess this is as good a time as any, especially since it's the first quiet time we've had together since you got here. And I apologize for that, by the way."

"Okay. From talking to your friends and family, I gather that you haven't ruled out having a relationship with another woman, or marrying again, but you don't want to date. So..." Sarah hesitated. "Um, how do you expect to meet someone and fall in love again, that is, if love really is in your future?"

"Well, I don't know. I guess the same way Vicky and I did it, the only other time in my life that I've done it."

"The girls showed me pictures of you and Vicky last night. You've always been very handsome and Vicky was gorgeous."

"Yeah, she sure was," Mike ignored Sarah's compliment of him. "And she was way out of my league it's amazing we ever got together at all...I was scrawny and shy and she was beautiful, popular and outgoing," Mike looked wistfully into the distance as he spoke about his late wife.

Sarah paused for a little while because she didn't want to push Mike too hard, as if interrogating him, but she wanted to know and, as he said, he had promised to answer all of her questions, she thought. The two sat silently on the couch for a few moments sipping their tea, and then exchanged some light, non-threatening conversation about Mike's company, and who his men were. Sarah was impressed with the skills and background of all Mike's men. They talked about Bob and Cindy Morton, and how Bob's recovery was going the first day after being shot the night before.

The oldies music continued to play low in the background, the computerized playlist automatically changing from artist to artist, song to song. Sarah sat at the far end of the couch from Mike and tucked her legs and feet up under herself again, her favorite way to sit. She watched Mike as he spoke, but only half way listening as her mind replayed the slide show of her rescue eight months before, watching the man sitting next to her now as he fought the terrorists and was shot. My God, she thought, he's just so frappin' *normal*.

"How did you and Vicky finally get together, Mike," Sarah finally asked, half out of genuine curiosity and half out of wanting to know Vicky's secret.

"Well, we had two classes together in 10th Grade and she talked to me a few times in class and after class. Pretty soon, a month or two into the school year, we accidentally met outside of school and then began hanging out together with groups of friends and ending up in the same place at the same time—school dances, football games, stuff like that," Mike paused and sipped his tea, still looking into the distance and not at Sarah.

"And then?" Sarah prompted.

"It just kind of evolved from there. We danced a few times in the gym after football games, talked in groups with other friends. Then she visited my house one night after school, I worked up the nerve to reciprocate and visited her house one night," Mike paused again, leaned forward on the couch and rolled his mug of hot tea between his hands, and thought.

As Mike and Sarah sat in silence for a few minutes, Mike thought about those first few days and weeks with Vicky, and smiled to himself inside. He was never under any delusions that Vicky was interested in a romantic relationship with him in high school. He knew she was a very nice girl, but way out of his league. At the time, Mike remembered, he just felt like Vick wanted to be friends with him even though she was probably dating some varsity football player, and that was enough for Mike back then, just to be friends with such a popular and beautiful young lady.

Jackson Browne sang softly in the background about "Running on Empty," a perfect metaphor for his life, Mike thought to himself, at least for his emotions. He explained to Sarah how he and Vicky were bored one Saturday evening while sitting around her kitchen table talking and playing cards with her sister and a neighbor, so they walked a block to the skating rink and how that was really their first date, and it was Vicky's idea, not Mike's.

"So, to this day, I've never asked a girl out," Mike admitted.

"Never?"

"Never. Well, after we started dating I did ask Vicky if she wanted to go places, so, I guess technically, I asked her out on dates but I've never just called a girl up cold and asked her out."

"Oh my," Sarah said. "So if it's not too personal or uncomfortable, what about your first kiss, how did that happen?"

"It never would have happened had it been left up to me. I was too shy and didn't know anything about girls or having a relationship with one, we were only fifteen," Mike paused and sipped his tea again. He wondered if it was a good time to have this conversation with Sarah or not, if he could handle it emotionally. He had never had this particular conversation with anyone and didn't know if he was ready. He took a deep breath through his nose as he sipped his hot tea.

"I was leaving her house one evening after playing cards, again, and," Mike paused and cleared his throat. "She kissed me good night out on the car port...planted a big wet one on me and then she said, get this," Mike interrupted himself and looked at Sarah, narrowed his eyes and smiled at her. "After the kiss Vicky said to me, there, now that didn't hurt a bit, did it," Mike shook his head slightly and chuckled as he remembered that first kiss from Vicky, his shoulders bobbing up and down.

"Wow, Vicky certainly knew what she wanted and went for it," Sarah laughed as Mike nodded.

"Did she ever say why you, why she picked you? I mean, because you said she was so far out of your league, which I don't believe because I saw your pictures, so, did she say why you?"

"I asked her once years and years ago and she said she saw something in my eyes...never said what it was, just something in my eyes."

Sarah knew what it was, what Vicky had seen in Mike's eyes because she saw it too. She leaned back against the arm of the couch and extended her legs toward Mike at the other end, causing her shirt to ride up her legs just short of her panty line, and pressed her toes against Mike's thigh as she nonchalantly feigned a stretch.

"So, you've been the man behind the eyes for sometime then, haven't you?" she said teasingly.

"I guess," Mike said with a hint of melancholy in his voice, and then sipped his tea again.

Sarah's beauty was not lost on Mike that evening. The dim lights bounced off her shiny blonde hair and perfectly accented her beautiful face. And he did notice that her shirt was mostly unbuttoned. Mike had always thought she was currently one of the most beautiful actresses in Hollywood and if she was at least ten years older, he thought to himself at that moment, he might actually try something. He turned his head away from her so she wouldn't see him smiling at himself, laughing at himself and the thought of *doing something* with Sarah Tomzewski. He didn't know what he might do because he'd never sat on a couch in the evening with a woman other than his late wife, but maybe something. He smiled at himself again and took another sip of his tea.

"So Mike, why do you still do, what you do—the rescues and all the operations, the missions?"

"I don't know," Mike replied as he shrugged. "I guess it has a lot to do with the way I was raised. I believe that if you have the ability, if I have the ability and resources to do something good then I have a responsibility to do it. That's for me and my responsibility; it's up to others to figure out their responsibilities."

Sarah let Mike's answer hang there in the air for a few moments without responding. She kept her toes on Mike's thighs and moved them slightly to gauge his reaction, she squirmed a little to adjust her position on the couch.

Sarah was amazed at how comfortable she felt with Mike even though she had really only known him for a day and a half, and was still finding out things about him, basic things. She couldn't believe how at ease she felt sitting on the couch with him and just talking about his life. There was nothing threatening, no pressure, and no judgment. There was just tranquility, orange chamomile, good conversation with a very nice, down to earth, and very handsome man. She realized at that moment that she had not built Mike Hampton up too high in her earlier delusions, before meeting him. He was everything she'd hoped, and more.

Mike unconsciously reached down and began massaging Sarah's foot with his left hand, the way he did for his wife when she was sick, as he stared off into the distance listening to the music. Sarah watched him, careful not to move because she knew he didn't realize what he was doing. She waited quietly for a few minutes and listened to the music herself as she sipped her chamomile.

"Well Sarah," Mike patted Sarah's foot as he spoke, clutched it for a second, then released it and stood. It's been a long two days so I think I'm going to hit the bed. I'm an old man, you know," Mike smiled a sarcastic smile at Sarah.

"Old man my foot. I don't know men half your age that could keep up with you," Sarah said. "But can I ask just one more question?" Sarah followed Mike into the kitchen with her mug and watched as he placed his mug in the dishwasher, turned and took Sarah's mug from her.

"Sure," Mike said as he closed the dishwasher, stood and leaned back against the kitchen counter.

"Is the real reason you don't want to date anyone right now because you miss Vicky and you're still mourning her passing?" Sarah said cautiously, her voice trailing up at the end as she watched Mike's reaction.

Mike looked down briefly, took a deep breath, crossed his arms, and looked back up. "No, that's not it, Sarah." Mike paused. "Our wedding vows said till death us do part, and death us did part."

"Vicky and I talked about it when she was first diagnosed with pancreatic cancer and the doctors told us she was terminal. She wanted me to date again, wanted me to find someone. It's just my bullheadedness, I guess. Well, that and the fact that I have absolutely no experience with women and I'm a coward about it," Mike smiled at Sarah again.

Sarah walked over to Mike and put her arms around him, gave him a tight, lingering hug and then a slow, soft peck on the cheek. She bowed her head slightly, keeping her cheek next to his.

"Good night, Mike, I had a great time today," Sarah said very softly as she released her hug and turned to walk away.

"What?" Mike said. "No punch in the arm this time?"

"Maybe tomorrow," Sarah turned and winked back at Mike as she answered, then turned back around, and walked up the stairs.

CHAPTER EIGHTEEN

"I no doubt deserved my enemies, but I don't believe I deserved my friends." —Walt Whitman

The June sun had barely crested the horizon to the east as Sarah woke up shortly after six in the morning to the smell of fresh coffee wafting up the stairs. She stretched her body down the length of the queen size bed in Mike's upstairs guest bedroom, curled her feet and toes, took in a deep cleansing breath, arched her back, stretched her arms and hands over her head, and let out a long satisfying sigh. She couldn't remember the last time she'd slept so peacefully through the night and awoke feeling so refreshed and ready for the day. She sat up on the edge of the bed and retrieved her hairbrush from the nightstand, and began brushing out her long hair as she silently reminisced about the day before...and the evening, smiling to herself as she brushed.

Sarah cleaned up for the day, dried her hair, put on what she felt was just the right amount of make-up, her skimpy blue bikini, the white cotton shirt from two days before, and skipped down the stairs to find Mike. She found him standing by the sink in the kitchen finishing the last of a fresh fruit smoothie, wearing a pair of black warm-up pants and a white tank top, tennis shows and white socks.

"Oh my gosh," Sarah said. "Have you been working out or something already?" she said as she walked into the kitchen toward the coffee pot on the counter next to Mike. She playfully bumped her hip against his. Mike feigned injury.

"Yeah," Mike said after pulling the plastic container of fruit smoothie down from his mouth. He let out a little chuckle at himself because he loved hearing Sarah's accent. "I usually get up between 4:30 and 5:00 and workout for about an hour or hour and a half, depending on how I feel. How'd you sleep?" Mike said as he reached into the cabinet and took down a coffee mug for Sarah.

"Wonderful," Sarah replied with enthusiasm. "Simply wonderful."

Mike poured coffee into Sarah's mug and passed her the cream and sugar. He dug into a drawer and retrieved a spoon for her.

"Good morning, by the way," Mike said as he bumped his hip against hers.

"Oh, good morning," Sarah said as she fixed her coffee.

I'm getting ready to do a little surfing if you want to join me...I know you took up surfing a couple of years ago out in LA. There's a storm several hundred miles off the coast pushing up a nice thigh to waist high swell, nice easy waves with no current running to make you work hard," Mike smiled as he gave Sarah the local surf report.

"I'd love to," Sarah said in between sips of her coffee. "Do you have an extra board?"

"I've got about five boards, but they're all long boards and I know you usually ride a shorter fun board. But the long board shouldn't be too hard to handle today because the waves aren't that powerful."

"That sounds fantastic. Do I need a wetsuit?"

"No," Mike said. "The water isn't that cold here in the summer like it is in California. You'd get too hot in a wetsuit."

"Cool," Sarah said playfully as she smiled at Mike and momentarily rose up on her bare toes and then back down again.

"I'll go wash up from my workout and change into my baggies and we'll head out in about fifteen minutes if that's okay," Mike said as he rinsed out his plastic jug and put it in the sink, and started out of the kitchen for his bedroom.

"Sounds good. That'll give me time to get a little coffee in me," Sarah said.

As Mike walked out of the kitchen and disappeared through the downstairs hallway toward his bedroom, it dawned on Sarah that he had several scars on both shoulders and biceps, some the size of nickels and one or two the size of quarters. There were two larger scars on the back of his shoulders, much larger. Most of the scars were round and looked like raised skin with rough edges and were the same color as his skin. But one scar on Mike's left shoulder still had a pinkish color to it, as if it was a newer scar. Sarah wondered if that was a scar from her rescue, if it was *her* scar.

Sarah realized it was the first time she had seen Mike wearing anything but a tee shirt, his long sleeved Under Armor, or a black fatigue blouse and had never really seen his muscular upper arms or shoulders before. She wondered if each scar reminded him of a time or a place. Did they remind him of specific situations, and how did he feel about them? Were the scars the *real* reason he wasn't dating, she wondered.

Mike, wearing his knee length black baggies with a red stripe down the side of each leg, a black rash guard shirt, and his slaps, found Sarah standing by the French doors looking out onto the pool deck. He handed her a rash guard and they walked outside into the warm morning air together, across the pool deck and out the back gate, stopping just momentarily at the storage room to grab two beach towels and two jugs of fresh water. Sarah took one of the jugs of water from Mike and reached for a beach towel.

"It's okay, Sarah, I got'em," Mike said as he walked down the steps.

"No," Sarah said, "I can carry mine," as she took the towel from Mike.

Mike shrugged one shoulder and rocked his head to one side, "Ok, if you say so."

Mike stopped at the bottom of the steps and knelt down, and reaching up under his deck, he retrieved two nine-foot long surfboards and a chunk of wax.

"Those are beautiful," Sarah said, "which one's mine?"

"You can use this one," Mike indicated the white surfboard with the black flames painted on it, his favorite. "It has more rocker in it so it's easier to catch the wave and it's also easier to maneuver. I'll use this green and white monster."

Mike placed a surfboard under each arm and turned for the beach.

"Excuse me, Mr. Hampton," Sarah said firmly. "I can carry my own surfboard, thank you very much," Sarah placed both hands on her hips as she spoke and gave Mike a look—that disapproving look that women sometimes give men.

"Oh, okay," Mike said. "I didn't mean to offend."

"No offense taken," Sarah said, intentionally bumping Mike playfully with her shoulder as she took the surfboard from him.

Sarah and Mike enjoyed an hour of surfing together, Sarah falling off her board often and Mike rarely falling, only when he tried to show off for Sarah. They teased each other and laughed while sitting astride their boards, bobbing up and down in the warm Atlantic water, and waiting for the next wave. There were no probing questions, no heavy topics to discuss, just fun.

The temperature gradually increased as the morning sun rose higher in the clear blue sky, but the water provided relief from the heat. Sunbathers began to gather on the beach, some families with small children from neighboring houses, others were local high school and college kids looking for a strand of beach without the hustle and bustle of the tourists farther south around the pier and the hotels. Sarah was impressed with Mike's surfing. She could tell he loved it and had been doing it for a very long time.

Sarah rode one more wave half way to the beach, and fell off her board again as Mike watched and laughed. She clambered back atop the long board and began paddling toward the beach. As the white water from another wave that broke behind her caught up with her and propelled her forward, she stood up on the board and rode it the rest of the way to the beach. Mike clapped and whistled, teased her.

Beth and Robin, sitting in their short beach chairs wearing baseball hats and sunglasses, clapped and hooted for Sarah as she walked over to them carrying her surfboard.

"What's up girl," Beth said to Sarah. "Looked like you were having some kind of fun out there with your man behind the eyes," she teased.

"Oh stop it, Beth," Sarah said as she laid her surfboard in the sand and pulled her rash guard shirt off over her head. She grabbed her hair in both hands, twisted it over her shoulder, and squeezed the salt water out.

"So," Robin said, "tell us about Mr. Hampton and your night with him. Anything in particular you want to talk about...anything fun," Robin said provocatively.

"No, Robin, nothing happened, nothing like *that* anyway. But I will tell you this, he is just such a normal guy—it's striking how *normal* he is. If you didn't know his background, what he does for a living, you'd just think he was any other guy walking around. It's all just so amazing to me. I've never known anyone like him," Sarah said as she laid her towel in the sand and plopped down on it in front of her friends.

Mike let a few good waves pass as he sat on his surfboard and thought. He liked waking up without a fuzzy head, no hangover. He liked waking up after an actual good night's sleep with no nightmares, no imaginary bad guys attacking him. And he liked spending time with Sarah, but thought it was going to be problematic. He feared getting too close to her because he knew it would never go anywhere, on the one hand, and risked damaging her reputation, on the other hand, being seen with an older man, a widower, and staying in his house. He also knew that at some point, if the two of them got too close, he would inevitably hurt her, at least emotionally.

He looked up at the sky and mumbled, "I think my life's starting to get complicated, Honey. And you know I don't like complications." Mike turned his board toward the beach, paddled for the next wave, caught it, and rode it all the way into the beach.

Upon reaching the dry sand of the beach, Mike reached down and removed the leash from his right ankle. He picked up his board and walked about fifty feet to Sarah, Beth, and Robin.

"Morning ladies," Mike said as he nodded to acknowledge Robin McKenna and Beth Mullaney.

"Good morning Mr. Hampton," Beth and Robin said in perfect unison.

"Nice fat lip and shiner you have going there," Beth said. "Anything you want to tell us about?"

"Not particularly," Mike said as Sarah shot Beth an evil eye for teasing Mike.

"Just temporary souvenirs from the other night."

Mike laid his surfboard in the sand next to Sarah's and picked up his gallon jug of fresh water. He took a long drink from the jug of water, swished it around in his mouth to get the salt-water taste out, turned away from the ladies, and spit it into the sand. Without taking off his rash guard first, as he would usually do if he was alone on the beach, he poured the rest of the jug over his head, careful not to splash his guests, and then dried off with his towel.

"So, what time is everyone else getting into town," Mike asked as he continued to towel off.

"About five," Beth answered.

"Good. If Angela did her job properly then there'll be a couple of limos there to pick them up and bring them to the house. What are you ladies planning for today?" Mike said as he sat in the sand a few feet from the three women, distancing himself a little from Sarah, which did not go unnoticed by her.

"Oh, we don't know," Robin said. "We were kind of waiting to see what you and Sarah had planned for today."

"I have to work this afternoon, have some meetings with law enforcement about the other night and some planning stuff to do for a meeting I have Friday up in New York," Mike looked at Sarah as he spoke.

"Oh drat," Sarah said. "I was hoping you could show us all around later today before everyone else gets here."

"I apologize, Sarah, I probably should have told you last night or this morning before surfing, but really didn't think about it until just now."

Mike did have an upcoming meeting in New York, but Angela was in-charge of putting it together and Mike would do all of his preparations for the meeting during the flight up. And, he could put FBI Deputy Director Craig Buckley and the other law enforcement agencies off another day or two, have his lawyers handle it if he needed, if he wanted, but he didn't want to. Something Mike had also failed to tell Sarah, was that there was another situation percolating somewhere out there in the world that he was probably going to have to deal with himself in a week or two, he and his men. A mission somewhere in West Africa that would be one of his most difficult, more challenging even than Sarah's rescue.

"Tell you what," Mike said. "You ladies take the Ford in the garage today and do whatever you want, look around town, sight-see, and just have fun. I'll take the BMW to my meetings. The Ford has GPS navigation with my address already plugged into it," Mike looked at Sarah.

"Okay," Sarah said, a little disappointed. "If you're sure you don't mind."

"Not at all, Sarah. My pleasure. Just use it like it's yours."

Mike picked up his and Sarah's surfboards and water jugs, paused, and looked at her to make sure he wasn't aggravating her by carrying them for her.

"Big country breakfast in about an hour if you ladies are hungry," he said as he slowly started walking toward the house, still waiting to see if Sarah was going to object.

"Okay," Sarah answered. "Thank you."

Mike thought to himself as he walked to the house. Even if he was ready for a relationship right now, Sarah certainly wasn't the one, she couldn't be the one because she was so damn young, he thought. "Nope," he muttered, "she's great and I love strong and confident women, but she's just too damn young."

CHAPTER NINETEEN

"Only the dead have seen the end of war." —Plato

It was a familiar and strangely comfortable feeling, and the fact it was so comfortable made him angry. As Mike Hampton stood in the shower with the nearly scalding hot water slamming into his face and rolling down his body over his scars, he felt himself becoming increasingly irritated and nervous, agitated. He mumbled and cursed the universe under his breath, shampoo dripping into his mouth.

He leaned forward and placed both hands on the shower wall in front of him and let the hot water slam into the top of his head, roll down his back and off his face as he looked down at the floor. He took long, deep cleansing breaths, exaggerated inhaling, and exhaling, pursed his lips and blew the air from his lungs, slowly moved his head from side to side under the water.

Mike felt his life closing in on him, suffocating him, but knew it was only in his mind, his own weakness, his own failings. He felt responsibilities piling up on him again, pressuring him, but knew it was nothing more than life itself, things every other person in the world deals with every day, just life. But even though he knew, in his mind Jekyll continued his struggle with Hyde.

Mike knew what he was about to do because it was as predictable as sunrise and sunset, and he hated it but felt powerless to stop it, and for that he felt shame. He was embarrassed to look in the mirror. He hated himself for it.

"A man should be able to control his own emotions for Christ's sake," he muttered, "his own mind."

He shook his head vigorously in a failed attempt to regain his composure as he reached blindly for the soap. He tried to clear his mind as he washed, remembering as he touched each scar. Without noticing, Mike began to scrub his body with increasing vigor, harder and then harder still, washing nonexistent blood from his skin—washing his soul. Images of bullets striking Bob Morton flashed through his mind; images of men writhing in pain, dismembered bodies—muzzle flashes in the darkness, the sound of children screaming in fear filled his ears, his mind. The smells filled his nose—sulfur, diesel fumes, urine, dirt, burnt bodies, the sweet scent of drying human blood, sweat.

His heart racing, breathing rapid and shallow, eyes closed, he scrubbed. He reached for the washcloth and scrubbed it across his chest and down his arms as if trying to remove paint from old wood, scrubbing faster still—chest heaving as the hot water struck his body like needles heated by flame. Steam engulfed the bathroom of his downstairs master bedroom.

"God damn it!" Mike said under his breath. "God damn it," he repeated in a full-throated voice as he scrubbed. "God damn it why can't I just be a normal fucking person!" Mike yelled at the universe and punched the tile in his shower.

Sarah Tomzewski, Robin McKenna, and Beth Mullaney collected their beach chairs, towels, and bags and trudged through the warm sand toward Mike's house one-hundred yards away, joking and laughing as they walked. Fans stopped them several times and the three actresses graciously posed for pictures with them and gave brief answers to questions.

The three left their beach chairs at the bottom of the wooden steps leading up to Mike's pool deck and walked up. They threw their damp towels onto three long white plastic deck chairs and dove into the warm pool to wash the salt water and sunscreen from their bodies.

"Oh my gosh," Beth said after five minutes in the pool. "What's that smell?"

"That's breakfast!" Robin said.

The three women got out of the pool, toweled off, put their shirts on over their bikinis, and walked through the French doors into Mike's dining room.

"Oh my God, he cooked for an army," Beth said.

Mike prepared a platter of sausage links and patties, fried potatoes with onion, a plate of bacon, and a plate of fresh cut fruit. A large white bowl of scrambled eggs sat in the middle of the table. The table was dressed neatly with three plates, silverware placed neatly atop cloth napkins, glasses of ice water, empty coffee cups turned upside down on their saucers, and two decanters of coffee, one decaf, and one regular.

Mike walked down the hallway and into the dining room dressed in a tailored gray Italian suit with a button down starched white shirt and a yellow tie, black dress shoes, and wearing his wire-framed glasses. He was carrying a leather brief case in his left hand as he adjusted his necktie with his right, and his long wavy brown and gray hair neatly combed back behind his ears and falling down the back of his neck over the collar of his suit coat.

Sarah stood in stunned silence.

"Oh my," Robin said.

"Hello again ladies," Mike said as he leaned down and put his briefcase on the floor near the door to the garage. "If you don't like scrambled eggs, I have enough time to make some eggs to order for you," he said as he stood and looked at Sarah.

"Oh," Sarah said. "This...this is fine...perfect," she stuttered slightly as she spoke.

"Okay then," Mike said as he walked toward Sarah.

"Here are the keys to the Ford Explorer in the garage," he said with a business-like tone in his voice as he handed her the keys. "Don't worry about locking up the house because...well...you know me, my guys are all over the place providing security for both houses so there's no problem."

"Okay," Sarah said as she looked at Mike, lost for more words.

"I hope to be back around seven tonight," Mike said as he walked toward the garage door and picked up his briefcase. "Catch up with you all then." Mike opened the door and disappeared into the garage.

"Good lord Sarah—that's one big old hunk of man candy right there!" Beth said.

"You better jump his bones before I do," Robin said as she filled her breakfast plate. "Hell, I'd leave my husband tonight for a shot at that," Beth and Robin laughed.

Sarah stood silent, not acknowledging her friends, fingering the car keys Mike gave her.

Mike drove his BMW M4 to the FBI office in Norfolk with the top down, and spent the rest of the morning and all afternoon answering questions and making an official statement about the operation his company conducted in Norfolk the previous Saturday night, his attorneys and Angela Montero in the room as well. The meeting was more pro forma than investigative because Craig Buckley, FBI Deputy Director for Counterterrorism, the State police, Norfolk police, and all the prosecutors knew and respected Mike Hampton. They respected the way he ran his company and knew everything that happened Saturday night was necessary. They also knew Mike's men had briefed all of them days before but lacked sufficient probable cause for law enforcement to take the necessary actions to rescue the girls before the Central American cartel sold them into the sex slave trade.

"You seemed a little on edge during the meeting, Mike," Craig Buckley said as he walked Mike out to his car.

"Just some crap on my mind, Craig, no big deal," Mike said. "Hey, you got a cigarette?"

"Damn Mike. I gave up smoking way before you did and you quite a couple years before Vicky passed. What's up?"

"Old habits, I guess. Hey, you remember when we were in the OSI academy together back in the 80's?" Mike said.

"Yeah, we had a blast. Why?"

"Nothing. Just feeling nostalgic," Mike said as he popped the trunk on his BMW and unceremoniously tossed his briefcase in.

"Give me a call next time you're around DC Mike and Peggy and I will have you over for dinner."

"You got it Craig, be safe."

Mike turned the music up in his car as loud as it would go as he drove from the FBI office in downtown Norfolk to the VFW post on Bowland Boulevard in Virginia Beach. He was able to drive without thinking because loud music always distracted him, unable to concentrate on anything but the song with the volume so high. He stopped at a local convenience store on the way for a pack of cigarettes, but didn't open it.

Mike parked in the VFW parking lot, took his suit coat off, and threw it in the backseat. He loosened the knot in his necktie and unbuttoned the top button of his shirt with one hand as he walked in the door.

"Scotch rocks," Mike said to the bartender in the VFW as he pulled the cigarettes from his shirt pocket, opened them, a put one between his lips. He searched his pants pockets for a lighter but forgot to buy one at the convenience store. After the bartender handed Mike his Scotch on the rocks, he walked to a small circular table in a dark corner of the club, sat by himself, and killed the drink in one long gulp. He motioned to the waitress for a refill as his other hand subconsciously tapped the unlit cigarette on the table.

Mike fidgeted in his seat, arched his back, and stretched his shoulders. Stretched his legs out under the table, and scanned the room for any friendly faces.

"Hey little brother, what's up with you?" Jim said as he limped over and sat with Mike.

"Nothing up here, Jim," Mike said. "Where's Pat?"

"Don't bullshit me, little brother. I know you too well and you don't kill a glass of Scotch like that unless you're on edge," Jim said as he sipped his beer and looked at Mike over the top of his glass.

Mike sighed, but didn't answer. He paid the waitress for his refill and gulped it down before she could make change and leave. Mike motioned for another as he swallowed.

"Going for a record?" Jim said as he glared at Mike.

Mike sat silently, cocked his head slightly to the right, and looked at Jim. He scanned the room again for people he might know, old friends.

"Okay," Jim said. "I'll just sit here and go drink for drink with you if that's what you want, but I'd rather have coffee." Jim reached up and motioned for the waitress.

"You don't want to talk, that's fine," Jim continued. "But it'll look kind of gay if we just sit here and stare at each other, so I'll talk."

"Well, aren't you the politically correct bastard in the house today," Mike said sarcastically as he continued to tap the unlit cigarette on the tabletop.

"That pretty little blonde actress really seemed to have a good time with you on our ride Sunday. Where's she at today?"

"Don't get in my ass about my love life, Jim. Leave that to Pat and my daughters—my sisters," Mike said.

"Well I'll tell you, little brother, that was about the most relaxed I've seen you since you moved up here from Florida—you looked good Sunday, had a little spring in your step and a smile on your face." Jim turned in his chair and took the coffee pot and two cups from the waitress, poured coffee in each cup.

Mike and Jim sat silently for several minutes, Mike listening to the music playing in the background, the low hum of voices across the room while Jim slurped his hot coffee. Mike rolled the empty Scotch glass around on the table between his hands for a moment, and then sat it to the side. He reached over and pulled the second cup of coffee over to his side of the table, ran his finger around the top rim, and then took a sip. He took a deep breath as he considered his next words.

Mike set the coffee down, leaned onto the table with his elbows, clasped his hands together out in front of himself, and hung his head. He was embarrassed and felt ashamed. Jim watched silently, knowing that Mike was in agony over something, and figured he knew what it was.

Mike finally broke down and told Jim what happened in the shower that morning, embarrassment permeating his voice. He told him about spending the last part of the evening on the couch with Sarah the night before and how good it felt, how relaxed he felt. Mike explained to Jim how easy it was to talk to Sarah, but how he felt bad about it because he had, as Mike put it, "adult thoughts" about her as she laid on the couch beside him in nothing but a shirt and panties, and she was younger than his daughters were. He shouldn't have thoughts about a young lady like that, he thought. He felt guilty.

"But the point is, I guess," Mike said to Jim, paused, and took another sip of coffee. "Whether she likes me or not, wants to be friends or more, I'll push her away like I do everyone else because I can't handle relationships anymore. The stress of a relationship, even a friendship, will build up and I'll push that pretty little girl away and hurt her feelings, and she doesn't deserve that. If it's any emotion other than anger or indifference, Jim, then I just fake it. Hell, I pushed Vicky away years and years before she ever got sick and passed away."

Mike hung his head again, took a deep breath, and let out a long sigh as Jim refreshed their coffee.

"Let me tell you something little brother," Jim said to Mike. We all have this emotional plate, see," Jim used his hands and arms to make a circle. "Like a big dinner plate. We plop stuff on our plate as the day goes by and then we clean that sucker off at night, just like washing dishes. Sometimes it's just as simple as getting mad at the boss or getting in an argument with our wife. Sometimes it's the kids screwing up or the dog taking a crap on the carpet, a call from a bill collector—something—but we scrape that crap off at night and wash the plate.

Sometimes though, sometimes a man sees or does something so bad that it stains that plate and he can't wash it off, can't scrub it off, like cops and firefighters, paramedics and such. Sometimes, guys like you running off all over the place on your escapades trying to save the world, just keep piling stuff on their emotional plate day after day after day and they never do get to scrape it off at all—never do get to clean that plate. So, you just fill that sucker up and keep on piling that crap up. That plate gets so stained you can't ever get all that crap off. You're eating off a dirty plate, Mike, a dirty plate. Then a cute little blonde actress comes along and smiles at you, tries to be your friend and you feel threatened because you just don't have any room for that on your plate—you got no place to put those emotions, hers or yours, so you can deal with them. So you bubble over and blow up in the shower. Every man in this bar's done it, even me. Nothing to be ashamed about, or embarrassed. Not around me anyway."

Jim and Mike sat in silence for a while, drinking their coffee thankfully replenished by the waitress. Mike thought about everything Jim said, really thought about it, and Jim thought about what to say next as he sat watching Mike.

"I'll tell ya, Mike. I'm not a psychiatrist and I don't play one on TV, but unlike you, little brother, I have been going to one for about twenty years and I still go to group once a week. And just like those old drunks helping each other in AA, us Vets have to stick together and help each other out," Jim stopped and sipped his coffee again.

Mike's cell phone vibrated in his pocket. He checked the watch on his left wrist as he retrieved the phone from his right pants pocket...*6:45 PM.* He looked at his phone and read the text from Sarah.

"*Are you still planning on being back around 7? I have a surprise for you.*"

Mike smiled, then chuckled quietly, and shook his head. "Gotta go," he said to Jim as he pushed back his chair and stood. "Thanks for the coffee and the chat and, believe it or not, Jim, I do listen to you and I do appreciate it."

"Any time little brother," Jim said as the two men shook hands.

Mike walked out to his car, leaving the pack of cigarettes and the single unlit cigarette lying on the table with Jim.

CHAPTER TWENTY

"Courage isn't having the strength to go on—it is going on when you don't have strength." —Napoléon Bonaparte

Sarah stood alone in Mike's dining room wearing her form fitting skinny jeans, white sandals with thin straps crisscrossing her slightly tanned feet and ankles. She left the top two buttons of her tailored white collared shirt undone; sleeves cuffed at the elbows and tail hanging loosely over her waist un-tucked. Her blonde hair parted on the left swept across her forehead and fell freely over her shoulders and down her back and looked as if it was windblown and teased.

She inspected the table she set for dinner, pointing at each traditional Polish food item and saying its name under her breath, checking its presentation. She nervously stroked and twisted her hair over her shoulder as she inspected the table, checked the clock in Mike's kitchen, and wondered if the food would stay hot until he arrived.

"Crap, quarter after seven," Sarah muttered as she poured a second glass of wine, pulled out a chair, and sat at the table, surveying the food again. She toyed with her plate and wondered why Mike hadn't answered her text.

It had been just over two years since Mike Hampton had to let someone know what time he'd be home from work or if he'd be home at all. His wife was gone, his four kids grown up and on their own, and he was accustomed to his freedom from relationship responsibilities. Cursed with the gift of introspection from his mother, he knew he was passive-aggressive and hated that about himself. He knew it was just part of his normal pathology and not part of his PTSD, and he usually tried to guard against it coming out, but usually failed. He took the scenic route home from the VFW, enjoying the warm Mid-Atlantic summer evening as he drove his BMW M4 through Virginia Beach with the top down after a stressful day.

Mike pulled his car into a convenience store, went in, and bought some mints to cut the smell of whiskey on his breath. He pulled his phone out of his pocket and toyed with the idea of texting Sarah that he was going to be later than expected, that he was still working—or that he was flying off somewhere for something. He thought about going by his club and jamming with the band a little, whatever band members might be there, but remembered the band's drummer, Bob Morton, was on death's door at the hospital. He also remembered punching the shower wall that morning and decided there was no way he could play his guitar, having broken probably at least one knuckle and maybe two on his right hand.

Sarah poured herself a third glass of wine, checked the clock again, and frowned, 7:25. "Crap," she muttered. Then, she pushed her chair back and stood as she heard the automatic garage door opener kick in with a whining jerk, the garage door opened. She walked around the dining room table and stood between it and the door leading to the garage, her arms hanging down in front of her, hands clasped together just below her waist.

Mike walked in through the door leading to the garage looking slightly disheveled, the top button of his shirt open, his yellow patterned necktie loose and askew, shirttail beginning to come out of his pants above his belt, his suit coat hanging over his left arm.

"Tada!" Sarah said as Mike walked in, raising her hands into the air and then moving them down in unison to point to the table, like a model displaying an exhibit, rising slightly up on her toes as she did so.

"Hi Sarah," Mike said as he threw his coat on the back of a chair near the door. "I apologize for being late," He pulled his Colt 1911 .45 out of its Bianchi pistol pocket holster and put it on the chair with his coat.

"No apologies necessary Mike," Sarah said. "I know you're busy and have a lot to deal with. Did everything go okay?"

"Yeah, fine," Mike said matter-of-factly. "What's all this?"

"This is a traditional Polish dinner. I thought I'd cook for you today since you've cooked for me a couple of times now, and you had to work today, so..."

"It looks great and smells delicious, but you really shouldn't have gone to all this trouble," Mike said.

"It was no trouble, Mike, I wanted to do it," Sarah answered. "Okay, you sit here," Sarah directed Mike to the head of the table, and then sat in the chair to his left on the side of the table.

Jesus. Is she nesting or really just being nice and trying to pay me back, Mike thought as he moved toward the chair.

"To start, I made *Zupa grzybowa*, a mushroom soup because, not to be nosy or anything, I dug through your refrigerator and saw that you like mushrooms," Sarah explained.

Mike nodded and tried to pronounce the name of the soup. Sarah laughed and repeated the Polish name for him, slowly. They repeated it together, slowly.

"The main course is *Zrazy zawijane*," Sarah spoke slowly again, because she knew Mike was going to try to repeat it, and he did. "Its beef rolls stuffed with bacon, gherkin, and onion," Sarah pointed to the platter with the beef.

"And over here is your side dish," Sarah said as she pointed. "This is *Kluski slaskie*, they're dumplings made from boiled potatoes. Oh, and I made a regular dinner salad to get some greens going. And lastly, for dessert, I made *Makowiec*, a sweet poppy cake." Sarah looked at Mike to gauge his reaction.

"It all looks and smells wonderful Sarah. And you look very nice this evening," Mike said in a low tone of voice without looking at Sarah, and then tasted his soup.

"Thank you, Mike," Sarah said, matching Mike's tone.

The two ate dinner together with Sarah doing most of the talking. She told Mike about her day, how she, Robin, and Beth went sightseeing around the local area and found a Polish deli and market on Kempsville Road just over the Virginia Beach - Norfolk city line. They especially liked Town Center on Virginia Beach Boulevard across from the Pembroke Mall, near Independence Boulevard, a place Mike showed her the day before when they went for their motorcycle ride. They liked the shopping, all of the different places to eat lunch, and the laid-back feeling. They really liked the absence of paparazzi.

Sarah was somewhat irritated at Mike because he insisted on helping with the dinner dishes. She wished he would let her pour him a Scotch, and then sit in his recliner and relax while listening to some of his classic rock music.

Mike didn't say it, but he insisted on helping with the dishes instead of relenting because he was uncomfortable with someone else cleaning up in his house, someone other than his maid service. He was uncomfortable with Sarah doing it, still wondering if she was nesting or being nice, repaying a debt she felt she owed him.

As they cleaned up, Sarah tried to tease and flirt with Mike, but he kept making excuses to walk away from her when she tried to bump hips or shoulders with him.

"Can I ask you a question, Mike?" Sarah said.

"I'll tell you what, Sarah," Mike answered as he leaned back on the kitchen counter, wiped his hands with a towel, and looked at her. "Please stop asking me if you can ask me a question. I told you a couple of times now that I'll answer all your questions."

"Oh, I'm sorry," Sarah said. "I don't mean to be a pain in your butt."

"You're not a pain in my butt, Sarah," Mike said with a fatherly tone of voice. "But I told you I'd answer *all* your questions and I meant that, you can ask me anything," Mike finished rinsing a plate and put it in the dishwasher.

"Okay," Sarah said as she scraped leftovers into the garbage disposal.

"Let's do this, though," Mike said. "How about I turn the tables on you and ask you a few questions. I mean, you know us fans and how we always want to know about the stars we like," Mike finally smiled at Sarah and lightened his voice because he knew he was being an ass.

"Okay," Sarah said, her own voice a little lighter.

"Why in the world—how in the world are you not married all ready or at least dating, in a serious relationship?" Mike said.

"My, my, why do you say it like that Mike, like I'm already an old maid or something at thirty five?"

"I say it like that because you are obviously a beautiful, sophisticated, glamorous, intelligent, and successful young lady and actress, you must have throngs of young men chasing you," Mike smiled again as he felt himself finally relaxing.

"Well, I was in a pretty serious relationship...um," Sarah paused and looked down. "The morning of the whole terrorist thing in LA, I found out that my fiancé cheated on me while I was shooting a movie on location in Toronto. I guess I was just gone too much and took things for granted, took him for granted."

"Jesus, what an idiot he is."

"He is Mike, or I am?"

"He is. It wasn't your fault. He entered a relationship with a beautiful and successful young actress that he knew traveled for work. If he couldn't handle it then that's on him."

"Thank you," Sarah said sheepishly.

"Good Lord it's almost nine o'clock, almost my old-man bedtime," Mike said as they finished cleaning up the dinner dishes.

"Would you please stop calling yourself an old man around me, *please*," Sarah insisted.

"Well, compared to you, your friends, and my kids, I'm an old man and that's just the fact of it."

"Stop it."

"Okay, but if you don't mind, I am going to go get out of these clothes and clean up a little for bed."

"Tea and chamomile on the couch tonight?" Sarah said.

"Sure, give me half an hour," Mike said as he turned and walked down the hallway.

Mike stripped down to nothing as he walked in his bedroom, walked into his master bathroom, and washed his face with cold water. He brushed his teeth and rinsed with mouthwash. He looked in the mirror and checked his teeth, and then ran his fingers through his hair. He reached into the medicine cabinet and grabbed his aftershave, then closed the mirrored door. He stopped and stared. "What in the hell are you doing, *dumbass*," he said to the man in the mirror. He put his aftershave back without using it.

Mike walked to his dresser, pulled out his black warm-up pants and white tank top, and dressed without thinking about his scars. He looked around and found his slaps under the bed. Angela Montero called from New York with her nightly update. She made the changes to his shared-calendar on his tablet, and briefed him on the telephone calls he needed to make the following day. She let him know that everything was ready for his meeting with the attorneys and accountants in New York scheduled for that Friday.

Mike walked back down the hallway, through the dining room and into the living room. He found Sarah sitting at the far end of the couch with her feet and legs pulled up under her, wearing the light blue button down shirt from the night before, the top three buttons open. Her hair lay across the front of both shoulders and she held her mug of chamomile in both hands at the far end of the couch, the shirt pulled up high on her thighs. James Taylor sang low in the background.

He found his mug of decaf green tea with honey sitting on the portable table at his end of the couch. He sat, grabbed his tea, and took a sip as Sarah watched, and noticed the shirt he was wearing. She had already decided that she would not ask Mike any probing personal questions because, in spite of his earlier protestations, she felt she had pushed too far and made him uncomfortable.

"So Mike," Sarah started with a lighthearted voice. "Are you finally officially-officially retired after the operation last Saturday night, or still just sort of retired?"

"Well, mostly officially retired. There's something still hanging and festering out there—something I might have to get involved with," Mike said and then sipped his tea.

They sat silently and listened to music for a few minutes, Sarah waiting to see if Mike would bring up a topic, ask her more questions about her love life, and Mike waiting for more personal questions from Sarah, still wondering if she was nesting or just being nice. It was the exact situation Mike feared and tried to avoid, one of the several reasons he hadn't dated since his wife passed away. He fidgeted in his seat, sipped his tea, and tried not to have "adult thoughts" about Sarah, something he was finding increasingly difficult to do.

Sarah stretched her legs down the length of the couch and pushed her toes against Mike's thigh as she had done the night before, as Mike stared into the darkness and listened to the music for several minutes, still not talking.

Sarah finally broke the silence and asked Mike how he was able to carry her during the last part of the rescue after the terrorists shot him in the arm, hip, and his ballistic vest, and then parachute off the top of the building. He explained to her about adrenaline, and the fact that his training with the former Navy SEALs, Special Forces soldiers and Rangers who worked for him had taught him focus and how to push through pain to accomplish mission objectives and goals.

Sarah set her chamomile down on the table at her end of the couch and sat up, now in the middle of the couch nearer to Mike.

"Mike, can I...I mean...I know I can ask anything but...," she slumped, her shoulders fell. She moved her right arm to the top of the couch and extended it toward Mike. Mike turned and looked at her as she moved closer still.

"I know it has to be a difficult subject for you, Mike. But you wore that shirt this morning and I thought I saw some scars on your arms and shoulders and I...I do have a question..." Sarah hesitated again.

"Just ask, Sarah," Mike said quietly, realizing for the first time what shirt he was wearing.

"There's one scar that's a different color than the rest, on your left shoulder, a little pinkish, and I was wondering...," Sarah paused again and in her mind, questioned her decision to ask Mike about the pink scar.

"Yes?" Mike said.

"Is that pink scar on your shoulder from my rescue Mike, is it *my* scar?" Sarah finally said.

"Yes," Mike said. "I have two, the one on my shoulder and this one on my hip," Mike pulled his shirt up and showed Sarah the still pink scar on his left hip, as Sarah moved closer still.

"Can I...um...do they still hurt?

"No."

"Can I...I'm sorry," Sarah whispered, her warm breath now on Mike's neck and shoulder. "I know this is probably morbid, Mike, but, can I touch them?"

Mike hesitated, he and Sarah now nearly face to face, her body slightly touching his.

"Yes," he said quietly.

Sarah reached her left hand up, shaking slightly, extended her index finger, and gently touched the pinkish scar on Mike's left shoulder. She circled her index finger around the edges of the scar, the entire circumference, her breath warm on the side of Mike's face and neck. She reached down, put her hand under Mike's shirt, and gently felt the scar on his hip, slowly, her right arm moving around Mike on the back of the couch. Sarah realized that Mike would carry *her* scars for the rest of his life. Mike turned his head slightly toward Sarah, their cheeks a mere whisper from each other.

Mike jerked slightly with surprise as his cell phone rang in the right hand pocket of his warm-up pants. He reached in a grabbed it, Sarah still gently massaging the scar on his left hip, keeping her face close to his.

"Hampton," Mike said as he answered the phone. He remained silent for two minutes as he listened.

"Okay, thank you. I'll be there in an hour or so," Mike hung up and placed the cell phone on the table next to his tea, moved Sarah's hand as he leaned forward on the couch, placed his elbows on his knees and clasped his hands together.

"What is it Mike?" Sarah said.

"Bob Morton just died."

CHAPTER TWENTY-ONE

"But the word of the LORD came to me, saying, Thou hast shed blood abundantly, and hast made great wars: thou shalt not build an house unto my name, because thou hast shed much blood upon the earth in my sight."
—1 Chronicles 22:8

Sarah tossed and turned all night, unable to sleep thinking about Mike and his men at the hospital to support Cindy Morton. She recalled Mike's rule—he doesn't *do* hospitals. She wanted to go with him, to be with him and support him, but he wouldn't allow it. She thought about what a nice man Bob Morton was and how she'd become fast friends with his wife, Cindy.

Sarah remembered from the cookout Saturday night how Cindy Morton told her about the fear all wives felt for their husbands in their line of work, and how they dealt with it. She thought about Cindy's admonishment not to show Mike her own fear, not to show any concern at all and now, Cindy Morton was living her worst fears.

Sarah thought about Bob and Cindy's two kids, but then her mind switched to images of Anne Campbell, seeing Mike for the first time as he entered that conference room dressed in all black, his face covered with a ski mask, kneeling in front of her and comforting her, his gentle touch.

Meeting Mike Hampton introduced Sarah to a world with which she was completely unfamiliar and that both excited and frightened her. She was baffled how the wives and kids could be so cavalier about it all, but knew it had to kill them emotionally inside. She cried in her bed for Cindy and for Mike.

Sarah heard Mike's garage door open and the loud pipes of his Harley pull in. Moments after the garage door closed, Sarah heard him walk into the dining room and toss his keys onto the table, landing with a jingling clank. She wiped the tears from her eyes and looked at the clock, 5 A.M. She considered getting out of bed and offering to make him some coffee or breakfast, but decided against it. The house went silent again as Mike walked down the hallway to his first floor bedroom.

Sarah heard footsteps walking up the carpeted stairs several minutes later. They stopped momentarily at the top, and then began again as Mike turned and walked the opposite direction from Sarah's room, down the upstairs hallway to his gym at the south end of the house. Sarah waited and then heard the sounds of exercise equipment.

Sarah waited several more minutes and then got out of bed. She quietly walked down the hallway toward the gym, paused at the partially open door, and looked in. Mike was moving at full speed on the elliptical, as if running a sprint, wearing only skintight black, thigh length, bicycle shorts, and tennis shoes. His arms and legs moved as fast as they could, ear buds in place with hard rock music at full volume, high enough that Sarah could hear the music very faintly from across the room and at the door. Mike's arms forcefully pumped the handlebars back and forth as his feet and legs rapidly moved up and down, running, his muscles bulging and straining against the resistance of the machine.

Sarah watched him; stared at his back as he ran on the elliptical, and noticed the scars she had not seen before when he wore his tank top shirt. Nearly his entire back was covered with very small, irregular shaped scars from old shrapnel wounds and five or six quarter-size circular scars with rough edges. A surgical scar started midway up the right side of his back, near his side, and traversed around to the front, crossing over the right side of his ribcage. There was a second surgical scar low on his back, to the left side, right at his waistline.

Sarah moved back slightly from the door, wondering if she should let Mike know she was there, or if she should leave. She wasn't sure if she wanted to stand there and cry as she watched Mike, run over to him and embrace him, or leave. She felt like a voyeur but watched anyway, unable to look away, frozen in place. Sarah wanted to touch each scar and ask Mike the story behind each one. She moved away from the door and walked back to her room.

Angela Montero sat at Mike's dining room table going over mundane corporate paperwork, Mike's daily calendar, and his call list, cancelling all of his appointments and conference calls, sipping coffee as she worked. Sarah walked down the steps at 7 AM after showering and preparing for her day, not knowing what that day would hold or how it would be.

"Good morning Angela," Sarah said as she walked through the dining room and into the kitchen for coffee. "It seems like you're down here more than in New York."

"Yeah, it works out that way sometimes. My husband hates it but Mike is such a great boss and the pay is way more that it should be," Angela put down her phone and sipped her coffee.

"He seems like he'd be a great boss," Sarah said as she walked over to the table and sat on the side opposite Angela. "He's such a wonderful man."

"Sometimes I wish he'd move his corporate operations down here from New York, or that he'd move to New York, but hey, what do I know? He dedicates one of his business jets for my travel and let's my husband and me use it when we take personal trips, so, all-in-all not a bad gig even with spending so much time away."

"He's such a wonderful man, Angela; I worry so much for him. And I think I screwed up and pushed him away," Sarah lamented. "I just, I just kind of lost myself and felt so comfortable with him, so natural, that...I don't know.

Being around him, I just feel like I've known him forever and everything just felt so right," Sarah abruptly stopped herself.

"Oh my gosh, where is Mike? Is he here? Is he going to hear us talking about him?" Sarah lowered her voice.

"No, he's not here. He's already back at the hospital with Cindy Morton and the kids helping them out. And let me tell you something, Sarah, and listen closely. Mr. Hampton likes you; he likes you a lot and respects you— always has. And that's exactly why *he* might be pushing *you* away, keeping you at arm's length...because he doesn't want to hurt you emotionally."

Angela routinely flew around the country and to Europe with Mike when he had to conduct contract negotiations himself, testify before legislatures in different states, Congress, and for other business and there were more than a few times when Mike had a little too much Scotch or Jack Daniels during the flights home and talked more than he usually would about personal matters.

Mike Hampton felt that he always hurt everyone around him, at least emotionally. He never physically hurt anyone, except the enemy, but he felt like he was poison to the people around him because of his PTSD. He often pushed people away and isolated himself, even from his family. Sometimes he just needed the temporary solitude, but sometimes he knew he was on the verge of letting his anger out and it was going to hurt those around him. Sometimes he isolated himself because he knew he was going to drink for a few days.

"You know, Angela, he told me about how he and Vicky first started dating, and about their first kiss. I kind of put myself in a position last night to kiss him, or for him to kiss me, kind of got a little ahead of myself I guess. But I was thinking about what he said when he described his first kiss with Vicky, how she just kissed him and..."

"Honey," Angela interrupted Sarah. "Vicky was dealing with a fifteen year old boy with raging hormones and you're dealing with a fifty-five year old man with dormant hormones and a whole lot of emotional baggage," Angela winked at Sarah and the two women laughed.

"I know," Sarah said and laughed again. "I know."

"And, not to mention his physical scars, he's very-very self conscious about those."

"I know. I saw more of his scars this morning."

"Let me tell you something else, Sarah. You're staying in his house and no other women, except relatives, have ever done that. You rode on the back of his Harley and no other women have ever done that. You've sat on the couch with him on two different evenings now, drinking tea and I assure you that no other women have ever done that! Mike really-really likes you and I think, in his own way, he is reaching out but he's afraid, well, he's afraid *and* naive when it comes to women. He's never been on a date as a grown man and that man can't tell if a woman is harmlessly flirting, or really interested, or just wants to be friends. And that man would never in a million years guess that a woman like you had romantic intentions for him."

"Like me?"

"Yeah, like you...so much younger than him, so beautiful. He sees himself as a burnt out old man with a broken body and no drop-dead gorgeous Hollywood blonde bombshell would ever fall for a man like that, like him, in his mind anyway. So, you might have confused and surprised him a little...okay, a lot. But he's also kind of a chauvinist. He believes in strong, independent, and liberated women but he also believes, probably, that you should find a nice young man your own age, get the house in the suburbs with the white picket fence, settle down, have a family, and build a life together, with someone your own age," Angela laughed.

"What should I do, Angela? I mean, I don't want to put you on the spot or anything, he is your boss, but what should I do?"

"Well, it took Vicky four months to land a fifteen year old Mike Hampton with raging hormones so, take your time. Stay close to him and be his friend. Realize he's going to try to push you away when you start getting inside his emotional comfort zone, and don't let him."

"Do I *have* four months with a man like Mike, Angela? He said there's possibly another operation in his future and the way he talked about it didn't sound too good. It sounded like it might be a bad one. What if..."

"Stay away from the "what if's, Sarah," Angela interrupted. "Just take it day-by-day."

Sarah helped Angela arrange the business papers and went through Mike's calendar while they continued to talk about Mike and his family.

Just before lunchtime, Beth Mullaney, Robin McKenna, their husbands, Adam and his wife and all of their kids walked up to Mike's pool from the beach and began playing, as Mike invited them to do days before.

"Oh my god I forgot they were coming over today!" Sarah said as she stood up from the table. "Mike will probably want some quiet time when he gets back."

"Its fine, Sarah," Angela said. "Mike needs to understand that life goes on even when people die, especially since he invited you all here. Ask them if they're hungry and I'll help you fix them some lunch."

"Are you sure?"

"Look honey, Mike respects it when people stand up to him, especially when he knows he's wrong. So if he gripes about them being here then just push back. Pick your battles, argue respectfully, but never be afraid to stand up to him. He respects it."

Sarah walked out and told everyone what happened to Bob Morton and that Mike was gone helping his wife. Robin and Beth thought they should take their families home in order for Mike to have peace and quiet when he arrived back home, but Sarah and Angela assured them it was okay to stay and enjoy the pool and hot tub. Angela, Sarah, and Robin went back into Mike's kitchen and started lunch.

"Good afternoon ladies," Mike said as he walked into the dining room from the garage. He walked straight through to the downstairs hallway without stopping, wearing his dark blue suit, starched white shirt, and red tie.

"Hello...goodbye...," Angela said as Sarah and Robin watched him walk through and disappear down the hallway. Angela nodded her head at Sarah in the direction Mike disappeared, and mouthed the word, "go." She nodded to Sarah again.

Sarah walked down the hallway to Mike's office and walked in as he was pulling off his necktie and unbuttoning his shirt, an open bottle of Jack Daniel's and a glass on his desk. He emptied his pockets and dropped everything on top of the desk, loose change rolling around and hitting the bottle. He looked angry. His teeth were clinched and grinding, the muscles in his jaws locked and slightly twitching, eyes narrowed almost to slits. He looked up and saw Sarah, poured a four-finger deep glass of Jack. Sarah walked over to his desk and stood in front of him. Mike took a deep cleansing breath as she approached, and thought for a moment.

"You know Sarah," Mike started and then paused. He clinched his lips together, looked down, and rotated his head to one side. "Sometimes, the death of someone close to you makes you think, it makes you think about your life and how you've lived it. It does with me anyway."

Sarah stayed silent, watching Mike and worrying for him.

"I'm tired. I'm really tired," Mike paused and looked down at his desk again, his face finally relaxed. "I'm tired of death but most of all, I'm tired of being so screwed up in the head...tired of hurting the people around me, the people I love," Mike looked up, directly into Sarah's baby blue eyes.

"Everyone needs someone to talk to, Mike, someone on their side," Sarah said with a soothing tone in her voice.

"I have Jim and Pat for that," he said as he slumped down in his leather office chair, leaned back and looked at the ceiling.

"That's not what I mean, Mike. I mean a partner, someone to share with, to be vulnerable with, someone to trust with your deepest feelings," Sarah said as she sat in the chair next to his desk.

"Yeah, that's what Jim and Pat said too," Mike paused again. "You know, I had a partner once, my wife Vicky. And all my problems started the year that I started pushing her away. I stopped letting her be my partner—I stopped being *her* partner. Everything just made me so damn angry and I was no good to her after that, no good to anyone."

Mike paused and drank his glass of Jack Daniel's in one gulp, then poured another.

"You know," Mike finally said after several minutes of uncomfortable silence. "My father really sucked as a dad and husband when he got home from Vietnam and I didn't understand why. He was just an angry man, angry about everything, the smallest thing. Then I had my *ah-ha* moment when I got home from working counterintelligence and counterinsurgency in the Philippines for three years and started getting mad at the slightest thing. I understood my dad better and we were able to repair our relationship. But that makes it all worse now," Mike stopped and stared into the distance.

"How does it make it worse?" Sarah said cautiously.

"Because I know, Sarah, I know what made me like that and didn't change it, didn't get help for it. I ignored it and felt like I could control it. It's one thing to not know and not understand, like my dad after Vietnam, but to let it consume you when you do know and do understand, I think that's just sinful, letting your ego overload your ass like that, it's negligent. It makes me feel stupid."

"Mike," Sarah said. "I don't know everything you're going through and feeling, what you feel like, but I'm beginning to feel screwed up in my head too. In LA, after you saved me, I couldn't sleep, ever. I started drinking way more wine than before and I just roamed my house at night, afraid to sleep, afraid the nightmares would come back and I almost lost my role in a movie because I was so angry and felt nothing was right. I felt everything was stupid and trivial. Nothing seemed important anymore. I thought it was so stupid when the director worried about my facial expression during a shot, how I cocked an eyebrow or the set of my jaw. How can that compare to what men like you go through, to what Cindy's going through—people are dying and that stupid director, how can anything I do compare?"

"That's all perfectly normal, Sarah, all normal emotions. And, it's exactly how I felt in my own little world. I still feel that way about things. But you do need to see someone. Don't wait around and let it consume you the way it has me. Don't let it ruin you." Mike fidgeted in his chair, feeling a little hypocritical giving advice he refused to follow himself.

"I'd better get back and help the girls with lunch," Sarah said as she stood. "Would you like some."

"No thank you," Mike said as he stood and walked around his desk. He walked up to Sarah and stood in front of her, close, looking directly into her eyes again. His chest and shoulders moved slightly up and down as he took a deep breath.

"I'll be in and out of the house the rest of the week helping Cindy and taking care of a few things," Mike said, "but I'd like you to do me a favor, if you would."

"Anything Mike," Sarah said. *"Anything,"* her voice low and sultry.

"Enjoy your vacation with your friends; enjoy the beach, the pool, that hot tub out there. Just relax and have a little fun," Mike smiled at Sarah and wiggled his eyebrows a little.

"I will Mike, promise. That is...if you promise to enjoy the hot tub with me one night."

"Deal," Mike said. "Tea on the couch tonight?"

"It's a date," Sarah said with a light-hearted tone in her voice and a smile on her lips as she turned to walk out of Mike's office.

"Mike," Sarah paused. "You're not ruined...people don't get ruined." Sarah turned and left.

CHAPTER TWENTY-TWO

"A friend is someone who knows all about you and still loves you" —Elbert Hubbard

Mike Hampton was standing at the window of his home office watching Sarah and the rest of his celebrity guests laugh as they played in the pool with their kids when he got the call from his corporate Current Operations Center, the office that monitors corporate operations worldwide 24-hours a day. The French government decided on their course of action to rescue their diplomat and his wife from the Boko Haram Islamic Terrorists in Nigeria. The French did not want to set a bad precedent by paying a ransom and they did not want to risk an international incident by using the French military to affect the rescue. They wanted Mike Hampton's company to conduct the operation.

Anticipating the decision because of failing negotiations, Mike's company prepositioned the six hundred foot corporate yacht in Monaco where it was fitted with a new hospital and surgical bay, took on weapons supplied by the French government, several rigid hull inflatable Zodiac boats, and everything else they needed for the operation.

Mike's senior operational managers, all retired or former Navy SEALs and Army Special Forces, handled the operational planning and coordinated with the Nigerian military and the South African mercenaries that work with them in their fight against Boko Haram. Other team members flew to France and drove to Monaco to oversee forward operations and planning.

Mike liked the plan, but worried about the operation, as he always did, but he was also excited. He could feel the adrenaline begin to pump in his veins again as he went over the plan in his mind. For the five-day cruise from Monaco to international waters just off the west coast of Nigeria, they would rig the yacht to look like a normal pleasure cruise with fifty men and women dressed casually and partying in case they were challenged by a foreign navy or coast guard. All of the men and women were former or retired military with combat experience around the world, and former Navy personnel trained in maritime security and ship's operations would crew the yacht. Mike would fly to France immediately after Bob Morton's funeral in two days.

Mike smiled to himself as he watched Sarah play in the pool with Robin and Beth's kids. What a wonderful young women, he thought, but so young, *so* young. He felt just like he did when he watched his daughters play with their kids in the pool. As a fan, Mike was glad that Sarah, and all her friends, was just as nice and down to earth as fans always hope celebrities are. He chuckled to himself about his adult thoughts and walked away from the window shaking his head. "Dirty old man," he muttered.

After the 800 milligrams of Ibuprofen kicked in and relieved the pain in Mike's right hand, the pain from punching the shower wall earlier, he changed into his cargo shorts, a patterned tee shirt, found his slaps under his bed, and took his acoustic guitar out onto the pool deck. He sat on the end of a deck chair close to the house as the five kids sat on the pool deck at his feet, and played all the kid's songs he could remember. The kids laughed and sang along with him to Jimmy Crack Corn, She'll be Comin' round the Mountain, and Mary Had a Little Lamb for the younger kids. He briefly checked the parents' faces for a reaction when he sang the Chuck Berry song My Ding-a-Ling to see if they would react as his younger sister had years before when he played it for her young boys.

"Probably inappropriate!" Sarah shouted over to him from the shallow end of the pool in her thick New Zealand accent as she laughed and clapped. She watched Mike as he played and sang with the kids. What a good man, she thought. Sarah enjoyed seeing Mike enjoy himself, especially after his stressful couple of days and Bob's death.

As the afternoon turned into early evening, Mike noticed Sarah, Beth, and Robin preparing to cook burgers and hotdogs on the grill. Sarah seemed to know exactly where everything was and had no problems navigating her way around the outdoor kitchen, giving Beth and Sarah instructions as the three women worked.

"I'll get that," Mike shouted over to Sarah as he stood.

"Nonsense," Sarah said. "We've got this."

"Come on, you guys are my guests, I'll cook dinner," Mike said.

"You just sit right there and relax, *Mr. Hampton,* and play some more guitar for the kids. We'll cook dinner," Sarah insisted as she walked over, handed him a beer, and smiled at him.

"Yes Ma'am," Mike agreed and sat back down. "But I'll do the dishes," he said.

"No you won't." Sarah said as she turned and walked back to the kitchen." And don't forget that we have a date tonight," Sarah shouted back to Mike over her shoulder as she walked away in her light blue bikini.

"You and Mike have a date tonight Sarah?" Beth said as Sarah walked back to the outdoor kitchen.

"He promised to enjoy the hot tub with me one night and I intend to hold him to it."

"Oh, moving a little fast, aren't we?" Robin said.

"No, we're not. And besides, one thing I've learned the past couple of days is that you never know how much time you have with a man like Mike Hampton," Sarah said as she began cooking.

The sounds of kids laughing and celebrities talking about their work filled the pool deck inside the eight-foot high wooden fence as Mike shared a glass of Scotch and some Cuban cigars with his new friends. He enjoyed getting the inside scoop on filming television shows and movies, and stories about Sarah's antics while on set filming. Mike had read interviews about Sarah's practical jokes on set and had watched some blooper videos from her work, but it was fun getting the firsthand stories from people who worked with her.

Robin, Beth, and their families left for their beach house next door as the blazing summer sun finally surrendered and allowed night to assume its rightful place. Sarah busied herself picking up the last remnants of trash while Mike put his guitar away.

"Put those baggies on mister, tonight is hot tub night," Sarah called out as Mike walked in the French doors, waving back to Sarah over his shoulder. "After my nightly phone call from Angela."

Mike went to his office and checked his email and messages, blindly shuffled papers around on his desk. Angela Montero called promptly at 9 PM and reminded Mike that she had already cancelled all of his appointments and phone calls because of Bob Morton's death, and there was nothing for him to do except make his final arrangements for Monaco and the operation. He would need to call his kids and his mother. He went to his room and changed for an evening in the hot tub with Sarah.

"Really Mike?" You're going to wear your rash guard shirt in the hot tub with me?" Sarah said as Mike walked out and stepped down into the built-in hot tub that shares a common wall with the pool, and sat on Sarah's right.

"Come on Sarah, don't give me a hard time. If I take my shirt off I might drive you crazy with this herculean body and all these muscles," Mike smiled at Sarah as she handed him a glass of wine.

"Oh you little flirt," Sarah laughed. "That's what I was counting on!"

Mike smiled and sipped his wine as he stretched his legs out into the hot tub. "Oops, excuse me," he said as his foot rubbed against Sarah's.

"Mike," Sarah started. "I know you're self conscious about your scars, Angela told me. But it's just you and me out here and its dark and..."

"I am self conscious about them Sarah and they're hard for some people to look at," Mike interrupted. "So instead of grossing people out I just keep my shirt on."

Sarah wondered if it was a good night to ask Mike about each of his scars and the stories behind them, but she dropped the subject for a few minutes. Mike teased her about some of her antics on set revealed by her former co-stars earlier that evening and listened as she told him about her experiences in Hollywood.

Sarah's Tomzewski's personnel story had always impressed Mike and he had a lot of respect for her. He thought it was amazing that she wasn't eaten alive by the backstabbing, cutthroat world of Hollywood when she first arrived as such a young actress ten years before. Mike didn't know much about Hollywood, but he did know that it was full of beautiful blonde bombshells that ended up as waitresses, or worse. It impressed him that he never saw negative coverage of Sarah in the news. She just went about her business, her life and career, without hitting the LA party scene, getting involved with drugs, or any of the traps so many of the other young stars fall into.

"Mike," Sarah paused. "Angela told me that you're going to France. She told me about the operation."

"She did, huh. Sounds like I need to send her to remedial OPSEC/COMSEC classes," Mike said with a little irritation in his voice."

"What's that?"

"OPSEC and COMSEC are military acronyms for operational security and communications security," Mike explained.

"You don't trust me? Don't think I can keep a secret?" Sarah sipped her wine.

"That isn't the point Sarah. The point is security, and only those people directly involved in the operation need to know about it. It's for everyone's safety."

"Well, don't get aggravated at Angela, but I already talked to her about going with you."

"Well that isn't happening," Mike said.

"I'm going and that's all there is to it," Sarah insisted.

Mike's face was deadly serious when he set his wine glass down on the pool deck and looked at Sarah. He took a deep breath, never taking his eyes from hers.

"You're not going Sarah," Mike said with a serious tone. "It's not safe."

"Am too," Sarah teased and poked Mike in the ribs with her finger, causing him to flinch.

"Look Sarah..."

"No, *you* look Mike Hampton. It's a party cruise and the ship will never been in danger. I already know that. The yacht will be safe in international waters while the operation is going on and you need people on that yacht just having a party, just enjoying a pleasure cruise for cover. Besides, Angela will be there and she isn't military or anything."

Mike didn't answer. The last thing in the world he wanted was for Sarah to go with him on the operation. He needed to be focused and not worrying about Sarah and her safety. He also knew that the mission wasn't going to be a typical hostage rescue, but actual combat in the jungles of Nigeria against a hardened enemy. He knew men were going to be wounded, killed, and their broken bodies brought back aboard the yacht and he didn't want Sarah to see that anymore than he would want one of his daughters to see it.

Knowing that she had two more days to convince him, Sarah let the subject drop. She and Mike sat in the hot tub with their wine and enjoyed looking at the stars. In between long periods of silence, she asked Mike about Vicky and their kids and he was more than happy to answer all her questions, anything other than talking about the operation or his scars. Sarah leaned her body against Mike's and put her right arm through his left.

"You know Mike, I know we haven't really known each other very long, but this would be the moment where you could kiss me if you want to," Sarah finally said.

"I can't Sarah. It wouldn't be right...you're such a young lady and..."

"Okay, I understand. But you can take that stupid shirt off," Sarah interrupted and laughed again to break the tension of her advances.

"Good lord Sarah...I see why you've done so well in Hollywood with those negotiation skills. I should hire you for my company." Mike laughed.

Mike gave in and took off his shirt. Sarah very gently touched the scars on his back as Mike told her the story behind all of them. Most of the small shrapnel scars were from long ago when Mike and his partner were meeting a counterintelligence informant in a bar outside Clark Air Base in the Philippines. Communist insurgents from the New Peoples' Army fired two RPG rounds into the restaurant and part of the building collapsed, killing the informant, and wounding Mike and his partner. Mike and his partner were wounded again by gunfire as they fought their way out of the building and back to the base.

Mike paused several times as he spoke, remembering the first occasion he nearly died. It was the time his kids told Sarah about several days earlier, when he had died twice during the day and was brought back to life first by the medics, and then by the surgeon. Sarah revisited *her* scars with her finger, thinking again how Mike would wear them for the rest of his life, however long that might be.

CHAPTER TWENTY-THREE

"But, instead of what our imagination makes us suppose and which we worthless try to discover, life gives us something that we could hardly imagine."
—Marcel Proust

Mike thought about Sarah and her insistence about going on the operation to Nigeria as he finished his morning workout slightly later than usual at 6:30 in the morning, cleaned up, and dressed for the day. There is no way in the world she's going, he thought to himself, no way. He could smell fresh coffee and sausage cooking as he put on his Levi's, his black Dingo boots, a white patterned tee shirt, and his black riding vest as he sat on the edge of his bed and dressed.

"Good morning Sarah," Mike said as he walked in the kitchen. "What's all this?"

"Oh, I made a traditional Polish dinner the other night so this morning I thought I'd make a traditional New Zealand breakfast," Sarah said with a perky tone in her voice as she poured Mike a cup of black coffee and handed it to him.

"Perfect," Mike said as he took a sip of the hot coffee. "Everything smells great."

"You just sit at the table and I'll bring you a plate."

Mike watched Sarah in the kitchen as she finished cooking breakfast and fixed his plate. She was wearing her skinny jeans that accentuated her athletic physique, brown leather boots over her calf muscles outside her pants, and the white spaghetti strap shirt, her long wavy blonde hair falling freely down her back. Nesting, he thought.

"Do you have plans with Beth and Robin today?" Mike finally said after a few minutes.

"No. They're just spending the day at the beach with their families and then wanted to come up to your pool again," Sarah said as she placed Mike's plate on the table in front of him. "You look like you're going riding today."

"Yeah," Mike said. "I thought you might like to take a ride up to Williamsburg and Yorktown and do some sightseeing today if you didn't have plans...hear the story of how we American's kicked your British ancestors' butt's twice," Mike chuckled and smiled at Sarah as he spoke.

"I'd love to, but they're not my ancestors," Sarah said curtly. "I was *born* in New Zealand but I'm German and Polish. Remember *buddy boy*?"

"I remember," Mike said. "So, what is all this on my plate, besides the eggs, I recognize eggs sunny side up."

"Well, you have two plump pork sausage links but they're seasoned differently than you're used to. Then there are sautéed mushrooms, some diced tomato, and some beans. And if you don't like beans for breakfast I made some hash browns on the side right here," Sarah said as she moved a small plate of hash browns toward Mike.

"Beans are fine, thank you. It all looks great."

Mike and Sarah cleaned up the breakfast dishes together and then walked out to the garage for their motorcycle ride. Mike went through the exact same routine as the first time he took Sarah for a ride; he put the helmet on her to protect her pretty little noggin and the glasses on her to protect those baby blues. He opened one of his saddlebags for Sarah to stow her purse, and then climbed astride the Fat Boy, motioning for Sarah to join him on back.

"You play at being so shy and naive, Mike, but you're really such a flirt," Sarah finally said as she put her arms around his waist and felt his Colt 1911 .45 neatly tucked into its pistol pocket holster fastened inside the top of his Levi's.

"Well if I'm a flirt I assure you it's completely by accident."

It was a beautiful and sunny late June morning as Mike and Sarah rode south on Atlantic Avenue and made the right turn onto Virginia Beach Boulevard. Mike drove his Harley to the entrance of the expressway for the trip to Interstate 64 and Williamsburg as Sarah leaned her body against his back and held on around his waist. She felt a contentment that was still so new to her.

Sarah enjoyed the hour and a half motorcycle ride with Mike but the beauty of Williamsburg took her aback. She hadn't really known what to expect and was shocked to find such a feeling of being out in the country with all the towering pine trees, some rolling hills, and the plush green grasses and shrubs. She loved the colonial architecture and how beautifully everything was restored and preserved, including the actors and guides playing the role of colonial citizens in 18th Century America. She hadn't known what to expect during the ride there, but certainly not what she found.

Sarah kept her right arm tucked into Mike's left arm as much as she could as they toured Williamsburg, and the two laughed as Mike recounted how it was an annual field trip for most of his school years growing up and the annual family trip. He felt as though he was almost as knowledgeable as the guides who worked there.

Mike told Sarah about other sites around Virginia he'd like to show her, including Thomas Jefferson's home at Monticello, Natural Bridge, Jamestown, and Luray Caverns. Before he realized it, Mike told Sarah about his entire childhood in Virginia before lunch as the two walked in the sun and laughed.

"Mike, you know I'm going to France with you, and on the yacht to Nigeria, right?" Sarah said as the two sat down for lunch.

"And you know that's a bad idea, right?"

"No, I don't know that Mike. In fact, Robin, Beth, and Adam want to go as a way to do character studies. We usually have technical advisors on set when we're filming and we do other research, but to watch you guys as you get ready and go out on this operation would be a gold mine for us. Adam always gets type-cast as a hard-nosed cop or military guy and it'd be great for him."

"Bad idea Sarah, it may not be safe. And something you haven't considered is our casualties. In every military operation, you calculate anticipated casualties, dead and wounded, and we anticipate at least twenty percent casualties on this operation—*at least*. Most of them will be brought back aboard the yacht after the operation and I don't want you seeing that—you don't need to see that, not after what you saw in LA when you were held hostage."

"I'm a thirty-five year old grown woman Mike, educated, intelligent, and successful in my own opinion and it's kind of presumptuous of you to tell me what I don't need to see."

Mike let out a sigh of exasperation and thought for a moment.

"You expect to be one of those casualties, don't you?" Sarah said after several minutes of silence.

"I don't know, I might be, but I don't speculate like that. But if my recent history is any guide, well..."

Sarah's fans interrupted their lunch conversation several times and each time, Mike excused himself and stepped away from the table so he wouldn't be included in any of the pictures. Several times Mike volunteered to take the pictures of Sarah and her fans himself; again ensuring he would not be included in them, even though he knew people had likely already taken pictures from afar that included him. Sarah very graciously signed autographs and answered questions.

Mike wasn't worried that his enemies or even people he might encounter on the way to Nigeria might recognize him. He was worried about Sarah's reputation, about people seeing her with such an older man and pictures making their way into the tabloids.

After lunch, the pair walked to Mike's Harley for the ride to Yorktown. Mike began his usual routine with Sarah's helmet, but she stopped him. She reached her right hand up and ran her fingers through his long wavy brown and gray hair, tucked it back behind his ear and gently rested her hand on the side of his face, rose up on her toes and gave him a lingering peck on the lips.

"What's that for?" Mike said.

"Because you're just such a wonderful man, Mike," Sarah said softly as she looked directly into his brown eyes, *those* eyes. "You're just so easy to be with and I'm so comfortable with you, always have been, since that first night in LA."

"You'd better be careful," Mike said. "Someone might take a picture of you doing that and sell it...then you're reputation will really be shot."

Sarah laughed, pulled her long blonde hair back into a low ponytail, and let Mike put her motorcycle helmet on for her, never taking her eyes away from his.

"You know Mike; age is just an artificial barrier, a social construct."

"Get on the bike," Mike said, feigning a slow, aggravated tone.

Mike and Sarah arrived home from their motorcycle trip just after dark. Sarah gave Mike a quick peck on the cheek and then hurried upstairs to change into her powder blue shirt for an evening of tea on the couch with him. Mike walked back to his office and checked his email and messages. Angela called with his regular 9 PM update. After speaking to Angela, Mike walked to his room and changed into his workout shorts and a fresh tee shirt for the evening.

He walked into the living room and let out a quiet grunt as he took his seat at the far end of the couch from Sarah, his decaf green tea with honey already on the small portable table. He stretched his legs from the long motorcycle ride and full day of walking, and rolled his head around to adjust his neck. He arched his back and rolled his shoulders to work out the stiffness. The lights were dim and classic rock music played low in the background. Sarah quietly held her tea with both hands as she sat at her end of the couch with her feet and legs curled up under her and watched him, wearing her light blue button down man's shirt, only two buttons fastened in the middle, the sleeves rolled up to her elbows.

"Tired?" Sarah finally broke the silence after several minutes.

"A little...you?" Mike said as he blew on his hot tea to cool it, and took a short sip.

"A little, but it was a wonderful day, Mike. I had a great time."

Mike nodded, the silence returned, and the two sat quietly. Mike moved his head back and looked up at the ceiling, closed his eyes and listened to the music while Sarah wondered what questions to ask him, if any, how much she should press her luck as she watched him. She new Mike was slowly letting her in but Angela's words reverberated in her mind, it took Vicky four months.

"You know Mike; I'm catching a little grief from my fans that follow me on social media because I haven't posted anything in a while," Sarah decided to start with something easy. "I was wondering..." she paused.

"You know the rule Sarah. You can ask me anything," Mike said with some exasperation and without opening his eyes or moving his head.

"I know. Beth and Robin have taken some pictures of us together, you and me, and I was wondering if you would mind me posting them on social media and introducing *my man behind the eyes* to my fans," Sarah finally said. "And some pictures of us surfing and on the beach have already been posted by fans, and people are wondering who I'm with...in the pictures, who you are."

"I don't mind Sarah. I know people are curious and you have a career to manage."

"Do you want me to watch what I say, to stay away from identifying you too much or where we are together?"

"No, you've successfully managed your career for a long time now, I trust your judgment, and I don't want to put any restrictions on you that might make things hard for you."

"Thank you."

The silence returned, only the music playing low in the background. Sarah moved her body and stretched her legs out, lightly pressed her feet and toes into Mike's left thigh. She watched him, thought about his scars and the stories behind them, and looked at the crow's feet around his eyes. Still such a paradox, she thought.

In the quiet moment, Sarah remembered going through Mike's businesses papers with Angela at the dining room table. The paperwork was mainly from Mike's charitable foundations and Sarah had no idea just how wealthy Mike was, and didn't really care other than normal curiosity, but the amount of money he routinely gives away astounded her.

After unexpectedly inheriting his fortune, Mike Hampton set up foundations to help wounded veterans and their families. He also set up scholarship funds for the kids of parents killed in war and education grants for inner city kids. He gave away millions of dollars to other more established foundations and charities. She knew Mike Hampton was a deeply caring and loving man—she again marveled at how such a tough and deadly man, such a serious man, could be so tender and gentle with his kids and grandkids, Beth and Robin's kids, and her. Sarah Tomzewski had never known a man, a person, like Mike Hampton.

"Mike," Sara said.

"Yes," Mike mumbled in a low, deep voice, beginning to doze off while holding his tea.

"I'm going with you to France and on the yacht," Sarah said softly.

"I know," Mike said, reaching down with his left hand, unconsciously patting and rubbing Sarah's foot again.

"Mike," Sarah said again.

"Yes," Mike continued to rub her foot and ankle.

"You know I'm not some eighteen year old little girl with a crush on the handsome older man who rescued her, right?"

"I know."

"Like I said before, Mike, I'm a full grown college educated woman who knows what she wants and why," Sarah said firmly but softly.

"I know."

Sarah stood and walked over in front of Mike. She leaned over and took his mug of tea from his hand, and gave him a kiss on the cheek.

"You'd better go to bed before you pass out on the couch Mike," she whispered, keeping her cheek next to his.

Mike inhaled deeply through his nose and let out a long, comfortable sigh.

"I know."

"I've fallen in love with you Mike," she whispered again.

CHAPTER TWENTY-FOUR

"The best mirror is an old friend." —Spanish Proverb

It was just after noon when Mike and his guests boarded the Airbus A-380 at Norfolk International Airport for the eight and a half hour flight to Paris after Bob Morton's funeral. Mike let Sarah and her friends know that the aircrew would give them a tour of the plane before the rest of his men arrived while he went to his office at the back of the plane on the second deck to start working.

"Can we talk for a minute Mike?" Sarah said.

"Not now Sarah, I have some calls I have to make and some work I need to do before the rest of the guys get here and we take off. The crew will show you around," Mike's voice was professional and business-like, serious and in control. He turned and walked up the sweeping staircase next to the bar near the front of the plane and disappeared from view.

Even the veteran actors accustomed to flying around the world in first class accommodations were impressed with the spacious Airbus A-380. The plane that can carry over eight-hundred people was configured to carry only 50 passengers, plus crew, for this flight to Paris, making it even more spacious and elegant. The lower deck was set up as an entertainment lounge with several horseshoe-shaped bars manned by a flight attendant bartender. There was a hardwood dance floor in the middle of the plane surrounded by several loveseats and couches along the sides of the airframe, and a few small circular tables.

The upper deck contained seating for the fifty passengers and Mike's office. Each seat could convert into a private bed with a television and headphones, and individual lighting controls.

The men and women who work for Mike added a definite air of excitement to the plane as they filed on. The men and women, mostly in their early twenties and thirties but also some older men in their forties and fifties, were dressed in everything from Hawaiian shirts and slaps to Western style shirts and boots, and they were boisterous and in a party mood. Sarah and her friends introduced themselves to the men and women as they boarded, hooting, and hollering, teasing and picking on each other as they ordered pre-flight drinks at the bars. The actors watched closely and listened to every word, beginning their character studies.

Most of the men and women who work for Mike Hampton work on different operational teams in different parts of the world, rarely seeing each other. They flew into Norfolk the night before for Bob Morton's funeral, and to stage for the operation to Nigeria. The older men in their fifties were from Mike's old tactical counterintelligence team in the Philippines from the late 1980s who went to work for him when he started his company several years before. They walked straight up the stairs to Mike's office.

Shortly after takeoff, the pilot keyed his intercom mic as the plane approached its cruising altitude.

"Good afternoon ladies and gentlemen and welcome aboard...this is your Captain. We will be cruising at an altitude of thirty-five thousand feet today for our eight-hour flight to Paris, France with an expected arrival time of 2 AM local. For our first time guests who may be unaware, this is a party flight and the bars will reopen as soon as we reach altitude and the smoking lamp will be lit—there will be Cuban cigar and cigarette smoke so if you're allergic or don't like it, well, we might be able to find you a parachute. Have a pleasant flight and thank you for flying with us."

Sarah and her friends signed autographs, took pictures with the men and women, and answered all their questions. Sarah was excited to meet more of the men who participated in her rescue and took advantage of the opportunity to ask them how they conducted the operation and what it was like. She also asked questions about Mike and what kind of a boss he is, what it was like to work for him.

Sarah found out days before how generous Mike was with his money, how charitable, but she had no idea he ran his company the same way. All of the men and women she spoke with told her how generous Mike is, about their retirement packages, how he helps them out personally and financially, and how he helped the families when someone was injured or killed. They also told her stories of fighting with Mike in the field, what kind of fighter he is. She didn't need another reason to be in love with Mike Hampton, but she felt herself increasingly drawn to him.

Mike and the older men walked down the sweeping staircase and to the bar at the front of the lower deck one hour into the flight. Mike ordered a Scotch on the rocks and lit his long Cuban cigar. He scanned the plane and watched his men and women dance to the modern music that he hated for a few minutes.

"Watch this Griff," Mike said to his old partner from the Philippines as Griff lit his own Cuban cigar. Mike leaned over and whispered to the flight attendant behind the bar.

Everyone stopped dancing and looked around curiously as the music abruptly stopped. Sarah stood on her tiptoes near the back of the plane and looked toward the front to see what was going on, a glass of Pinot in her right hand.

The sound of a steel slide quickly running down the string of an electric guitar sounded over the speaker system and Lynyrd Skynyrd began singing "Call Me the Breeze" as everyone clapped and started dancing again.

"Yeah baby—the Boss is in the house!" one of Mike's men standing next to Sarah shouted.

"I'll teach these young bastards what good music is if it kills me," Mike said to Griff as both men laughed and puffed their cigars.

Sarah walked around the party in the middle of the plane toward Mike, keeping her eyes on him as she walked. As she approached, Mike waved his hand vigorously in front of himself to dissipate the cigar smoke.

"Hey handsome," Sarah said in a playful voice as she walked up to Mike and put her hand on his arm, leaned her body against his. "Buy me another drink?"

"Hi Sarah," Mike said as he took Sarah's empty wine glass, gave it to the flight attendant and ordered a refill.

"Sarah, this is one of my oldest and closest friends, Griffin Howard, one of my old partners from the Philippines" Mike introduced Griff and Sarah.

Griffin Howard was an imposing man at 6 feet, 4 inches tall, and two-hundred fifty pounds, and a few years older than Mike, already sixty. His hair was snow white and cut to military specifications. His face was red from decades of drinking too much and Mike thought he would make the perfect Santa Clause at any kid's party if he grew a beard. He and Mike worked counterintelligence and counterinsurgency together for two years in the Philippines and saved each other's lives several times. They lost count of how many times one had saved the other, and who owed whom a drink for the last save.

Griff walked with a limp due to an injury he received while working for the Colorado State Police after he retired from the Air Force. He stepped in a gopher hole and blew out his right knee chasing a murder suspect through a field in 1999.

"Excuse me Sarah, Griff," Mike said after having the flight attendant refill his Scotch. "I'm going to go mingle with the guys a little."

Sarah was somewhat surprised at Mike's abrupt departure as she watched him walk off, high fiving his men and shaking hands as he walked toward the back of the plane.

"Don't worry about him Sarah," Griff said. "He always get's moody before an operation. Takes him a while to get his mind right and his game face on and he's worried about everyone who works for him."

"Tell me about him Griff, about his past," Sarah said.

"Let's go upstairs to Mike's office where it's quieter," Griff said.

Griff turned and got one bottle of wine and one bottle of Scotch from the flight attendant, turned and limped toward the stairs. Sarah followed as the pair walked up the sweeping, curved staircase to the upper deck, down the length of the plane to Mike's office in the back.

Mike's office was spacious and included a double bed, a closet, a private bathroom with a shower, and a work area with a desk. There was a computer affixed to the floor under the desk, two large flat screen monitors, and a telephone on it. Sarah and Griff sat in the two leather chairs next to Mike's desk. Griff opened the wine for Sarah and the Scotch for himself, refreshed each of their drinks, and snuffed out his Cuban cigar as he apologized to Sarah for the stench.

"Let's see, where to begin," Griff said as he leaned back in the chair and thought.

"Just start anywhere you want Griff and tell me about him."

Over the course of the next hour, Griff told Sarah about Mike. Griff arrived in the Philippines to work counterintelligence as a special agent with the Air Force Office of Special Investigations after Mike had already been there for about nine months. The first murders of American military personnel by the NPA communist insurgents had already happened in October 1987, while Mike was the new non-commissioned officer in-charge of tactical counterintelligence. It happened on Mike's watch and his office had no idea the threat level was even elevated, much less that assassinations were about to happen. It was Mike's job to know, he felt, and to warn command authorities so they could plan and prepare, but he didn't know and couldn't warn them.

After the October '87 killings, Mike took it personally and changed the way his office did business. With no experience or training in counterintelligence, having been an undercover narcotics agent in Alabama before going to the Philippines, Mike decided to start handling his counterintelligence informants like low-life drug informants and attacking counterintelligence as he would any narcotics investigation. His plan worked, but command officials failed to take what Mike believed to be necessary precautions and the NPA assassinated more American military and civilian personnel. Mike took that personally because he felt he hadn't fought hard enough to convince command authorities to take more precautions.

"I watched Mike change right in front of my eyes that first year I knew him," Griff said. "He started getting angry and impatient. He argued with everyone, even me. He almost lost his whole career over it. He worked day and night trying to collect threat information and dragged my sorry ass all over the Philippines getting me involved with all kinds of crap. He started drinking hard too—hard. Mind if I light another Cuban Sarah?" Griff interrupted himself.

"Oh no, not at all. Please do," Sarah said as Griff got up from his chair and started to pace Mike's office while thinking about the old days in the Philippines with Mike. He stood several feet from Sarah as he lit his cigar and gave it a few puffs, waving the smoke away as he exhaled.

"Three of us got to the Philippines after Mike was already there and, even though we out-ranked him and were agents longer, he kept us alive by teaching us counterintelligence and about the threat we faced," Griff said seriously. "He taught us how to run our host-nation informants, our assets."

Sarah watched Griff closely as he talked and paced. She could see the love and concern for Mike in his face and hear it in his voice. Griff loved Mike like a brother.

"That man downstairs, Sarah, risked his career and his life to save American servicemen in the Philippines," Griff said as he pointed at the floor for emphasis, his Cuban cigar between his fingers. "He broke international law, U.S. Law, Philippine law and Air Force regulations and went out on counterinsurgency operations with different Philippine Army intelligence units and got into some shit, excuse my French. He took me with him a few times but there were times he went by himself because he knew it was going to get real bad and he didn't want any witnesses or anybody else getting hurt."

Griff paused and continued to pace as Sarah watched, intrigued as if watching a television show or movie, hearing about a man who doesn't really exist, a character scripted by a screenwriter, someone her former co-star Adam Levi might be type-cast to play.

"Griff, I don't mean to get too personal but..." Sarah hesitated. "Does your time in the Philippines and the other stuff you've seen and done affect you the way it does Mike?" Sarah finally said.

"You mean PTSD?" Griff said.

"I guess, I mean...I don't know much about it and..."

"Look Sarah," Griff interrupted himself as he walked over and sat back in his chair.

"Some people get PTSD and some people don't, and nobody knows why. And, it's different for everyone who does get it—it manifests differently in everyone. That's why there's a social stigma with it and people with PTSD feel embarrassed and ashamed, wondering why did they get it and people they served with didn't? I do know that it rewires your brain. I don't get nightmares and duck and cover if an electrical transformer blows up, but hell, I divorced my wife, married a little Filipino girl, and fell head first into the whiskey bottle. I have uncomfortable thoughts during the day, intrusive thoughts. I still search my mirrors for potential threats behind me when I'm driving, leave space between me and the car in front of me when I stop at a traffic light, and feel uncomfortable in certain situations," Griff laughed a nervous laugh as he spoke and then puffed his Cuban cigar.

"Let me tell you something else Sarah. Some of those men and women downstairs are going to be killed and crippled in a few days and that's going to take a huge chunk out of Mike's soul...a huge chunk," Griff said as he puffed his cigar. "We all have this locker room bravado going on and act as if we don't care, like death is just a normal part of what we do. But the fact is, we do care because we're human. And Mike Hampton cares more than most Sarah; he cares right down to his bones. We all swallow it because that's what we're supposed to do and we keep doing what we do because that's what our dead expect us to do—to keep going—to keep serving—to get the damn mission done!"

Sarah felt herself start to cry, but held it together. She poured another glass of wine and drank it in one gulp. She felt like she needed to leave the office and go downstairs, find Mike and just hold him, kiss him.

CHAPTER TWENTY-FIVE

"The idea of waiting for something makes it more exciting"
—Andy Warhol

Sarah loved everything about Paris, the food, the art, the nightlife and even the weather. She traveled Europe extensively for her acting and modeling careers as well as vacations. Being fluent in Polish and German, mostly fluent speaking French made her travels around France and all of Europe fairly easy and she hoped to have an opportunity in the future to show Mike around, take him skiing in the Alps, and show him her parents' hometown in Eastern Germany, or even their ancestral home in Poland.

Days before when she first found out about the mission, Sarah had the fleeting thought of asking Mike to fly to Paris a day or two early with her and meet his men there, but then remembered Bob Morton's funeral. She took a deep breath to enjoy the Paris air and wrapped her sweater around herself against the cool morning air as she stepped off the bus and walked toward the train station.

Mike stood next to Angela Montero in the darkness as she checked off names on her clipboard as his men and women staggered off the buses and into the train station at 3:30 in the morning after the thirty-minute ride from Charles de Gaulle Airport. Mike was satisfied with the assistance of the French government ensuring everything ran smoothly and the transition between the flight and the train ride to Monaco was seamless.

Angela and Sarah boarded the nearest train car and sat in the second seat back from the front of the car on the right. Mike and Griff boarded last and sat in the front seat on the left. Mike nodded at Sarah as he boarded. He took papers out of his briefcase, put his wire-framed glasses on, adjusted the overhead lighting, and began going over paperwork with Griff as Sarah watched.

Sarah was already familiar with Mike's business demeanor and his "serious face," but this was the first time she had witnessed his current manner. Mike seemed disciplined and more serious than ever. He walked with his shoulders back and straighter and he interacted with Griff not as an old friend, but as a business partner or military planner discussing the serious business of war. His jaws were tight as he peered through his glasses at the paperwork, and over them at Griff, his brow furrowed. His sentences were short and curt as he spoke, his voice somehow different.

"How in the world does he do that Angela?" Sarah said in a quiet tone. "How does Mike switch so easily from father, grandfather, and friend one minute, to business professional or lethal fighter the next?"

"Well, I think everyone can switch back and forth to be who they need to be given a certain situation. The titans of Wall Street run billion dollar multinational companies during the day and then go home to their families or play golf with friends on the weekends."

"Oh I get that, Angela. But there's such a wide gulf between the Mike Hampton that grills steaks for friends or plays guitar and sings for five year olds, and the man I see sitting there right now. Or the Mike Hampton that takes me on motorcycle rides and shows me around Williamsburg. How in the world does he do that? I don't know, maybe I'm making too much of it but, it's all such a paradox to me."

The train car suddenly jerked and swayed as it began to pull out of the station in the early morning darkness for the seven-hour trip to Monaco.

"You don't have any context sweetie because you haven't spent any time around military men and women. Some guys are sergeants or chiefs during the day at work and then take that crap home at night, but many don't. And Vicky wouldn't let Mike bring that crap home at night. As he got deeper into his military police career and made sergeant, he started becoming a harder man and trying to be a sergeant with Vicky and the kids but she put a stop to that real fast. She was a strong woman and Mike's partner...he loved her very deeply."

"You're right, I guess, I have no context."

"I'll tell you something else Sarah. You think you have acting chops? Sweetie please...Mike has been a cop, an undercover narcotics agent and a counterintelligence collections specialist and that man can be anything or anyone he needs to be, when he needs to be. Like when he's with you, he tries to act all aloof but I know that man has the biggest crush on you—at least a crush—but he just can't get over your age difference. And that's if he can even understand if, and why, you have romantic feelings for him in the first place. Like I told you the other day, he'd never in a million years believe that a woman like you would be interested in a man like him. Never."

Sarah relaxed back into her seat and drifted off to sleep, hoping her nightmares from LA would not return while she slept in public.

Robin McKenna, Beth Mullaney, and Adam Levi paired up with some of Mike's men and women who they thought were interesting character studies and might help them play future roles better in movies and television. They had a great time partying on the flight from Norfolk and made fast friends with Mike's men and women, intrigued by how relaxed and comfortable they all were knowing full well what they were on their way to do and the dangers involved.

The sun cresting the horizon over French villages along the countryside began to wake everyone up on the train after a short nap. After some brief stretching and a few sips of bottled water, and a breath mint, Mike invited Sarah and Angela to breakfast with him and Griff. The four made their way through three passenger cars and into the restaurant car. Sarah was happy for the invitation and glad to see that Mike looked somewhat more relaxed, and she was curious to see the interaction between him and Griff.

Sarah slid into the booth first and Mike slid in beside her, teasingly pushing his body against hers. Angela slide into the booth opposite Sarah and Griff slid in opposite Mike as the train car gently swayed on the tracks. They exchanged mundane conversation about how they slept, what they might like for breakfast before Griff began to reminisce about the old days with Mike.

Sarah and Angela laughed and snorted, used their hands to hold coffee and food in their mouths as Griff told old stories about working with Mike in the Philippines, funny stories, and not stories about gunfights, terrorist bombings, or times in the hospital.

"Yeah Griff, we definitely had some great times together," Mike said with a little nostalgia in his voice. "But, we're old men now and more than just a little broken, you old gimp," Mike teased Griff.

"Oh stop it Mike," Sarah said as she poked Mike in his left side with her right elbow, causing him to wince slightly. "I told you to stop saying that around me."

"What'd I say?" Mike said innocently.

"I told you to stop calling yourself old around me Mike," she said with some aggravation.

"Well, facts are facts," Mike said matter-of-factly as he nodded at Griff.

"Oh my god, help me out here Angela, Griff," Sarah said.

Angela smirked at Mike. Griff smiled at him and chuckled under his breath because he knew Mike was about to be taken to task by Sarah, and deservedly so. He remembered several times in the Philippines when Vicky took Mike to task for acting foolish or drinking too much.

"This man right here can run circles around any man I know my own age," Sarah patted Mike's shoulder as she spoke. "He goes horseback riding, skydiving...and not the normal kind of skydiving, what's that other kind you do with those Navy SEALs?"

"HALO jumping, high altitude, low opening," Mike said.

"Yeah, that. You ride your Harley, surf, snow ski, water ski, jet ski, hike, camp." Sarah paused for a breath and to think as Angela and Griff kept laughing. "Really, you own that bar and restaurant and play in the band there on weekends when you're not off traipsing around the world rescuing damsels in distress like me, and don't you think for a moment that I didn't notice what a sweet singing voice you have and how well you played guitar the other night Mike Hampton...You are young at heart and young in age but have the maturity not to sag your pants off your butt and turn your baseball hat around backwards for crying out loud!" Sarah nodded sharply to place an exaggerated period on the end of her summation.

Mike hung his head and shook it slightly, smiling to himself.

"So you just stop calling yourself old around me."

"Yes Ma'am," Mike said as he looked back up, smiled with the corner of his mouth, and winked at Griff.

It was a beautiful sunny summer morning in Monaco-Ville, Monaco as the train pulled into the station at precisely 11:30. The group disembarked and walked toward the buses for the short ride to Digue de L'Avant Port and the corporate yacht. Mike and Griff met several of the advance men from the forward deployed team as they exited the train. Sarah stood with Angela as Angela began checking names off on her clipboard again, the long line of hung-over men and women slowly filing past them in the bright sunshine toward the buses. Some of the men and women wore sunglasses while others used their hands to shield their sore eyes from the bright sun.

Sarah sat with Beth, Robin, and Adam on the bus to catch up with everyone and find out how they were enjoying their trip thus far. They were all excited and eager to tell Sarah about the people they met and things they'd learned. They were all astounded by the maturity level among the men and women who worked for Mike, the party flight to France notwithstanding. Robin and Beth were particularly impressed with the level of maturity among the men, none of them hitting on the two actresses, trying to "cop a feel," as Mike would say, or acting inappropriate in any way. The men all remained perfect gentlemen even after drinking too much.

Sarah and her friends looked in awe as they got off the bus on the long pier and looked at the six-hundred foot sleek white yacht. They hadn't really known what to expect but it certainly wasn't what they were looking at. All of the crew was dressed in formal white naval attire with short sleeve shirts, long pants, and white shoes. Some of them busied themselves with work on the yacht while others walked down the gangway to meet everyone. Sarah noticed the name in large metallic green block letters, "VIC."

"Vicky's favorite color was green," Angela said as she walked up next to Sarah.

"Oh," Sarah said slowly, the reality of what was happening hitting her with new force.

Crewed by eighty men and women, *The Vic* was seventy feet wide at her beam with six decks above the waterline and a helipad on the bow. There was a swimming pool and hot tub near the stern of the ship and the main deck had a spacious and elegantly appointed lounge that doubled as the main dining room and bar. Long, formal, sweeping staircases lead up from the lounge to the upper decks and to the lower decks where most of the private cabins were located.

Sarah and her friends admired the opulence as they boarded the Vic and looked around the main lounge, the smell of lunch wafting through the air. Crew members dressed in cocktail service attire with black vests over white shirts, black pants and black shoes, assisted the kitchen staff in setting the buffet line, the lounge filled with circular and square tables. Lunch would include lobster tails, shrimp, fresh caught fish, filet mignon, fresh sliced roast beef, and ham, fresh fruits, and several types of vegetables.

"Would you ladies and gentleman like to see your cabins and freshen up a bit from your trip, you have a little time before lunch?" The chief steward asked Sarah and her friends.

"That would be wonderful," Sarah said.

The group followed the chief steward through the lounge and down the elegant staircase to the deck below. They walked down a wide long hallway past other cabins to theirs near the bow of the ship. Robin and Beth shared a cabin while Adam Levi shared a cabin with Griff. The chief Steward escorted Sarah farther down the hallway to her suite next to Mike's cabin.

Sarah heard the PA system crackle to life as she walked into her cabin, and cringed when she heard the words.

"Attention ladies and gentlemen...all squad leaders and fire team leaders report to the Combat Information Center for initial briefings after lunch at 1300 hours. The CIC is located aft on deck 3," the anonymous voice commanded.

Sarah was quite impressed as she looked around her cabin. There was a beautifully dressed queen size bed nestled between two wooden mahogany nightstands, lamps perfectly placed, a ship's phone on the nightstand to the right of the bed. A fifty-five inch flat screen television hung on the wall directly across from the foot of the bed, with a beautiful mahogany dresser beneath it. Next to the television was a set of doors leading into the cedar-lined walk-in closet where Sarah found her luggage. She walked across the cabin and admired the elegant bathroom, a double vanity with make-up lighting, a separate shower, and Jacuzzi bathtub to the side. She walked back into the main cabin and found a note addressed to her lying on the desk.

Sarah,

I know this hasn't been much of a vacation for you, as I promised, and I apologize for that. I also apologize that it probably isn't going to get much better. We probably won't see each other very much over the next couple of days, except in passing, and I can't promise to make it up to you in the future. Please enjoy the cruise with your friends, and I will see you at least the last two nights before we reach our destination, that I can promise."

Mike

Sarah folded the note back up and returned it to the envelope as she thought what beautiful penmanship Mike has. "It's been a wonderful vacation Mike," she whispered.

CHAPTER TWENTY-SIX

"I think Heaven will be like a first kiss."
—Sarah Addison Allen

The Vic slowly and carefully got underway just after lunch. The captain navigated her south by southwest away from the port in Monaco and toward the Strait of Gibraltar. Mike and Griff joined the senior leadership from the forward deployed team, two squad leaders, and eight fire team leaders in the CIC after having a private lunch together in the yacht's wardroom, the officer's dining room. Mike dropped his brown leather-bound folder on the desk at the front of the room while Griff found a comfortable chair nearby.

The CIC was a large room filled with electronic equipment—a large bank of flat screen television monitors three rows high and five screens long above a long shelf-type work area ran the length of the wall. Radio microphones, telephones, and notebooks were prepositioned on the shelf. Four chairs sat empty and pushed up under the shelf working area. The lighting in the room was low to allow better viewing of the video monitors.

"As you are all aware, this is a rescue mission into the jungles of Nigeria, 4.5 miles to the interior from the coast," Mike's senior operations manager began the briefing. An assistant brought the bank of video monitors online to display maps and other significant information for the briefing.

"We will be conducting the rescue operation against approximately 450 Boko Haram terrorists according to our latest intel. We will operate in two squads comprised of four, five-man fire teams each, supporting Eagle 9-9 and Eagle 9-7 as they acquire the hostages. Each fire team will be set up with a fire team leader, a rifleman-grenadier, machine gunner armed with the SAW, and assistant machine gunner. We will use helmet cams and gun cams and transmit a live feed with audio back here to the CIC.

At 0100 hours, five days from now, the yacht will breach Nigerian national waters with a wink and a nod from the Nigerian government, move within an acceptable distance of the coastline, and deploy the Zodiacs with the squads, Eagle 9-7, and Eagle 9-9. The two squads will infiltrate though the beach here and meet two scouts from the advance team," the briefer pointed to a location on the map displayed on one of the video monitors. "The scouts will lead you to the Boko Haram base, moving east by northeast separately, using different tracks, here and here.

South African mercenaries supported by the Nigerian military will infiltrate the area from the south, here, and from the east, here...we're hoping, anyway." The room erupted in laughter as Mike and Griff smiled at each other. Third-world host nation police and military forces had let them both down in the past.

"They'll begin diversionary attacks on the camp to draw attention away from us. There also may be, hopefully, some air support and medivac available from the Nigerian Army."

"Eagle 9-4," the briefer turned and pointed at Griff, "will command the CIC and work the communications, call sign *Eagle Actual*. Gentlemen, this is just your initial brief, there will be more over the next couple of days. Please study the information in the packages we handed out at the beginning of this briefing. That's it for today."

"Hey Frank," Mike called to his senior operations manager.

"Yeah Boss?"

"If we have a wink and a nod from the government and they're supporting us in this operation, then why aren't we just going in with them?"

"They want to maintain some plausible deniability Boss, and not mix their forces with us. It's already well known that they work with South African merc's, but they don't want to get linked to us."

"Got it, thanks."

"Roger that Boss."

Mike and Griff left the CIC and started toward the bridge of the yacht to meet with the captain.

"Sounds like they got over their hangovers and got the party started upstairs," Mike said to Griff as they walked down the hallway toward the stairs.

"Yep, you going up to join Sarah and her friends, do a little dancing or something," Griff teased and shook his hips.

"No, still got things to do," Mike said as he started up the stairs, Griff limping along behind him.

"That little girl sure has it bad for you," Griff said as he patted Mike on the back.

"Yeah, so I'm told Griff...so I'm told."

Afternoon gave way to evening, and evening finally to night as the yacht sailed toward the Strait of Gibraltar and Mike finally finished his last meetings, briefings, and telephone calls. He went to his cabin, poured himself a Jack and coke, and headed for the shower to clean up from the day.

Sarah and Angela sat together at a small round table in the main lounge and watched young girls take turns dancing with Adam while young men took turns dancing with Robin and Beth as the live band, men and women who worked for Mike, played classic rock songs. Sarah occasionally signed more autographs, posed for more pictures, and answered questions as she sipped her wine. Every now and then, she gave in and agreed to dance with one several of the young men.

"Are you sure that Mike won't mind if I post these pictures on my social media Angela?" Sarah said.

"He won't mind at all Sarah. Remember, this is nothing but a pleasure cruise."

"You know Angela, the fans that follow me on social media went crazy the other day when I posted pictures of Mike and me in Williamsburg, pictures of him standing by his motorcycle. They went nuts over getting to see my *man behind the eyes* and learning that I finally got to meet him."

"I know, he mentioned it to me on the plane," Angela said.

"Oh I hope he wasn't upset," Sarah said with concern.

"Not at all," Angela laughed. "He got a kick out of it, even though he couldn't understand all the fuss over it, over him."

"My fans are so sweet and concerned about me, some of them too sweet if you know what I mean."

"Yeah, the weirdoes and stalkers."

Everyone in the crowded lounge turned toward the stage and clapped when the music stopped. They hooted and hollered as Mike Hampton walked onto the small bandstand dressed in his tight fitting, faded Levi blue jeans, black Dingo boots, white surfer tee shirt, and black motorcycle vest. Sarah craned her neck trying to see over the crowd, turned her head from side to side trying to see through the crowd. Mike placed his tall cup of Jack and coke in the cup holder affixed to his mic stand, picked up an electric guitar, put the strap over his head, and let it rest on his left shoulder. He strummed a "C" chord once to check for tuning and volume.

"Test, check," Mike said into the microphone to check its volume.

"Why that little...," Sarah said as she stood and walked toward the small bandstand at the front of the lounge wearing her gray skinny jeans, royal blue loose fitting blouse with the spaghetti straps over her shoulders, and flat white sandals with the thin straps that crisscrossed her slightly tanned feet.

"Okay, I haven't done this in a while so let's see just how bad I can embarrass myself," Mike said as he turned to the band. Mike's employees clapped again, hooted and hollered.

The crowd cheered loudly as Mike and the band began to play an upbeat blues song. He dropped more than one note as he played and sang slightly off key, but the men and women who work for him loved it and started dancing wildly to the music.

Sarah moved to the front of the crowd and watched Mike as he played and sang. She watched him move to the music as he played, watched him move as she hadn't seen him move before, sliding his pick across the strings during parts of the song for the exaggerated notes. She marveled at how relaxed Mike looked. It was a side of him she had never seen, and she liked it. She loved it. Mike noticed Sarah watching, and smiled and at her as he sang. He sipped his Jack and coke between songs and made eye contact with Sarah. He nodded his head toward the dance floor and mouth the words "go dance Sarah." She nodded back and mouthed the words "I will."

Mike played upbeat blues and classic rock songs for the next hour and a half as everyone danced, ate and drank. Sarah watched and then finally danced with some of the young men, but stayed close to the bandstand where she could see Mike and she knew he could see her. Every so often, Sarah took pictures of Mike with her cell phone and posted them on her social media, captioned, "Mike, my man behind the eyes." Within minutes, thousands of her social media followers expressed their approval and congratulated her.

Mike placed his guitar back on its rack, took his drink from the holder on the mic stand, walked over to Sarah, and winked at her as he placed his drink on a small round table.

"Pardon me Ma'am," he said in a proper tone of voice. "May I have this dance?"

"Why yes you may," Sarah said, feigning a Southern accent.

Mike took Sarah's right hand in his left hand and placed his right hand low on her left hip. They slow danced to the music as Sarah stared into his eyes. She inspected every part of his face, but kept going back to his eyes. She marveled at how revealing they were, especially since she knew so much about him now.

"My Mr. Hampton, you are a wonderful dancer," Sarah said as she moved closer to Mike and tightened her left arm around his waist.

"Thank you Ma'am, and so are you," Mike said as he allowed her to move in closer.

Mike and Sarah danced to three songs, and then walked to the back of the lounge and sat at one of the larger tables with Griff, Angela, Beth, Robin, and Adam. Sarah sat next to Mike on his left, remembering his daughter's admonishment not to sit on his "gun side." Cindy Morton's words also reverberated in her head, "Don't show him your fear or concern; he won't be able to do his job."

Plates of seafood hors d'oeuvres, drink glasses, wine bottles and cell phones filled the middle of the table. A steward brought over two bottles of Champaign, opened them, and poured each person a glass as everyone ate and drank.

"So how long have you been playing and singing Mike?" Adam said.

"Oh let's see," Mike looked up at the ceiling and thought. "I guess I started playing guitar when I was in about the 5th Grade, and I studied music theory in high school. I sang for family and friends off and on, and have been in a few garage bands, nothing big."

"You did great tonight," Robin said.

"Thank you Robin. The old voice is a little ragged after drinking and smoking for so many years, but what the hell, it's fun," Mike said.

"Well you sounded great and still have good range in your voice," Beth said.

"That's probably the alcohol talking," Griff laughed before he could get the words out.

The group of friends sat at the table eating and drinking until midnight, when the group began to dissipate. Robin and Beth excused themselves first and walked to their cabin. Griff finally excused himself about fifteen minutes later and Adam ten minutes after Griff.

"If you're not ready to head back to your cabin Sarah, come with me for a minute. I want to show you something," Mike said.

"Okay."

Mike stood and took Sarah's right hand in his left hand, and walked toward the stern of the ship. They walked down a couple of flights of stairs to the first deck above the waterline, and out onto a rectangular platform on the aft of the ship that ran the entire width. The platform was made for swimmers enjoying the ocean and launching jet skis. Mike pushed a button and turned off all the lights except the ship's required running lights. He walked Sarah to the end of the platform near the water. She took her hand from his and put her arm around his waist for security, and he placed his left arm around her waist.

"This is so beautiful Mike, and so romantic," Sarah said.

"It is. I love how the Moon lights up the water and the low sounds of the engines kind of moaning, the sound of the ship moving through the water, it's nice, relaxing," Mike said.

The two stood on the platform arm in arm and watched the wake of the ship, the moonlit waters, in silence for several minutes. Sarah leaned her head over and placed it on Mike's shoulder, slightly tightening her arm around his waist.

"Mike. You know the other night in the hot tub when I told you it would be a good time to kiss me?" Sarah whispered and broke the silence.

"Yes."

"I'm so glad now that you didn't."

The two stood in silence for several more minutes enjoying the view, their bodies gently bobbing up and down and swaying from side to side as if one with the ship. Sarah slowly turned to face Mike, never removing her arm from around his waist. She put her other arm around his waist as she faced him, and he placed his other arm around hers. Mike moved close to Sarah and looked down into her eyes. He lightly brushed her cheek with the back of his fingers, pushed her hair behind her ear, and gently laid his forehead against hers.

"Are you sure," Mike whispered.

"Yes," Sarah whispered.

Mike pulled Sarah in tighter, tilted his head slightly and very gently placed his lips on hers, gave her a lingering peck, and then pulled his lips just a breath away.

"Yes," Sarah whispered again.

Mike kissed Sarah deeply and passionately in the moonlight for what seemed like an eternity to them both as they held each other, their hands gently caressing each other. Mike ended the kiss and moved his lips slightly away again, his forehead against her forehead, and then finished with another lingering peck. They hugged tightly for a moment, and then Sarah moved back to Mike's side, the two arm in arm.

CHAPTER TWENTY-SEVEN

"Love will find a way through paths where wolves fear to prey." —Lord Byron

The warm Mediterranean sun peeked through the porthole in Sarah's cabin as she stretched out in her bed and smiled, remembering the view from the back of the ship, the moonlit Mediterranean Sea, Mike's kiss, his embrace, the embrace she felt the night of her rescue. She sat up, walked into the bathroom, sat at the double vanity, and looked into the mirror as she began brushing out her long blonde hair, still smiling to herself. She took deep comfortable, contented breaths as she recounted the previous evening in her mind. She wished Mike had stayed the night with her, or at least stayed for a little while, but understood why he couldn't, why he wouldn't. He simply walked her back to her cabin and kissed her goodnight, and for now at least, that was enough for Sarah.

Sarah worried a little as she recalled things Griff and Angela said to her over the past few days; that Mike was concerned about staying focused, keeping his head in the game, getting his game face on and not becoming distracted. She also recalled Mike's words that her rescue mission was big but this mission was going to be combat, war. Sarah feared for just a moment that she might have become Mike's distraction. Everything military was still so new to Sarah, the fears, the seriousness, the attitudes, everything still such a paradox.

Sarah cleaned up for the day and dressed in her shortest blue jean shorts, her white sandals, lose fitting white see-through blouse, her light blue bikini under her clothes. In the hallway, she briefly put her ear to Mike's door to see if he was inside, but there was no sound. Sarah left only slightly disappointed, knowing how busy Mike was, and found her way to the lounge for breakfast.

Mike and his senior staff discussed the operation and all the required coordination over breakfast in the wardroom. He expressed his concerns and asked Griff to set up a conference call with their contact in the Nigerian government and Craig Buckley, FBI, for later that day. Mike instructed Frank Banner, the senior operations planner and operational manager, to have two additional squads, another forty men, fly into the Nigerian capital from the U.S. He was happy to hear that the advanced long-range reconnaissance team was successfully inserted into the operational area and relaying current intelligence back to the CIC aboard the yacht, but didn't like what the intel revealed.

"Did you kiss that little girl last night? She sure does have the hots for you, "Griff said as the two men left the wardroom after breakfast and made their way toward the CIC.

"Yeah...yeah I did and I think I'm starting to regret it."

"What the hell is there to regret? You can really be such an idiot sometimes Hampton," Griff said as he shook his head.

"I have to stay focused Griff; I have a bad feeling about this op."

"Damn Hampton. I watched you focus so hard in the Philippines that you just about pushed Vicky and everyone else away. The colonel almost fired and court-martialed you for insubordination that day you argued with him and threw your badge at him. Remember that?" Griff said with a hearty chuckle.

"Yeah," Mike grunted and then laughed with Griff, shaking his head as he remembered the incident.

"What were you, a twenty-something year old staff sergeant then?" Griff snorted again as he laughed.

"We were ten feet tall and bullet proof back then, full of piss and vinegar—nothing could hurt us—young, dumb, and full of cum like those young men upstairs right now," Griff smiled at Mike.

The two men walked quietly for a few minutes with their memories of the old days fresh in their minds.

"I don't want to sound like a girl or anything, Mike," Griff said as they stood outside the door to the CIC. "But you're allowed to be loved you know, and that little girl genuinely loves you. Don't end up old and alone like my limp old ass buddy."

"So I'm told Griff, so I'm told," Mike said as he opened the door to the CIC and walked in.

Sarah ate breakfast with her former co-stars and told them about her evening with Mike. She occasionally looked off into this distance and spoke wistfully as she described the moonlit sea and told them about the kiss. She took a deep breath through her nose and let out a long contented sigh.

"Oh my god Sarah, did you take him to bed?" Robin said playfully.

"No, I did not," Sarah answered sharply. "Well, okay, I wanted to but he wouldn't," she confessed. "But I will tell you this...that was the best damn kiss I've ever had but Mike apologized and said he was out of practice—he apologized!" Sarah put her hands to her mouth and laughed.

"Dang, was there anything awkward or clumsy about it?" Beth said.

"No, not at all, and that's the thing, it was absolutely perfect, just perfect in every way. It was tender, gentle, loving, and passionate. It wasn't aggressive or animalistic the way some younger guys do it, trying to devour your face or something—he didn't shove his hand down my pants, grab my butt, or fondle my breasts or anything. It was just a very tender and loving kiss, a tender and romantic moment."

"Did he use the L word?" Robin teased again.

"No, and I didn't either."

"Oh, but I'll tell you this," Sarah continued. "I don't know when he did it because I never saw him do it, but that sneaky little man—Mr. Undercover agent—somehow—got a breath mint in his mouth while we were walking from the lounge to the platform downstairs! I know because his breath was so fresh when we kissed and I remember that about his breath from the rescue. I remember wondering how in the world that man had such fresh breath during a hostage rescue and even took the time to worry about it in the first place!" Sarah laughed as she remembered.

"It's the little things," Beth said as everyone laughed again.

Mike Hampton walked into the lounge dressed in a form-fitting white polo shirt that revealed his "V" shaped muscular torso, khaki pants, and brown deck shoes. He stopped at each table to spend a few moments with the men and women who work for him. Some of them gave him high fives and some simply shook hands with him. He patted a few on the back as he stood and spoke to them, making small talk and some jokes, everyone around him laughing as he talked.

Mike could see Sarah at the large table near the back of the lounge with her friends from the corner of his eye and waved to her, used his index finger to indicate he'd be there in a minute.

Some of Mike's men were beginning to focus on their mission and asked him questions about it. He assured them that they would receive a full briefing before heading out, in plenty of time to prepare properly, and reminded them to write their letters home in case the worst happened. He looked at them and nodded in a fatherly way as he spoke.

Mike eventually made his way through the lounge to Sarah's table at the back, pulled an empty chair over and sat next to her.

"Hey stud muffin," Robin said as Mike sat down, and then laughed.

"Good morning Sarah," Mike said as he leaned his left shoulder against Sarah. "Good morning everyone," Mike smiled and nodded as he greeted everyone else at the table.

Sarah placed her right hand on Mike's left thigh under the table and gave it a little squeeze, careful not to show too much affection around Mike's men.

"Sarah, I'm going to be pretty tied up all day every day until we get where we're going, but how about this, how about tea downstairs on the platform tonight at around 11:00?" Mike offered.

"That sounds wonderful Mike. I miss our nightly tea and talks."

"Me too," Mike said and smiled at Sarah.

Sarah and her friends spent the day in the pool and hot tub with some of the men and women on Mike's team, while Adam Levi spent most of the afternoon in the ship's gaming center playing video games with others. All four of the actors began to wonder if each person they spent time with and talked to would be one of the ones killed or wounded. Like Sarah, the other actors had never spent any real time around the military, veterans, or even first responders, police and fire. Adam had the most experience because directors and producers always typecast him to play those sorts of roles in movies and television shows.

The feasts fit for royalty at each meal impressed the actors. Every meal included platters of fresh seafood of every kind, steaks, freshly carved roast beef and ham, fresh vegetables and fruit. The meals were as good and beautiful as any gourmet meal on any cruise ship, or in any gourmet restaurant. The tables in the lounge were always perfectly dressed with white tablecloths, expensive silver flatware, and cloth napkins.

The band played off and on during the day and night with different people taking turns on the instruments and singing, and an automated playlist took over while the band was on breaks, and there was always at least small groups of people dancing. There was a continuous party atmosphere to the cruise, just as Mike wanted.

Sarah walked back to her cabin at 9:30 to prepare for her "tea and talk" with Mike on the platform. She went through her clothes in the walk-in closet and selected her outfit for the evening. She chose looser fitting designer blue jeans, an elegant white long sleeve blouse to protect her from the chilly Atlantic air and her brown sandals. She picked just a couple of gold rings for different fingers, a gold toe ring, and a gold necklace with a Crucifix hanging between her breasts. After showering and dressing, Sarah took the long walk to the back of the ship, engaging people in small talk along the way, went down several flights of stairs, and found Mike sitting on a plush white leather loveseat crew members installed for them earlier, one cup of orange chamomile and one cup of decaf green tea with honey sitting on a small table.

"Well, good evening, you look comfortable," Sarah said as she walked up behind Mike.

"Good evening Sarah," Mike said as he stood, motioned for Sarah to have a seat.

Mike handed Sarah her cup of orange chamomile as she sat, took his tea from the table, and sat to her right. They sat quietly for a few moments enjoying the view of the moonlit Atlantic Ocean from the back of the ship. Plankton caused the churning wake from the ship to fluoresce in the moonlight, the low hum of the engines in the background. Sarah leaned her body against Mike's, he put his arm around her and pulled her close.

"How was your day Sarah?"

"It was wonderful Mike. How was yours?"

"It was good, got a lot done, made a lot of good progress."

The two sat quietly again and sipped their tea. Sarah snuggled closer against Mike as if literally trying to get in his skin, her head resting gently on his shoulder.

"It's so beautiful out here Mike, the most romantic thing I think I've ever seen," Sarah said as she moved her body slightly against his.

"Yep," Mike said.

"I know I'm not supposed to say this Mike, and I don't want to ruin the evening." Sarah hesitated. "But I spent all day with the men and women who work for you, who are going on the operation with you and... I'm getting nervous.

"Me too," Mike confessed.

"You are," Sarah said with a little surprise as she leaned her head to look up at Mike.

"Everyone gets nervous Sarah, scared. And if they say they don't then their either stupid or lying and either way, you don't want to go into combat with them," Mike gave Sarah a deep and gentle kiss.

Sarah sighed deeply and rested her head back on Mike's shoulder. They sat and watched the ship's wake in the moonlight for another ten minutes without talking, just enjoying each other's physical presence, the view and fresh air, Sarah occasionally squirming her body against Mike's.

After setting his empty cup on the small table, Mike took Sarah's cup from her. He turned in his seat, brushed Sarah's cheek with his hand as he looked into her baby blue eyes, and gave her a gentle peck on the lips. He kept his face close to hers, close enough that Sarah felt his warm breath very lightly on her face. He kissed her passionately but tenderly for a minute, finishing with another gentle peck. He brushed her face again with his hand and let her blonde hair linger between his fingers.

"Are you still sure," Mike whispered.

"Yes," she whispered back as she reached up and removed the lipstick smudge from his lower lip with her thumb.

Sarah and Mike sat together another fifteen minutes, his arm around her and her head laying on his chest just in front of his shoulder, her left hand gently rubbing the other side of his chest.

CHAPTER TWENTY-EIGHT

"Love is the master key that opens the gates of happiness, of hatred, of jealousy, and, most easily of all, the gate of fear." —Oliver Wendell Holmes, Sr.

Mike and Sarah didn't see each other very much over the course of the next two days. They spent two more evenings together having tea on the back platform of the ship, and kissed romantically. Mike walked Sarah back to her cabin both nights, kissed her at the door, and said goodnight, never going in. Without speaking about it, they both knew that the fourth night aboard the yacht having tea together would be their last, at least for a while. Sarah hoped they would have tea again the night after the mission, and prayed for Mike's safety.

During the fifth day at sea, Griff broke Mike's rule and gave the actors a tour of the CIC. He briefed them on its purpose, his job, and showed them a row of cushioned chairs in the back of the room where they could sit and listen to the operation over the radios and watch the live feed on the video monitors if they thought it would help their character studies for future roles, and if they thought they could handle it, handle the violence that was sure to be involved.

Sarah was hesitant at first, but discussed it with her friends and decided they would like to watch the operation from Griff's perspective. Sarah decided that she had to watch, come what may.

The actors noticed a distinct lack of activity aboard the yacht that last day, and Angela told them that final preparations were in full swing. The men were writing what was possibly their last letters home, video chatting with loved ones in the computer center, and studying their briefing packages. Some were cleaning and checking weapons, checking all their gear while others were in deep meditation or prayer, each person doing what he or she felt they needed to do in order to prepare.

There was less alcohol the night before in the lounge, less drinking, and there was no drinking on the final day to ensure everyone was properly hydrated and sober. The ship's two trauma surgeons, nurses, and medics busied themselves in sickbay ensuring everything was ready.

Sarah and her friends ate lunch and dinner together in a mostly empty lounge and exchanged mundane conversation, each afraid to express their fears. The ladies swam in the pool and enjoyed the hot tub as Adam visited the gaming center again. He watched the few men and women in the gaming center with him, and engaged in pleasant small talk. For the first time since the cruise began, Adam detected an ominous feeling aboard the yacht, a sense of foreboding.

Beth and Robin found Sarah sitting on her and Mike's loveseat on the platform after sunset. They walked down and joined her, one woman sitting on each side of her. They sat quietly for several minutes enjoying the view, each woman holding one of Sarah's hands.

"So this is the scene of the crime," Robin finally tried to lighten the mood.

"Yes," Sarah said softly as she choked her emotions back.

The three women sat on the loveseat for thirty minutes as Sarah recounted her nights on the platform with Mike, still speaking softly, her voice just barely louder than the soft hum of the ship's engines. She described for them again, how she felt when Mike rescued her and she looked into his eyes for the first time, those eyes, and what it was like to be in his arms the first time when he carried her over the broken glass and parachuted off the top of the building. She talked about the long eight months looking for him, wondering who he was and what he was like, her voice cracking as she spoke. She laughed slightly as she told her friends about Mike bringing wine and those tiny little bread sticks with cheese to her rescue, the ones his grandson likes.

"*Attention all operational personnel...attention all operational personnel...report to the main lounge at 0030 hours...that's twelve-thirty in the morning for our civilian guests,*" the anonymous voice crackled over the PA system startling Sarah, Beth, and Robin. Sarah gasped, took a long, deep breath, and exhaled nervously. Beth and Robin put their arms around her and held her.

At 11:00 that night, Mike sat at the desk in his cabin writing on ship's stationary, all of his planning meetings, conference calls, and preparations completed. He paused, reached down into a desk drawer, and took out a picture taken several years before of him and Vicky. He took out another picture, a group photo of his kids and grandkids, sat it next to the first picture, and continued writing. He placed the pictures back in the desk drawer.

Mike's clothes and weapons for the operation lay neatly on his bed. The uniform for the operation was jungle camouflage with an olive drab, brownish green tee shirt. His weapon of choice was the silenced M-4 rifle, his Colt 1911 .45 for high up on his hip, and his Glock .40 for the holster low on his right thigh. His ka-bar knife already attached to his ballistic vest. Mike finished his writing and began to dress.

Sarah walked to Mike's cabin at eleven forty-five that evening, hesitated momentarily in the hallway, and then knocked on the door, not knowing if he would be there or not. She halfway hoped he wouldn't be there, wouldn't answer his door, but at the same time, wanted to make sure she saw him and talked to him before he left.

"It's open," Mike shouted from inside his cabin as he finished tying his second boot.

"Mike?" Sarah said cautiously as she opened the door and walked partially in.

"Sarah, come in," Mike said as he stood, wearing his fatigue pants, boots, and brownish green tee shirt, his muscles thick and tight as if he just finished one thousand push-ups. "Is everything okay?"

"Yes Mike. I just...I didn't know if," Sarah paused and glanced over to the weapons on Mike's bed, and then down at the floor. "I didn't know if..."

Mike walked across the cabin to Sarah and took her face in both hands, raising it to look into her eyes. He used his thumb to brush away a tear from each of her eyes as he held her face. He leaned in and gave her a gentle peck on her lips. He pulled away and then gave her another, more lingering peck, and then brushed another tear with his thumb. He ran the fingers of both hands through her hair, smoothing it, and brushed her bangs across her forehead. He leaned in and kissed her deeply, passionately as he put his arms around her and held her tightly.

"I'm glad you're here," Mike whispered as he held her and Sarah tightened her grip on him as if she was not going to let him go.

"Hey, I've got an idea," Mike said as he leaned back and looked at Sarah.

"Yes?"

"You're one of those Hollywood types, and a girl, so you know make-up. Right?" Mike said with a playful tone of voice.

"Hollywood types," Sarah punched Mike in the left arm.

"Yeah, you know make-up so why don't you help me put on my war paint?" Mike said.

"I don't know anything about that camouflage stuff," Sarah said as she looked at the tubes of camouflage face and body paint lying on Mike's desk.

"Come on, it's easy," Mike said as he took Sarah's hand, turned and walked toward the desk.

Mike pulled up a second chair for Sarah and they both sat in front of his desk. He showed Sarah the camo sticks and explained that each stick has two colors, one at each end, and that he was using the jungle camo—black and olive drab. Mike demonstrated how to apply it for Sarah and described the theory behind breaking up the lines on his face and masking his facial features. They both laughed as they painted his face, Mike occasionally making funny faces at Sarah as they worked and giving her quick pecks on the lips as she leaned in to apply the paint. Mike playfully smudged some of the paint on Sarah's face.

When she thought she was finished, Sarah stepped back and inspected their work. She cocked her head from side to side and looked at Mike thoughtfully. She narrowed her eyes and furrowed her brow. She walked back over to Mike, moved her legs to the outside of his legs and sat in his lap facing him as she had done moments before they base-jumped off the roof of the building in LA months before. She put her arms around his neck and kissed him deeply.

"Thank you," she whispered.

"For what?"

"For letting me help with your war paint," Sarah said and kissed him again.

The two stood and Mike walked over to his bed to finish dressing. Sarah helped him button his fatigue blouse and put his ballistic vest on. He reached down, picked up his two handguns, and holstered them as Sarah watched closely. He leaned over and kissed Sarah, leaned back down and picked up his rifle.

"Well, time to go to work," Mike smiled at Sarah. "Don't hold dinner," he teased.

Sarah took another deep breath, kissed Mike, and the two walked out of the room together.

Mike and Sarah heard the briefing already underway as they crested the top of the stairs to the main lounge. Forty heavily armed men dressed in the same way as Mike, faces painted, sat around the tables in the lounge in silence as they listened to their last briefing before leaving for the mission. Mike squeezed Sarah's hand and motioned with his head for her to join her friends near the main bar to the left middle of the lounge, and walked to the front of the lounge to join Frank and Griff.

"My god Sarah, have you heard any of this briefing, have you heard what they're going to do, and how?" Robin said as Sarah walked up to her.

"I don't need to," Sarah said softly.

"What's that on your face?" Beth said as she reached over to clean Sarah's face.

"It's Mike," Sarah said as she pulled her face away from Beth's hand. "Just leave it."

"And without further adieu," Frank said as he wrapped up the briefing. "The Boss."

"Good morning," Mike began. "First off, I don't want anyone to worry; I'm not going to give you one of those damn, long winded, rah-rah Saint Crispin's Day speeches, or talk about Valhalla. You all know what we're here to do, how we're going to do it, and you know how I feel about you.

Second, remember, shoot—move—communicate...shoot and scoot, shoot and scoot! Oh, Bill? Where's Billy?"

"Here Boss," a young man in the back of the lounge raised his hand.

"Watch your crossfire and don't shoot your battle buddy in the ass," Mike chuckled.

"Yes Sir," the man said.

"Now, do any of you have any questions for me?"

"Play the song Boss!" one man shouted from the back of the room.

"Yeah, play the song!" Another shouted.

"Oh my god, watch this," Sarah said to her friends. "I've seen this once before at Mike's house the night Bob Morton was shot."

Mike silently scanned the room, tried to make eye contact with each man. He looked over his right shoulder and motioned with his right hand. As a slow, mournful drumbeat began, followed by a crying guitar, every man in the lounge stood and looked to the floor. They all began to sway their bodies in almost perfect unison as Phil Collins sang "In the Air Tonight." Slowly, the men reached to their sides and took the men's hands standing on each side of them. Sarah silently watched Mike, her eyes again welling up with tears. Beth and Robin reached down and took her hands as they both began to cry with her. Adam Levi stood silently, amazed, his mouth slightly open.

As the song built to its crescendo, Mike raised his head and opened his eyes. He looked at Sarah with a blank expression on his face, his game face behind the war paint, and then gave her a slow wink and a nod, as if promising everything would be okay. One by one, Mike's men walked to the front of the lounge as the song continued to play and dropped an envelope on the table in front of him, and then shook Mike's hand.

"Their last letters home," Angela whispered to Sarah and her friends.

After each man shook Mike's hand, they turned and walked down the staircase at the back of the lounge, disappearing from sight. Mike shook hands with Griff and Frank, pulled two envelopes from the lower pocket on the left side of his fatigue pants, and dropped them into the middle of the table. He turned and walked toward Sarah. Mike moved his rifle to his back as he approached her, placed his left hand on her hip, and kissed her deeply, passionately, and then looked deeply into her eyes while cleaning the smudge of camo paint from her lip without saying a word. He shook hands with Adam and nodded. Then nodded to Beth and Robin, turned and walked to the stairs, handing Angela a third envelope as he walked.

Angela escorted Sarah, Beth, Robin, and Adam downstairs one deck to a point where they could all look down onto the platform below, Mike and Sarah's platform. They watched as men gathered on the platform and then disappeared back into the yacht, into the first deck above the waterline. Moments later, inflatable rigid hull Zodiac boats deployed from a large opening in the side of the yacht that Sarah and her friends had not noticed before.

All of the men, including Mike, were gone within fifteen minutes, the Zodiacs disappearing into the darkness in groups of twos and threes.

After the men were gone, Griff and Angela escorted Sarah and her friends to the CIC, manned by Griff and three other men. The video monitors were on but there was no video. Frank busied himself filling out a checklist and making notes in a large binder. Griff explained that there would be radio silence and no video until the Mike and the men actually made it onto the beach in approximately twenty minutes...twenty minutes of silence, Sarah thought.

"Coffee's fresh and hot, gonna be a long night," Griff said to Sarah's group.

"I think I'd rather have a shot of whiskey or tequila," Adam said.

"Wine," Robin and Beth said in unison while Sarah remained silent.

"Sorry ladies and gentlemen, no alcohol tonight, bar's closed," Griff said. "Coffee's fresh and hot."

Griff poured two cups of coffee and limped over to Sarah.

"You okay?" he said as he handed her a cup of coffee."

"Yes, I mean...I don't know...I just feel like the next time I see Mike will be at his funeral," Sarah said very quietly.

CHAPTER TWENTY-NINE

"Come on you sons of bitches, do you want to live forever?!" —Sgt. Maj. Dan Daly, USMC

The Zodiac boats with Mike and his team raced through the dark toward the Nigerian coast, arriving at 1:30 in the stifling hot and humid morning. They met two men from their scout team who were already ashore. Fifteen men immediately deployed along the tree line for security while the rest of the men pulled the boats ashore to cover.

"*Eagle Actual, Eagle Actual, Eagle 9-9, comms check,*" Mike said into his radio mic as he knelt in the sand just in front of the tree line.

"Read you five by five Eagle 9-9, how me, over," Griff answered as Sarah stood from her chair in the CIC at the sound of Mike's voice and looked on.

"*Read you five by and limping along, Eagle Actual,*" Mike joked.

"Asshole," Griff said as he chuckled but not keying the radio microphone. "Copy, Eagle 9-9," he finally answered once he stopped laughing over Mike teasing him about his limp.

"*Eagle Actual, bringing up my body and gun cams now, over,*" Mike said.

Griff turned to Sarah and pointed to the video monitors to the top left marked "B-99" and "G-99." A clear green picture appeared on both monitors revealing dark shadowy figures moving around the beach and advancing into the tree line, Mike's men.

"Eagle 9-9, your cams are hot and clear, over."

"*9-9 copy, Actual. See you when we get home.*"

"Safe travels, Eagle Actual out."

Sarah moved her chair closer to Griff so she could see the monitors better, but making sure to stay out of everyone's way. She and her friends kept their eyes glued to the monitors in the dimly lit room. Adam made his way to the coffee pot, and quietly offered to make a cup for Beth and Robin, but they declined.

"Wow, I don't know what it is but Mike really sounds different on the radio," Beth said to Sarah.

"That's his *work voice*," Sarah laughed as she tried to mimic Mike's voice. "I've heard that voice before, during my rescue."

Mike and his men put their night vision goggles in place and began moving into the Nigerian jungle for their four-mile trek to the Boko Haram base camp, lead by the two men from the scout team who they met on the beach. They moved slowly and carefully, continuously watching for trip wires and other signs of booby traps, as well as native wild life. Mike estimated it would take him and his men approximately four hours to make it to their destination, arriving sometime around five that morning. The timing had to be precise so they arrived right before the Nigerian Army and South African mercenaries began their diversionary attacks against the camps, hopefully waiting for Mike's go ahead to start.

Sarah fidgeted in her chair, got up and walked toward the back of the room, always listening for Mike's voice over the radio. She made herself a cup of coffee and sipped it nervously, her hands slightly shaking. Griff walked back and joined her, made himself a cup of coffee.

"You okay Sarah?" Griff said.

"Yes, I'm okay Griff. Thank you. I've seen Mike fight before and I know what a capable man he is...just a little nervous, not too bad."

"You know Sarah, I've known Mike Hampton a very long time and we were in some pretty tough spots before, some worse than this I think. And there's nobody I'd rather be in a fight with than him," Griff said.

"I know Griff. I just know that he's tired of getting hurt. He joked with me the other night about it, about needing his little plastic donut ring to sit on if he gets shot in the butt again. He was so funny about it all," Sarah laughed as she recounted Mike's story for Griff, and sipped her coffee.

"I'd say that before Mike met you Sarah, the odds of him coming back alive from this operation were pretty slim because Vicky's gone and his kids are grown. Now though, with you in his life, I'd say the odds are in his favor because he's got something to come home to, someone to come home to. Don't get me wrong Sarah, its going get bad, going be a fight and I can't promise Mike will be okay. But I do think he'll make it out alive...he always does."

"Thank you Griff, that's so sweet of you to say. But I really am okay, I promise. I hate it when Mike gets hurt, but I've watched him get shot, close up, and he bounces right back and keeps fighting. It was the most incredible thing I think I've ever seen."

"It's going to be about four hours before the show really starts if you folks want to get some sleep," Griff said to everyone.

"No," Sarah said."

The radios remained silent for hours as Mike and his men made their way through the jungle. Only the green video feed showing trees, underbrush, and feet gave Sarah any information. Griff reached into a drawer in one of the cabinets in the CIC and tossed a deck of cards across the room to Adam. The four actors played games of Spades and Hearts as they drank coffee and made light conversation about their latest film and television roles.

Angela Montero walked into the room and over to Griff. She leaned over and whispered to him for a moment. Griff nodded in agreement. Angela laid her purse and small briefcase on the floor and walked over to Sarah holding a brown leather folder, and sat next to her.

"Sarah, this is for you," Angela said as she pulled a white envelope from her folder. "It's Mike's letter to you in case, well, you know, in case he doesn't make it back. I'm not supposed to give it to you yet, but what the hell, I mean let's face it, I do so many things that Mr. H doesn't want me to do anyway. I just ask that you don't read it unless..."

"I know what it is," Sarah said as she looked at Angela. "And I appreciate your concern but I really don't think I should take it right now Angela. Mike doesn't want me to have it yet and there really is no need for it right now. But thank you."

"*Eagle 9-9, all Eagle units...hold in place...cams on...snipers out,*" the radio in the CIC crackled to life with the sound of Mike's voice. Sarah stood from her chair and looked at the video monitors. She glanced at her friends and mouthed the words "here we go," and looked back at the monitors with mixed emotions.

"*Break-break, Eagle Actual, Eagle 9-9, over,*" Mike said.

"Eagle 9-9, Eagle Actual, go ahead, over," Griff answered.

"*Eagle Actual, Eagle units approaching objective, negative contact so far, over.*"

"Actual copies, 9-9, standing by."

The CIC came to life as gun and body cameras lit up all fifteen video monitors in front of Griff. The three men sitting next to Griff along the shelf-like counter opened their three ring binders of checklists and readied their grease pencils. Countdown clocks were set. Adam put the cards away and Sarah walked across the room toward Griff and the other men.

Fifteen more minutes passed before the sound of Mike breathing came over a different speaker as he turned on the audio feed on his body camera. Sarah watched his gun camera footage intently and could tell that he was crawling through high thick grass under tall trees. She looked at another monitor for one of Mike's men's camera and saw him crawling. I shouldn't be here, she thought. I have to be here.

"*Allied Actual, Allied Actual, Eagle 9-9, over,*" Mike said over the radio.

"*Eagle 9-9, this is Allied Actual, go ahead,*" a man with a thick South African accent answered.

"*Allied Actual, make it rain baby - light'em up!*" Mike said over the radio.

"*Allied Actual copy, Eagle 9-9, start the party,*" the South African accent answered.

Within a minute, the sounds of war filled the CIC. Griff and the men sitting with him worked to adjust the incoming volume on the radios. The video monitors filled with views of explosions rocking a clearing in the jungle filled with a few permanent structures, but mostly rows of tents and some grass hut type structures. Fires began to burn, everything with the night vision green hue first made familiar to everyone by the news media during Operation Desert Strom in 1991.

Sarah's mouth went slightly dry and her heart began to pump faster with excitement and anticipation. She was nervous for Mike but she also knew that the beginning of the operation meant it would all be over soon. Even more than worrying about Mike, Sarah worried for his men she had met over the past several days on the yacht, such young men, she thought. She knew how Mike felt about them, how much he loved them and he would be deeply hurt if any one of them was killed or seriously injured.

"Don't worry everyone, Mike's going to be fine," Sarah looked back and said to her friends. "He'll be fine. I'm fine." Sarah returned her attention to the video monitors.

"*Eagle 9-9 to all Eagle units...hold what you got, hold fire...hold...patience,*" Mike said to his teams.

The open audio feeds from the gun and body cameras on Mike and his men picked up every sound, every explosion, and every gunshot. Bright greenish and white flashes streaked across the video monitors as the fighting intensified. Mike and his men came under heavy small arms fire as some of the Boko Haram fighters tried to escape to the west toward Mike and his men, toward the ocean.

"*Engage,*" Mike shouted to his men. His men opened fire and Sarah, Beth, Robin, and Adam could see Boko Haram fighters in the distance going down wounded and killed.

"*Billy!*" Mike shouted. "*Billy! Get some 40 mike-mike on that machine gun on your 1 o'clock—take that rat bastard out!*" Mike ordered.

Billy fired two 40-millimeter grenades at a Boko Haram machine gunner 100 yards away on his right.

"*Atta kid,*" Mike shouted.

"*Eagle Actual, Eagle 9-9,*" Mike said over the radio.

"*Eagle 9-9 and 9-7 moving north along the tree line to position bravo—beginning extraction, over.*

"Copy 9-9," Griff answered Mike.

Sarah watched the video monitors for Mike's gun and body cameras intently. She could see that Mike was jogging through a tree line, the Boko Haram camp, and a clearing to his right. He fired his M-4 rifle intermittently as he ran, breathing hard, and occasionally cussing, the sound of his feet trampling the grass, fallen leaves, and sticks. Explosions continued to resonate through the speakers, bright flashes streaked across the video monitors, many in Mike's direction, splintering tree bark around him, close to him.

Sarah remembered the doorframe in the conference room splintering around Mike as the terrorist fired at him and shot him, during her rescue. She remembered how horrified she was at the time, trying to crawl over to Mike, but how he bounced right back. She suddenly realized at that moment, that Mike was mad that they shot him instead of afraid or scared. She smiled to herself at the memory.

Mike's squad leaders assumed command and directed their men in the fight, repositioning their fire teams and directing fire as they moved into the outskirts of the Boko

Haram base camp. Men yelled over their open audio feeds, congratulated each other as their shots found their marks.

As Mike and Eagle 9-7 moved toward the building where their intelligence indicated the two hostages were held, they encountered 10 Boko Haram fighters trying to retreat, and engaged in a fierce firefight. Mike and his partner moved toward the enemy as they fought, and became separated. They continued to fight separately, communicating over their radios and using hand signals.

Sarah tensed slightly as she heard Mike grunt over his open audio feed. The monitor for his body camera went dark and his gun camera fell and then focused on nothing but tall grass.

"Eagle 9-2, this is Eagle 97...Eagle 9-9 is down, repeat, Eagle 9-9 is down, move up and support, copy?

"Eagle 9-2 copies 9-7."

Beth and Robin were stunned—they watched Sarah, walked over to her and held her hands.

"I'm okay," Sarah said rather matter-of-factly.

"Hold what you got, 9-2 and 9-7, I'm fine," Mike said. *"Just got the wind knocked out of me."*

Sarah turned and smiled at her friends. "He's okay," she whispered.

The Boko Haram commanders soon realized that Mike and his men were behind them attempting a hostage rescue. They directed more of their fighters back through the camp and around the tree line to engage them. Fifty Boko Haram fighters attacked the right flank of the Eagle units with rocket propelled grenades, old Soviet era heavy machine guns, and small arms fire. Mike's squad leaders repositioned their fire teams to repel the repeated attacks.

Mike realized that he and Eagle 9-7 needed to make their way to the target building and the hostages before their guards assassinated or moved them. They completed the firefight with the 10 terrorists and moved toward the building, but became separated again. Mike fought his way through the clearing and toward the building. Four Boko Haram fighters rounded the building and opened fire on him. He shot two, but the other two were able to rush him as he reloaded.

"*Boss is in a knife fight in the clearing,*" someone shouted over his open audio feed. "*Anybody got a shot?*" the man yelled as he turned his gun camera toward Mike.

Sarah watched the gun camera video in silence, her body moving in unison with Mike's, discretely shadow boxing with him as he fought. Bright flashes of light continued streaking across the screen, the sounds of gunfire and explosions resonating through the room. She watched as Mike fought the two terrorists. She tensed again as one of the terrorists pulled a pistol and fired several shots at Mike in rapid succession, striking his ballistic vest. Sarah worried as Mike fell to the ground. He pulled out his Glock .40 and fired, striking the two terrorists and killed them.

Sarah smiled again as Mike scrambled to his feet while bullets impacted the ground around him and the cinderblock building in front of him, cement shards flying into the air. He took cover at the corner of the building, squatted, and reloaded his Glock with a fresh magazine, then his M-4 rifle. Sarah's mind flashed back to Mike fighting and moving during her rescue, looking at her and winking while pausing to reload. Men continued to scream and shout over the open audio feeds of the cameras as the squad leaders barked out instructions over their radios.

Sarah continued to watch Mike intently. She listened to his heavy, labored breathing over his audio feed. Eagle 9-7 joined Mike at the corner of the building and Sarah watched as they stood and rushed inside. Bright flashes of light in rapid succession shown through the windows of the cinderblock building as Mike and Eagle 9-7 fought the terrorists guarding the two hostages. Within just a couple of minutes, Mike emerged from the building with a man and a woman, but Sarah noticed that Mike was limping. Eagle 9-7 emerged from the building a moment later and the four squatted at the corner of the building again, momentarily taking cover.

"*Eagle Actual, Eagle 9-9, acquired two, begin egress,* Mike said, his breathing even heavier than before. "*Damn it,*" Mike whispered to himself, transmitting over his audio feed.

"Copy 9-9," Griff answered. "Eagle Actual to all Eagle units, begin egress procedure."

Sarah watched the video monitors as Mike and Eagle 9-7 began moving the hostages across the clearing toward the tree line, Mike limping behind the other three, occasionally turning and firing. Sarah saw Boko Haram fighters closing in on Mike.

"*Eagle 9-7 plus two...we're pinned down in the tree line!*"

"*Eagle Actual, Eagle 9-3...our right flank is under pressure and turning, Eagle 9-1 and 9-4 are cut off...*"

"Shit's getting sideways on us," Griff mumbled under his breath.

Sarah watched as the Boko Haram fighters continued to close on Mike's position, firing at him as he limped toward the tree line, his breathing heavily labored, grunting as he moved. His body camera went dark again as he went down wounded just short of the tree line. Sarah could tell by Mike's gun camera that he was crawling toward the trees, breathing rapid and shallow. Several rocket-propelled grenades exploded close to him. He crawled just inside the tree line, turned, and engaged the enemy fighters.

"*Eagle 9-7, Eagle 9-9,*" Mike drew deep heavy breaths as he talked into his radio.

"*Go 9-9.*"

"*9-7, get those two out of here, I'll cover your six,*" Mike said, the sound of gunfire and bullets impacting trees all around him, his words truncated and interrupted by his breathing.

"*Allied Actual, Eagle 9-9.*"

"*Go ahead, Eagle 9-9,*" the thick South African accent answered Mike.

"Sure could use a little air support from those helicopters about now," Mike said.

"And where would you like it, 9-9?"

"Light up the tree line baby—light it up."

"Roger that, Eagle 9-9, light show in 5."

Mike's men fought their way back away from the tree line to the west, toward the beach, engaging the enemy as they moved, and the Boko Haram fighters moved into the tree line. Mike crawled as far as he could to engage the terrorists to help his men evacuate, but the incoming fire on his men was still too heavy for their retreat. Several of the terrorists turned their attention to Mike, pouring heavy fire into his position, hitting him several times in the legs, the arms, and his ballistic vest. One round penetrated under Mike's vest through his armpit and collapsed his lung.

"Eagle Actual, Eagle 9-2...we're not getting out of here without that air support on the tree line, incoming fire is too heavy, copy?

"Eagle Actual copies, Eagle 9-2, air support is incoming but Eagle 9-9 is still in the tree line, anyone got a location on him?"

"Negative, Eagle Actual."

Eagle 9-9, Eagle Actual," Griff said into the radio. There was no answer.

"Eagle 9-9, Eagle Actual," Griff repeated.

Sarah remained stoic as she listened to Griff try to contact Mike. Her friends walked up behind her and placed their hands on her shoulders. Robin gently took Sarah's hand as everyone realized what might have happened.

"Eagle 9-9, Eagle Actual," Griff repeated again, but again, Mike didn't answer.

Sarah looked at the monitors, Mike's two cameras were black...no picture at all, his audio feed was silent, no heavy breathing. She watched another monitor as Eagle 9-2 scanned the tree line with his gun camera around Mike's last known position. The camera showed the heavily increasing volume of in-coming enemy small arms fire, and rocket-propelled grenades. The gun camera stopped scanning and Sarah was able to see a small group of Boko Haram fighters firing into, and advancing on, a position to their right. Approximately fifteen yards from the enemy fighters, a lone pistol fired back at them.

"Eagle Actual..............Eagle 9...Eagle 9-9," Mike's voice was weak, breathless.

"Go ahead 9-9," Griff said.

"Griff...get that god damned air support on this tree line brother so these guys can get the fuck out of here," Mike whispered into his radio mic as he struggled for breath, firing three shots from his Colt 1911 .45 as he spoke.

"Eagle 9-9, Allied Actual," the South African accent broke in before Griff could answer Mike. *"Air Support in one...are you clear of the tree line?"*

"Just put it on the tree line Allied Act...," Mike ran out of breath before he could finish his sentence. *"Put it on the tree line."*

"Are you clear, Eagle 9-9?" The South African accent insisted.

"Negative Allied Actual," Mike drew in a deep breath and coughed. *"And I can't get clear...I'm down, Allied...I'm down."*

"Dear God," Beth said as everyone listened to Mike. "Dear God," she repeated.

Griff moved his chair back and stood, looked at Sarah and Angela. Sarah stood frozen with her right hand over her mouth, her eyes wet. She breathed deeply to brace herself, to collect herself, her shoulders rising and falling as she inhaled and exhaled.

"No," Sarah mumbled very quietly. "Please God, no..."

"Hey Griff," Mike said very weakly into the radio mic.

"Yeah Mike?" Griff answered.

Mike did not respond.

"Go ahead Mike," Griff repeated. "Mike? Eagle 9-9...this is Eagle Actual, over," Griff called into the radio.

Eagle 9-2's gun camera showed the tree line light up with explosions from the rockets fired by the helicopters.

"NO!" Sarah screamed as if ordering the helicopters to stop.

The helicopters fired another volley of rockets as they made a second pass and raked the tree line with heavy machine gun fire.

"NO!" Sarah screamed as she collapsed onto the floor crying, her friends struggling to hold her up. "NO! My God NO!"

CHAPTER THIRTY

"A strong woman builds her own world. She is one who is wise enough to know that it will attract the man she will gladly share it with." —Ellen J. Barrier

Sarah argued and demanded to stay in the CIC in case there was any news about Mike or his body, but her friends finally convinced her to go back to her cabin with the ship's doctor. She refused to let the doctor sedate her. She was shaky on her feet, but able to walk back toward her cabin under her own power. Sarah took deep breaths as she walked and smoothed her clothes with her hands. She ran her fingers through her long hair and then fixed it in a ponytail. She took deep breaths and threw her shoulders back as she walked in front of the others. She had her meltdown, she decided, and it was time to get it together.

"I'd rather go to the lounge for some coffee and breakfast, wait for Mike's guys to get back," Sarah said to Beth and Robin as they reached her cabin door.

"Are you sure?" Beth said with surprise.

"Yes," Sarah said confidently. "We should be there when they get back. The men who aren't wounded will probably want to celebrate their successful mission. Hell, some of the wounded men might want to celebrate too and we should be there," Sarah insisted. "And if they're upset about Mike, well, then we should be there for them. They've known him a lot longer and been through a lot more with him than we have."

The three women turned and walked to the lounge together, Sarah leading the group.

Adam Levi stayed in the CIC monitoring the radios with Griff, waiting for any news about Mike, but there was none. All of Mike's men, including the walking wounded and two hostages made it back to the Nigerian coast and left in the Zodiac boats. They estimated it would take 20 minutes for the boats to make the return trip to the yacht. According to Eagle 9-7, there was still too much enemy activity to search for Mike's body and another rescue and recovery mission might be required. The primary mission for that day was to rescue the hostages and get them to safety, and they accomplished that mission.

Different Eagle unites radioed the condition of wounded men to the ship's medical staff from the Zodiac boats. The medical staff charted the information and prepared emergency medical services on the back platform of the ship and in sickbay. Ship's crew had stretchers ready, IV fluids, and all the medical equipment necessary to treat the expected number of casualties. The head paramedic set up the triage area just inside the lower deck of the ship past the platform.

Sarah, Beth, and Robin walked into a lounge buzzing with activity. Ship's crew dressed in their short black vests readied a buffet table with a gourmet brunch including lobster tail, shrimp, roast beef, ham, and there was an omelet and pancake station at the end of the long table. Bottles of Champagne, wine, and whiskey adorned several tables in the middle of the lounge, along with buckets of ice.

"Is there anything we can help with?" Sarah said as she walked over to the chief steward.

"No thank you, Ms. Tomzewski. But you ladies can have breakfast anytime you're ready."

"Thank you, but we'll wait for the men to get back," Sarah said. "I would like a good stiff drink though, if you don't mind, maybe a double Jack and coke please?"

"Yes Ma'am, of course." The chief steward motioned for a waitress.

"*Attention all personnel, attention all personnel,*" the ship's PA system crackled to life. "*The flight deck is hot for immediate helicopter departure,*" the anonymous voice announced.

Adam Levi ran into the lounge just as Sarah finished her first double Jack and coke, at 7: 30 in the morning, Robin and Beth were on their second glass of wine, the three women having decided they had enough coffee during the night.

"He's alive Sarah, they found him, and he's alive, hurt bad and barely alive, but alive," Adam said as he struggled for breath.

"Oh my god, how is that possible—we saw it—we heard it...how?" Sarah spoke excitedly.

"He's alive Sarah," Adam repeated himself, regaining his breath. "The Nigerians and South African mercenaries secured the camp and found Mike in the tree line, almost dead but alive—hurt bad—he was covered by three dead terrorists and they think the dead terrorists absorbed most of the hits...but he's alive!" Adam said. "He's unconscious but alive," Adam reached over and drank Robin's glass of wine. "They just sent the helicopter for him."

Sarah sat back in her chair; her shoulders slumped, looking at Adam in disbelief. She nervously took a sip of the second Jack and coke the waitress set on the table in front of her. Sarah heard a commotion toward the back of the lounge. She and her friends walked back, down two flights of stairs, and watched as the men in the Zodiac boats began returning to the yacht.

Sarah watched with pride as the young men she had grown to know over the previous five days climbed out of the Zodiac boats and onto the ship's platform, and into the opening on the side of the ship just foreword of the platform. Some of the men had bandages tied around an arm, a leg; one had a bandage around his head as the ship's crew helped them aboard. The two hostages, the

French diplomat and his wife, boarded the yacht first, before Mike's men.

The ship's medical crew checked each man in the triage area even if he did not appear wounded. The doctor checked each man's eyes and ears for signs of traumatic brain injury, asked each man a series of brief questions, closely listening to his response for clarity and accuracy. As the doctor medically cleared each man, another crewmember stowed the returning man's weapons. Sarah and her friends kept watching until each man was safely back aboard the yacht, happily greeting each one that walked up the stairs toward the lounge with a hug and kiss on the cheek.

Sarah saw the ship's helicopter approaching from the east through the glare of the morning sun. She turned and ran up the stairs, through the lounge and up the sweeping staircase. She ran down the long hallway toward the door leading out onto the helipad just as more medical staff from sickbay ran out of the door. Sarah stood just outside the door and watched as the helicopter landed, ensuring to stay out of everyone's way. Robin, Beth, and Adam joined her moments later. Griff limped out behind them.

The paramedics took Mike off the helicopter on a stretcher. He was naked except for his underwear, his body covered with blood, dirt, and soot from the fires. One man held an IV bag over Mike's body and squeezed it as they rushed Mike toward the door into the ship. Sarah noticed several large red welts on Mike's chest, his neck, and head bandaged. His eyes closed, blood oozed from his ears, nose, and mouth. Mike had a small slicing wound on his forehead, a gunshot wound in his right shoulder, both legs, and arms.

"BP sixty-two over forty-one," the paramedic shouted over the sound of the helicopter's engines winding down. "Pulse weak and thready, pupils responsive, respirations shallow and weak, no breath sounds on the right."

Sarah followed the medical staff to sickbay and tried to go in the door behind them.

"No Ma'am," the nurse said as she motioned for Sarah to stop.

Sarah's friends caught up to her and Griff followed behind them.

"Come on Sarah," Griff said as he opened the door to sickbay and ushered Sarah inside.

"Clear!" the doctor shouted as he applied the defibrillator to Mike. "Charging!" The doctor shocked Mike a second time.

"Nothing," the nurse shouted.

"Clear!" the doctor tried again as Sarah and Griff watched, Griff's arm around Sarah.

"I've got a pulse!"

"Get him into surgery—we can't wait till we get him stabilized," the doctor ordered as a second doctor, the paramedics, and nurses continued to work on Mike.

The doctor motioned for Griff and Sarah to join him in the hallway. Robin, Beth, and Adam gathered around Sarah to support her and listen to the doctor.

"Look, Ms. Tomzewski. We have to get Mr. Hampton into surgery right away and I can't make any promises...hell, he should be dead already," the doctor stopped and regrouped, looked down and then back at Sarah.

"We're going to do everything we can and I can't tell you how long surgery will take...we won't know until we get in there and see what we're dealing with. But, he's a strong man, physically fit and in great shape."

"I know doctor," Sarah reached out and put her hand on the doctor's arm. "I know you'll do everything you can and, as Mike would say, the facts are what they are."

The doctor nodded and walked back into sickbay. Sarah turned to her friends, her eyes welling up. She took a deep breath and swallowed her emotions.

"Do you want us to stay with you Sarah," Beth asked.

"No... Thank you. You guys go up there and celebrate with those young men and women, if they're celebrating. Dance with them, sign autographs if they want, take pictures, and post them on social media. If they're not celebrating because they're worried about Mike, then console them. I'll stay here and wait because someone should be here if Mike wakes up," Sarah said calmly and confidently.

"I'll stay with her," Griff said. "

The captain turned the yacht to the north to leave Nigerian national waters and rendezvous with the French Navy to repatriate the diplomat and his wife. Angela Montero and Mike's senior staff coordinated with the French government to transfer him to the French Navy for more advanced medical care and possible medical evacuation to the U.S. military hospital in Germany, if he lived through surgery. Angela contacted Mike's eldest daughter and passed on the news of his condition.

Robin, Beth, and Adam walked into the lounge just as the party started. Mike's men and women sat around the tables eating and drinking as the band played classic rock and blues songs. It was raucous and loud in the lounge with laughter and occasional cheers as the men talked to each other about their individual successes during the fight. They teased each other about taking cover during in-coming fire, and close calls.

Sarah's friends went table to table talking to the men and women, and drinking with them. Robin and Beth danced with the men who asked, while Adam made plans to meet several of the men in the ship's gaming center during the return voyage home. The actors were in disbelief, and simply couldn't understand how Mike's men and women could be so exuberant because they had never been in a life or death situation, a life or death struggle themselves. They marveled at the young men and women.

Sarah only picked at the food Griff ordered for her as they talked about Mike and how they met, waiting for news from the doctors. Sarah told Griff about growing up in New Zealand and her acting career. She took short naps off and on in her chair over the next twelve hours as the two waited in the hallway outside sickbay. She prayed that Mike would live, but knew the odds were against him. Sarah was nervous, but not scared. She knew how strong and determined Mike was, and knew what he survived in his past. She also knew that if he died, she at least had his kiss.

"Ms. Tomzewski," the doctor said to Sarah as he walked out of sickbay. "Mr. Hampton is alive. I don't know how, or why, but he's alive, at least for now."

"Okay," Sarah said. "What now?"

"Now we wait and try to keep him stable. We're having a little trouble getting his blood pressure to stabilize. He's hurt pretty bad and we found a lot of internal damage once we opened him up. There's no way he should have survived those wounds—that much damage—he lost more blood than any human should be able to lose, but...he's still alive. The nurses and medics are finishing up his bandages and we're going to keep him sedated for a while...I'm not going to transfer him to the French Navy unless we get him stabilized, we have everything here that they have aboard their ships so we can do just as much for him as they can, and, everything that can be done has been done. It's up to him now and...."

"Can I see him," Sarah interrupted the doctor.

"Give it about ten minutes, Ms. Tomzewski. Let the nurses finish cleaning him up and bandaging him and then Griff can take you in, but I want to stress one more thing; the next 48 to 72 hours are critical. If he survives that long then he might have a chance, might."

"Thank you, Doctor, thank you for everything."

"Yes Ma'am."

CHAPTER THIRTY-ONE

"One by one she slew her fears, and then planted a flower garden over their graves." —John Mark Green

The ship's sickbay was a series of very large interconnecting rooms on the second deck above the water line toward the aft of the ship. There were ten beds for sick and injured, a nurse's station, stainless steel medical shelving, cabinets, and all the modern medical equipment and devices one would expect to see in any American hospital. To Sarah's right as she walked in the door was a large area partitioned from the rest of the room by a light green floor to ceiling curtain. Nurses and medics tended to five wounded men laying in the row of beds to Sarah's left. She smelled the antiseptic and disinfectant as she walked in.

Griff started to walk Sarah over to the area with the floor to ceiling curtains, but she stopped him. She wanted to walk over to the men in the beds first, so Griff escorted her over. Sarah talked to the men and laughed with them as they told her stories about their mission, teasing each other about getting wounded and the type of wounds they suffered. They also talked about Mike, "The Boss," as they called him. They told Sarah how he fought and how much they love and respect him. Sarah touched each man's arm as she listened, and gave each a kiss on the cheek.

"Will you gentlemen please excuse me? I want to go see Mike now," Sarah said to the five men. She waived to the men and nodded before turning to walk toward the curtains with Griff.

"You ready?" Griff said to Sarah as they paused briefly outside the curtains.

"Yes."

Griff moved the curtain aside for Sarah, and they walked in together. Two nurses were tending to Mike, watching the monitors, and charting his vitals. Gauze and bandages nearly covered his entire body and a sheet covered his lower body. One tube extended down Mike's nose, the ventilator hose extended down his throat, one IV in his right hand and another in his left arm. Chest tubes extended from both sides of his upper torso. Tight gauze bandages covered his entire head, part of his face, and neck. Sarah glanced at the monitors, not knowing exactly what to look for. She stood another moment, listening to the machine breathe for Mike.

Sarah put her hands to her mouth as she realized she was starting to chuckle. Unable to control herself, she began to laugh quietly and looked at Griff, her hands still over her mouth. She felt disrespectful, but was powerless to stop her laughter. She glanced at the nurses to check their expressions, and they smiled back.

"Are you thinking what I'm thinking?" Griff said.

"Oh my God," Sarah laughed. "He's really in the wrong line of work for a man who hates needles and hospitals so much," Sarah said through her laughter as she removed one hand from her mouth.

Griff reached outside the curtain and pulled a recliner in, placing it at the head of the bed for Sarah. She took a deep breath as she sat and looked at Mike, her shoulders rising and falling.

"Griff, does the ship have a library? I want to read to Mike," Sarah said.

"Not a very good one, but there's a few books lying around if that's what you're looking for."

"Well, if you get a chance, could you ask Robin or Beth to get my tablet out of the bag in my cabin and bring it to me? I have some books on there," Sarah said as she reached over and carefully took Mike's left hand in hers, looking at the nurse for approval."

"Sure."

Sarah leaned over closer to Mike's bed and began talking to him. She told him about his men returning to the yacht and the wonderful young men wounded during the mission and sharing sickbay with him. She assured Mike that the rest of his men were fine and celebrating upstairs with Beth, Robin, and Adam. She talked to Mike almost continuously for the next five hours before she fell asleep exhausted, her head lying on the side of Mike's bed.

"Sarah," Griff whispered as he gently shook Sarah's shoulder to wake her.

"Sarah, he whispered again."

Sarah stirred slightly on the side of Mike's bed and then sat up in her chair, looking over to check Mike as she sat up rubbing her eyes.

"I'm sorry to wake you Sarah, but the doctors are on a conference call in the CIC with Mike's family and they're asking for you."

"Oh, okay. Will you sit with him while I'm gone Griff? I don't want him to be alone."

"Sure."

Sarah sat next to Mike's doctor inside the CIC, Mike's family on the speakerphone.

"Hello everyone," Sarah said when there was a break in the conversation.

"Hi, how are you Sarah," Mike's daughter asked.

"Well, you know...it is what it is," Sarah said.

"Sarah, Mom is here with us and she has a favor to ask you," Mike's eldest sister said.

Sarah stiffened in her chair. She hadn't met Mike's mother yet, or even talked to her before. She hoped she could choke down her own emotions while speaking to Mrs. Hampton because, she thought, she had no reason to be any more emotional than Mike's mother might be.

"Hello? Sarah?" Mike's mother said.

"Yes Mrs. Hampton, I'm here."

"My daughter was wrong Sarah. I have two favors to ask you," Mike's mother said in a professional, business-like tone of voice.

"Yes Ma'am?"

"The first favor is for you to make sure you take care of yourself, and I want you to promise me. Griff told me that you've been by Mike's bedside for hours now and I want you to promise me that you'll take care of yourself. Mike is a strong man but right now, he's in the doctor's care—my son might live and he might die, we don't know. But we do know that you need to take care of yourself. And I know how much he loves you because I can hear it in his voice when we talk, so if that man wakes up and finds out that we haven't made sure you took care of yourself then we're all in trouble and there's going to be hell to pay. Now promise me," Mike's mother said.

"Yes Ma'am...I promise."

"The second favor may be a little tougher Sarah. I need you and Griff to make sure they bring my son home to Florida. You don't let them stick in him some third world hospital, don't give him to the French for crying out loud, and for God's sake don't let them take him to Germany again! He was so mad when Bob Morton put him on that plane to Germany last time. You make them bring that man home to his family. If my son dies then I'll bury him, and if he lives, then you marry him. You understand me Sarah?"

Sarah was speechless, her jaw dropped and her eyes widened as she sat and stared at the speakerphone in the middle of the table.

"Sarah?" Mrs. Hampton said. "Sarah honey?"

"Yes Ma'am...I'm here..." Sarah cleared her throat. "I understand, Mrs. Hampton."

"Mike's brother is working with the Orlando Regional Medical Center to build a fully equipped hospital suite in Mike's house on Merritt Island. The man has more money than God so there's no problem equipping it and staffing it around the clock. The captain told me it'll take about five or six days to get the yacht within helicopter range of Central Florida and we should know more about Mike's condition by then. Okay Sarah? You make sure they bring him home."

"Yes Ma'am," Sarah said, still stunned by Mrs. Hampton's words. Sarah left the room and made her way back toward sickbay, stopping to talk with some of Mike's men as she passed them in the hallway. As she walked down the stairs and rounded the corner into the hallway leading to sickbay, Sarah saw Griff sitting in a chair outside the door. She paused, took a deep breath, and walked down the long hallway.

"Hi Sarah," Griff said with a tense look on his face as he stood to greet her.

"What happened Griff?" Sarah said nervously.

"We don't know yet Sarah—stroke or cardiac arrest and they've been working on him for about thirty minutes now. They rushed me out of the room so I don't know what the final problem was, what the diagnoses was," Griff said.

Sarah nodded at Griff as she sat in one of the two chairs. Griff sat next to her, and they waited, Griff holding Sarah's hand. They talked for an hour about Mike's condition and Sarah's conference call with his family. Griff was aware of Mrs. Hampton's desires, and agreed that the only hospitals currently within flight distance for the helicopter were third world hospitals, and that wouldn't work. He already spoke to the captain about sailing times to different ports, or within flying distance of different hospitals, and agreed none of them would work.

"Well, Mr. Hampton's alive again...for now anyway," the doctor said as he walked out of sickbay and into the hallway.

"What happened?" Sarah said.

"Mr. Hampton's heart is weak and he went into cardiac arrest. We're still having trouble keeping his BP stabilized. I hate to be cliché, but everything is very touch and go right now and will be for quite some time."

"Can I go back inside now, Doctor?"

"Yes Ms. Tomzewski, go on in."

Sarah stayed at Mike's bedside, usually only leaving for brief trips to the bathroom. Griff, Angela Montero, and her former co-stars took turns sitting with her and talking, concerned about her emotional and physical health. They tried to bring her food, but she only ate a little salad and parts of sandwiches, always refusing to take a break and go upstairs to the lounge for a drink or a few dances. She did leave Mike's bedside a few times to visit with the other wounded men, but never left the sickbay completely.

"Good morning Doctor," Sarah said as the doctor walked in to check on Mike.

He checked with the nurses about Mike's progress that first night, and seemed pleased. He checked Mike from head to toe and documented his findings in Mike's chart. He checked the numbers twice against Mike's numbers from the day before.

"Well, it isn't much Ms. Tomzewski, but he's made some progress over night...fingers crossed?" the doctor motioned to Sarah.

"Fingers crossed," Sarah said as she copied the doctor's gesture.

"His heart is still pretty weak but his lungs are incredibly improved. I'm happy with that progress," the Doctor smiled at Sarah.

Mike's condition continued to go back and forth, and there were two more medical emergencies during the second day after Mike's surgery. During each medical emergency, a medic pulled Sarah's chair away from the bed to allow nurses and doctors to attend to him. Each time Sarah walked out into the hallway and waited to hear if he was alive or dead, and what caused the medical emergency. Each time she went back in and sat by his bedside. She thought about Vicky sitting at his bedside in the Philippines, and his kids visiting, and wondered if that's why Mike hated hospitals.

Sarah continued to read to Mike, and told him a few jokes, laughing to herself each time. She recounted their short time together and told him how she felt each step of the way as they got to know each other, how she fell in love with him. The nurses showed Sarah how to wash Mike's face, how to clean the area around his IV, and how to help them move him when they changed his sheets. She liked being involved with his care, but more than anything, live or die, she wanted him to wake up so she could look at his eyes again, *those eyes*, even if it was for just one last time.

During the overnight hours the fourth day after Mike's surgery, the doctor took Mike off the ventilator because his condition unexpectedly improved and he was able to breathe on his own. Sarah watched Mike closely and slowly fell asleep sometime after midnight with her head lying on Mike's bedside next to his waist and holding his hand.

Sarah stirred at four in the morning. She stretched her shoulders, lifted her head off Mike's bed and craned her neck, stretched the stiffness out of it. She fluttered her eyes to focus, opened them wide and then narrowed them again.

"Oh my God!" Sarah said loudly. "You're awake," she lowered her voice as she looked at Mike, remembering where she was and not wanting to disturb the other wounded men."

"I love you Sarah," Mike whispered, his throat sore from the ventilator tube. "I love you." His eyes welled with tears and began to close as he spoke.

"I love you too Mike Hampton," Sarah said, as she leaned close to Mike and took his hand back in hers. "I'll get the nurses."

"Wait," Mike struggled to talk. "Wait."

Sarah froze and held Mike's gaze when he reopened his eyes. Mike very weakly ran his tongue around his lips.

"Kiss me Sarah," he finally whispered.

Sarah leaned in and gave Mike a lingering kiss on his lips, and then pulled back to look into his eyes. "Are you sure," she whispered.

"Yes," he whispered back.

Sarah leaned in and kissed Mike deeply and passionately, carefully holding his hand as they kissed. She finished the kiss and kept her lips close to his so that he could just feel her warm breath, and then gave him a lingering peck.

"I love you," Mike whispered again. "Still on the boat?"

"Yes, we're on our way to Florida."

"You too?"

"Yes," Sarah nodded her head slowly. She leaned in and very gently kissed Mike again, and then moved her face around to Mike's bandaged ear. "To paraphrase your mum, I'm not leaving you until either she buries you or I marry you, Mike Hampton."

A NOTE FROM THE AUTHOR

Between eleven and twenty percent of Afghanistan and Iraq War veterans experience Post Traumatic Stress Disorder (PTSD), about twelve percent of Gulf War Veterans and as much as fifteen percent of Vietnam Veterans.

According to the Department of Veterans Affairs, approximately twenty-two military veterans commit suicide each day, about 8,030 per year. For a little context, between the years 2001 and 2016, 2,392 American military members lost their lives in Afghanistan. Between 2003 and 2011, 3,836 military members lost their lives in Iraq. Sadly, it appears safer to go to war in our modern times than to come home from war. This story is for them and their families.

"The Last Mission" contains fictionalized versions of PTSD events that my late father, my little brother, and I experienced in our lives over decades as well as actual conversations we had with each other and other people over the years.

My father was a veteran of the Korean and Vietnam wars. My little brother is a disabled Desert Storm veteran diagnosed with chronic PTSD. Like my dad returning from Vietnam, I returned a different man after working tactical counterintelligence collections in the Philippines against the Communist New People's Army (NPA) during three very violent years.

As those first few years home from the Philippines went by, I began getting angry at simple things, little things, felt agitated and anxious for no reason, and was just always on edge. It has worsened over the years because I have never sought help. In fact, it wasn't until sometime in the early years of our new century that I even believed in this thing called PTSD. I went from not believing, to why me and not him, why not them? From there I began to experience shame and embarrassment for somehow being too weak to control my own thoughts and actions, my own mind. Remembering that knowledge is power, I did my research and no longer feel shame or embarrassment. I still have my anger and anxiety, but I am much better.

Since PTSD can be acute or chronic, and manifests differently in different people, it can be difficult to diagnose and accurate statistics are elusive. It can be mild and subtle in some people, manifesting as recurring intrusive thoughts during the day making it hard to concentrate and causing problems at work or in other aspects of life. In others, however, it can manifest as severe flashbacks, exaggerated reactions to loud noises or large crowds, and be completely debilitating.

According to the Mayo Clinic, "Post-traumatic stress disorder (PTSD) is a mental health condition that's triggered by a terrifying event—either experiencing it or witnessing it. Symptoms may include flashbacks, nightmares and severe anxiety, as well as uncontrollable thoughts about the event.

Many people who go through traumatic events have difficulty adjusting and coping for a while, but they don't have PTSD—with time and good self-care, they usually get better. But if the symptoms get worse or last for months or even years and interfere with your functioning, you may have PTSD.

Getting effective treatment after PTSD symptoms develop can be critical to reduce symptoms and improve function."

If you believe you or a loved one may be living with PTSD you can learn more about it by visiting the Mayo Clinic and VA websites. If you believe a veteran in your life may be at risk of harming himself or herself, you can call the Veteran's Suicide Hotline at (800) 273-8255.

Steve

www.ingramcontent.com/pod-product-compliance
Lightning Source LLC
Chambersburg PA
CBHW031309170626
46807CB00001B/351